C, M

APACHE AMBUSH!

Flames lanced from gun muzzles as the Apaches opened fire. Shifting sands formed into ghostly gray figures that rose up and pumped slugs into the posse in a blistering cross fire at close range.

All was chaos. There were shots, shouts, the screams of horses and men. Bullets thudded deep into flesh.

Sheriff Pitts was blown out of his saddle. A bullet tore off Rex's nose along with the rest of his face. Wilmot threw up both his arms when he was shot and flipped over backward like a tin target in a shooting gallery . . .

Slocum figured it would be a good idea to follow his guns, so he kept on going and dove out of the saddle headfirst. A bullet whizzed through the space he had occupied a split-second earlier . . .

**This book contains a preview of
the exciting new western novel
Sixkiller by Giles Tippette.**

OTHER BOOKS BY JAKE LOGAN

JAKE LOGAN

SLOCUM'S WAR

BERKLEY BOOKS, NEW YORK

SLOCUM'S WAR

A Berkley Book / published by arrangement with
the author

PRINTING HISTORY
Berkley edition / May 1992

ISBN: 0-425-13273-0

A BERKLEY BOOK® TM 757,375
Berkley Books are published by The Berkley Publishing Group,
200 Madison Avenue, New York, New York 10016.
The name "BERKLEY" and the "B" logo
are trademarks belonging to Berkley Publishing Corporation.

PRINTED IN THE UNITED STATES OF AMERICA

10 9 8 7 6 5 4 3 2 1

No Sunday west of Newton
and no God west of the Pecos.
             —Old frontier saying

1

Captain Darby stormed out of the wheelhouse to find out why his ship was going nowhere fast. He was the skipper of the steam barge *Laura Lee*, now moored at the port of Dos Rios, West Texas, where Blood River meets the Rio Grande. Cargo and passengers were stowed on board, steam pressure was high, black smoke poured from the stacks, but the *Laura Lee* stayed tied up at the docks.

Darby scowled at the still-lowered gangplank and the securely fastened mooring lines. A half-dozen dock workers milled around with their hands in their pockets. "Prepare to cast off!" Darby shouted at them.

They shifted uneasily, shuffling their feet, but they made no move to obey.

"What's wrong with you men?" Darby demanded, thunderstruck. "Are you deaf?!"

"We ain't deaf, Cap'n," volunteered a spokesman for the group, "but this fellow here says he'll shoot anybody that lays a hand on a hawser."

1

"I will, too," said a man who stood apart from the dockers. A smooth-faced man in a tan suit, clean white shirt, and black shiny boots, he was dressed like a dude but he carried himself like a gunfighter. His empty hands rested at his sides, but his jacket flap was swept back clear of his holstered gun.

Darby said, "This some kind of joke, mister?"

"You boys think I'm joking?" Tan Suit said. The dockers shook their heads. "Joke, hell!" one of them muttered.

"It's no joke, Captain," Tan Suit said.

"What's your game, damn you?"

"Just holding the boat for a few latecomers. As soon as they get here, we'll all be on our way."

"The hell you say!" Captain Darby exploded.

The mate, Mr. Peavey, ducked into the wheelhouse. The cabin boy, Fluke, stood staring in slack-jawed stupefaction. The passengers on deck looked for cover, but were afraid to move for fear of triggering fireworks.

Skippering a riverboat on the Border was no job for the fainthearted. At one time or another, Captain Darby had tangled with marauding Indians, Mexican *bandidos*, Texas badmen, and mutinous crews. A six-gun was stuffed into the top of his pants, hidden under his brass-buttoned navy-blue coat. His hand drifted to his middle, seemingly toying with a button. Fingers crept inside the coat, touching the gun butt.

"Behind you," Tan Suit said.

Deckboards creaked behind Darby, making him break out in a cold sweat. Something tapped him on the shoulder. Hardly daring to breathe, he turned his head, expecting to see a gun pointed at it. Instead, he saw— greenbacks.

Greenbacks. Dollars. Paper money, lots of it, held clenched in a black leather fist. Money in the gloved hand of the woman who stood behind him.

She was a big dish-faced woman, built like a black-smith. She wore a prim black bonnet, veil, and mourning clothes. A slovenly teenage girl stood beside her, smirking. She wore black, too.

"For your troubles," the woman said, fanning the money in Darby's face.

Mr. Peavey came back out on deck, carrying a shotgun. Tan Suit laughed once, without humor.

"Hold the boat a little while longer and the money's yours," the woman said. "Take it!"

Captain Darby reached a decision. "Belay that scattergun, Mr. Peavey. We won't be needing it," he said.

"I'm not so sure, Skipper," the mate said, but he lowered the shotgun when he got a good look at the money.

"Go on, take it," the woman said.

Darby took it. "Smart move," Tan Suit said.

The captain counted the money. It added up to one hundred dollars. That kind of money was hard to come by honestly—or dishonestly, for that matter. Pocketing it, he turned to face the woman and said, "Captain Cornelius Darby at your service, ma'am."

"I'm Mrs. Jones. This is my daughter, Pearl," she said, pointing to the girl beside her, "and you already met my boy, Neville."

Neville was Tan Suit. He acknowledged the introduction by flipping Darby a casual salute with the hand that wasn't his gun hand.

Mrs. Jones said, "We're waiting on some of my kinfolk. They're late, but they'll be here directly, I promise you that."

"Yes, ma'am," Darby said.

Fluke, the cabin boy, still stood frozen in place, eyes popping, mouth hanging open. "You're catching flies," Mrs. Jones said to him.

"Huh?"

She cupped his chin and lifted it, shutting his mouth. "That's better," she said.

She set off along the companionway with Pearl in tow. The girl's puffy white face still showed its babyfat, but the rest of her was all grown up. Her wickedly curved body threatened to burst the seams of her tight, frayed black dress. She caught Darby eyeing her and stuck out her tongue at him.

Fluke gaped once again.

The mate drew Darby aside, saying low-voiced, "I don't like it, Skipper. This is a bad business, and a bad bunch, too."

"But their money is good, Mr. Peavey."

"There is that," the mate agreed. "How much did we get?"

The "we" was not lost on Darby. "I didn't count it yet," he lied.

"Well, count it now, and split it, too, before any of it strays."

"Greed is an ugly thing, Mr. Peavey."

"I'm not greedy, Skipper. All I want is half, and not a penny more."

"Damn you for a double-dyed rogue—"

"Now, now, Skipper, don't be greedy."

Darby did some more grumbling, but he paid up. It was worth it. This trip would be dangerous enough without his having to worry about a discontented first mate, too.

As for Fluke, he didn't get a cent of the money. He was a trifle slow-witted and wouldn't know what to do with it, anyway.

A half hour or so dragged by before the latecomers arrived. A team of four black horses, yoked in tandem, drew a long black carriage through the riverfront streets and down to the pier. Hoofs and wheels clattered over the planks of the dock.

Fluke said, "Wuh—What kind of wagon is *that*, Mr. Peavey?"

"A corpse-wagon, you poor fool," the mate said.

The hearse was a long, tall, narrow black box on wheels. A dour, bareheaded undertaker held the reins. His stovepipe hat was perched on the head of the man who sat beside him, a wolfish, raggedy man with a rifle held across his knees.

Neville Jones said, "You're behind schedule, Pink. Any trouble?"

"Nope," the wolfish man, Pink, said. "Just running late, is all."

"You'd be late for your own funeral!"

"Can you think of a better thing to be late for?"

Standing at the rail of the *Laura Lee*, Mrs. Jones called down, "Time's a-wasting, boys!"

Pink hopped down from the driver's box. The undertaker stayed put. "Well, let's get to it," Pink said.

He and Neville went to the back of the hearse. The rear door opened from the inside, and a body tumbled out. A body, and a bottle. The bottle was empty and skittered over the side of the dock and into the water. The body looked like a heap of dirty clothes, but it was a man, and a live one at that.

Groaning, he raised himself on his arms. Thatched white hair showed from under his battered, shapeless hat. He wore greasy brown leather chaps, boots, spurs, and a gun.

Pink swore. "Drunk again! Dammit, Tewk!"

The oldster made a gurgling sound. Neville caught a whiff of him and stepped back quickly. "Man, he reeks! Ma's not going to like this," he added in an undertone.

"I swear he didn't have a bottle on him," Pink said.

"He probably hid it in the hearse ahead of time. Trust that old rummy to think of a trick like that."

"He was too quiet on the trip. I should've known something was wrong. . . ."

Tewk gurgled some more. "What's he saying?" Pink demanded.

"He said he'll be all right once he gets on his feet," Neville said.

" . . . Yup," Tewk said, nodding, blinking his watery eyes.

Pink grabbed a handful of the back of the old man's collar and hauled him upright. Tewk's gun fell out of the holster, but it didn't go off. He leaned against the hearse, holding on to it to keep from falling.

"You dropped something," Neville said, picking up the gun and sticking it into Tewk's holster.

"Thanksh."

"You can thank me by not breathing on me," Neville said.

He and Pink wrestled a coffin out of the hearse. It was an oblong black box with brass handles and fittings, and it was heavy, too heavy for the two men to handle. Breathing hard, Pink said, "Hey, undertaker, get your lazy ass down here and help us out!"

The undertaker hopped to it, not liking it much. The three of them hefted the coffin and carried it up the gangplank of the *Laura Lee*. Using Pink's rifle as a crutch, old Tewk managed to stumble aboard under his own power.

Captain Darby took off his cap as the coffin was carried past him. "My condolences, ma'am."

"Thank you," Mrs. Jones said, dry-eyed under her veil. She held tickets for Pink, Neville, and Old Tewk, as well as for Pearl and herself. One-way tickets for Redrock at Drowned Canyon at the source of the Blood, sixty-five miles from the river's mouth here at Dos Rios.

She'd reserved two adjoining cabins near the port bow. Darby scared up a pair of wooden trestles, which were put in the larger cabin. The coffin was laid on top of them.

While the others were busy, the undertaker sneaked off the ship. He climbed up into the driver's box of the hearse and lashed the horses with a buggy whip. Scared and hurt, they leaped forward in wild flight. The hearse hurtled away from the waterfront and was soon soon out of sight.

Pink said, "Can you beat that? Man was in such an all-fired hurry to get shut of us that he forgot his hat! Not that I was gonna give it back, anyway."

Nothing kept the *Laura Lee* from casting off now. The steam engine chuffed and chugged. There was a thud, a lurch, and a shudder; then the paddle wheels began to turn. Spinning blades cut the water, churning up a wake. The dock retreated, the shoreline slipped away, and Dos Rios fell behind as the steamboat started up Blood River.

Mrs. Jones and her brood were crowded around the coffin, all of them but Old Tewk, who stank too badly to be allowed into the cramped cabin. He sat outside, slumped against the bulkhead.

Emmeline Jones was known to the Pinkertons and to various police departments along the Gulf Coast as Ma Jones, Widow Jones, and the Black Widow. She had five grown children, sired by five different husbands, each of whom was now dead. Neville was her first-born, Pinkney her third, and Pearl her youngest. They were all killers, Pearl included.

Emmeline Jones stood over the coffin, running her meaty hands back and forth across the lid. "Open it up. I want to take a look," she said.

"I'll keep watch," Neville said. He exited the cabin, closing the door behind him.

The air grew thicker, closer, but nobody seemed to mind, or even notice. Their attention was focused on the coffin, where Pink's strong, sure hands picked open the brass fastenings. He wedged his Bowie knife blade-first under the lid and pried it open.

A Gatling gun lay nestled inside the quilted satin-lined coffin.

"Shoots five hundred rounds a minute," Pink said at last, breaking the silence. "Now, ain't that the prettiest corpse you ever did see?"

2

A speck of motion disturbed the vast emptiness of the plains under the big Texas sky. The speck was a man, a walking man. His name was John Slocum and he wasn't much of a walker. His bowed legs showed he spent most of his time in the saddle. Now, he was carrying one.

He was walking instead of riding because of pure dumb luck—all bad. He'd been riding south when a rattlesnake spooked his horse. The horse bolted, stepped into a gopher hole, tripped, and fell, throwing him.

Slocum managed to kick himself clear and escaped being pinned under the animal when it went over. He hit the ground so hard, he felt as if he'd been knocked into next week. He landed flat on his back and saw stars and couldn't get up for a long while. When he finally did stand up, he was light-headed and shaky and nearly fell down.

He was bruised up pretty badly, but nothing was broken. The horse wasn't so lucky. It had a broken leg. It lay on its side, whinnying, eyes rolling, its three good legs pawing the air. One shot put it out of its misery. Slocum's misery was just beginning.

He was alone in hard country west of the Pecos. Flat, sun-baked prairie stretched out and away from him in all directions, almost as far as the eye could see. The flats lay between two mountain ranges, the Glass Mountains, far to the north, and the Santiago Mountains, far to the south. And me in the middle, thought Slocum.

The dead horse's eyes were already filmed over, glazed. Slocum used his knife to cut the saddle loose. It took him a long time to do it because he was still weak and sick from the fall. His ears rang and his bones ached. He was a lean, rawboned type, able to take plenty of physical punishment, but that didn't mean he wasn't hurt.

He'd been traveling light and fast, with no excess baggage. In addition to the saddle, he had a rifle, two Colt revolvers, a foot-and-a-half-long Bowie knife, two bandoliers, a few boxes of ammunition, a bedroll with a rain slicker rolled up inside of it, and a pair of saddlebags containing various odds and ends. He had two canteens that were almost full, and a couple of pound blocks of jerked beef and pemmican. If he hadn't had the food, he'd have cut a few flank steaks off the horse—but he did have it. Starvation wasn't a problem, but there were many other ways to die out here.

He was the tallest object in that expanse of hard-packed grassland dotted with scrub brush. The only sign of human habitation was the faint trail, not even a road, by which he had come. Ahead, it arrowed southeast across the plain, vanishing in a haze at the horizon where the blue-gray ridge of the Santiagos rose. Somewhere in those mountains lay the well-watered grazing lands of the Blood River basin.

Slocum shouldered his saddle and gear, pointed himself at the southeastern sierra, and started walking. He had a long walk ahead of him. Too long, because tomorrow was April 16 and he wouldn't be able to get where he was going in time to stop the slaughter. But he didn't know that yet, and even if he had, there wasn't a damned thing he could have done about it except to keep on doing what he was doing—namely, walking.

He soon learned the truth of the old Texas saying "A man afoot is no man at all." The rugged Big Bend country through which he now trudged was only a small part of the state, but it was as big as West Virginia. He also learned that cowboy boots aren't made for walking.

He wanted to put plenty of ground between him and the dead horse. Carrion would draw the buzzards, and they in turn were likely to attract a different breed of scavengers, of the two-legged variety. In these parts, any stranger was a potential enemy until proved otherwise.

Slocum left the trail and followed a parallel course a quarter mile to the left of it. It was a slight precaution, but it increased his chances of seeing riders on the trail before they saw him. He couldn't afford to overlook any possible advantage, no matter how slight.

It was a mild spring day for the area; the temperature at midday barely reached eighty-five degrees Fahrenheit. Slocum slogged onward for a long time, and when he finally looked back, the dead horse was out of sight. The mountains didn't seem any closer, though.

The saddle slowed him down, but he resisted the temptation to get rid of it. It wasn't much, but it was the only saddle he had and it wasn't in his nature to give up anything that was his without a fight. Besides, if he ran into trouble, he could take cover behind it. It wasn't much, but it was the only cover available in this empty immensity.

He kept moving. Sometimes, when he was too tired to take another step, he stopped and stood resting in place. He didn't put down the saddle and he didn't sit down. If he put down the saddle, he might not have the strength to pick it up again. If he sat down, he might stiffen up and be unable to rise. So he just stood around waiting for the weakness to pass until he could walk again. As the hours wore on, the periods of weakness grew shorter and more infrequent.

The flatland wasn't as empty as it seemed to be at first glance. There were snakes, centipedes, scorpions, grasshoppers, field mice, jackrabbits, prairie dogs. Buzzards, too.

The buzzards were up ahead of him, a fair piece of distance away, but the high-flying birds could be seen from a long way off. They soared on the thermals, wheeling around in the air, circling something dead on the ground.

Slocum swung out even farther away from the trail, then curved cautiously back toward it. The ground wasn't entirely level, and he used what dips and draws and hollows there were to cover his approach. An hour passed before he reached the spot where the buzzards circled directly overhead.

He found two dead men stretched out behind a boulder some twenty yards off the trail. Cowboys, from the looks of them. One was a grizzled old trailhand; the other was so young that he hadn't had his first shave yet. They'd been gunned down, blasted at close range with about five slugs per man. Their pockets had been emptied, turned inside out. Their guns were gone and so were their boots.

Horse tracks and trail sign told most of the sordid story, to those who knew how to read them, and Slocum could guess the rest. The cowboys had been driving a supply wagon when they crossed paths with three riders from the north. The riders were gunmen, killers. The cowboys never had a chance. They were cut down in cold blood, right in the open.

The corpses were robbed, loaded into the back of the wagon, and dumped behind a rock. The killers took the wagon with them and rode south, toward Blood River.

Slocum even knew who the killers were: Bill Rigdon, Whiteface Ames, and Choey Bravo. Three no-goods, born to hang. Not if I catch up with them first, Slocum thought.

He'd been trailing them all the way from Big Spring. They were murderous devils who'd just as soon backshoot a man as look at him, but that didn't mean that they couldn't handle their guns if they had to. Bill Rigdon was lightning-fast on the draw, maybe even faster than Slocum. Slocum didn't intend to put it to the test. When it was time for the showdown, Slocum would come after him with a rifle, not a gun. Rigdon's fast draw wouldn't do him much good then.

Of course, he had to admit that he was a long way off from catching up to Bill Rigdon and company. He was a long way off from anywhere and without a horse to get there. He wasn't dead, though, not like these two fellows.

Bill and the boys hadn't ridden hell-bent for leather a couple of hundred miles, from Big Spring to Big Bend, just to shoot down two ranch hands who probably couldn't scrape up more than a few dollars between them. And why steal the wagon?

Because the gunmen were part of something big, something due to happen tomorrow, April 16, in the Blood River basin.

"Looks like the boys got a head start on the festivities," Slocum said.

The bloodstains were mostly dry. Slocum figured that the shootings had taken place at mid-morning. It was mid-afternoon now. He'd better get moving. There was nothing he could do here.

He'd put down the saddle earlier, before sneaking up on the death site. It took some effort, but he found that he was able to hoist it up across his shoulders. His strength was returning.

Buzzards are cautious creatures. They'll watch a body for a long time to make sure it's dead before moving in to feed. Slocum's arrival had scared them away from the dead men, but they returned when he had left the scene.

The mountains didn't seem much closer, but the table-land began to tilt upward, rising toward the foothills. The terrain grew more irregular, rugged, shot through with dry draws and creek beds. A series of long, gently sloping ridges formed a natural stairway climbing into higher country.

The only part of Texas with mountains, and me without a horse! Slocum thought. He saved his breath for the climb. It was hard work, but at least there was plenty of natural cover here, unlike the plains, where he'd felt so nakedly exposed. He shunned the valleys as much as possible, keeping to the high ground, moving just below the ridge tops so as not to skyline. He hadn't forgotten Bill Rigdon and the boys, or their victims on the flats a couple of thousand feet below.

He followed the main trail, keeping some distance from it. He didn't see the killers or anybody else. From time to time, he ventured down from the ridge to read the sign on the trail. Fresh-cut wagon wheel tracks showed the killers had come this way, and not too fresh horse manure indicated that they were a good six, seven hours ahead of him.

He crossed the divide into a plateau that stretched out for many miles, bounded by the Del Norte Mountains on the west and the Santiagos on the south. It was well-watered country, many-veined with streams and creeks. Covered in new spring grass, it looked lush in comparison to the arid plains. Good grazing land. There were sure to be ranches in the vicinity.

The light was failing; the sun was going down fast. Purple shadows rolled down from the sierra, flooding the canyons, washing across the plateau. Breezes blew up, cool ones, tugging at Slocum's garments.

He knew he'd better make camp before darkness fell. The sun set, but there was still some light in the sky when he finally found a place to his liking. It was a hollow, three feet deep and six feet wide, hemmed in and hidden from casual view by some man-sized boulders. Slocum made damned sure there weren't any snakes nesting in it.

He dined on jerked beef and water while the stars came out. It had been a hot day, but the night was cold. He wrapped himself in a blanket. He would have liked to light a fire, but he couldn't risk its being seen. The rocks and the sides of the hollow shielded him from the worst of the bone-chilling winds blowing down from the mountains.

A yellow half-moon came up. Slocum slept, using his saddle for a pillow.

He woke at first light. His body was so stiff and cramped, he felt as if he'd died sometime during the night and just didn't know it. He stomped around for a quarter hour, chafing life and warmth into his limbs. His breath steamed in the frosty morning air, haloing his head with a cloud of ghostly vapors.

What he wouldn't give for a big breakfast of steak and eggs and home fries, all washed down with a quart or two of hot black coffee! He breakfasted on jerked beef and water.

Rummaging around in his shirt pocket, he found the remnants of a half-smoked cigarillo and a match to light it with. So he sat on his saddle with his back on a rock and had a smoke. It cheered him, and after that the day didn't look quite so bad.

Then he remembered that the day was April 16.

Whatever was going to happen would happen today. Maybe it had already started. He'd better get started, too.

He hoisted his burden, set his face to the southeast, and started down the slope.

He was hurting more today than yesterday. The numbness had gone away. He felt as if he had been worked over, head to toe, by railroad roustabouts armed with ax handles. Sleeping on the hard cold ground hadn't helped his aches and pains, either.

"By God! Somebody's going to pay for this," he said. Said it many times, while walking many a footsore and weary mile.

Dew shimmered on the grassy fields, soaking the bottoms of his pants legs as he plodded along. The morning air was fresh and bright for the first hour or two after sunrise. The last cool breeze stopped blowing and died at around half past eight. The sun burned off the dew. The air was still, hot.

Insects buzzed and hummed. The hotter it got, the louder they got, until the racket seemed almost deafening. That wasn't all bad, though. Insects were in tune with their surroundings. If they should suddenly fall silent, it would send Slocum a danger signal.

Sweat poured out of him. His long strides kicked up dry, fine dust that settled on him and got in his nose. He came to a creek, soaked his head in the water to cool it off, topped off his canteens, and continued his trek. When the noonday sun reached its peak, he rested for an hour in the shade of a tree. Trees could grow here on the plateau, unlike the plains.

He resumed his journey an hour or so after the sun passed its zenith. He wasn't as cautious about hugging the ground cover as he had been. He was feeling ornery. He found himself half-hoping that somebody would take a shot at him so he could shoot back.

In early afternoon, he came to a fork in the main trail. One branch kept on going southeast toward Blood River; the other went due south, disappearing in a wild broken country of arroyos, canyons, and high hills. Trail signs showed that the killers had taken the wagon down the south fork, into the badlands. Those lonely wastes were the haunt of outlaws, misfits, and fugitives. No posse would be foolish enough to invade that lawless land, whose gulches and ravines and blind corners made it a bushwhacker's paradise.

Bill Rigdon must have a damn good reason for riding into there.

Slocum took the other branch, the one that forked toward Blood River. Far in the distance rose Steeple Peak, a landmark feature of the Sawtooth Mountains, pointing the way to Notch Pass, the gateway to the Blood River basin.

He crossed the Maravillas Creek on an old stone bridge that had been built by the Spaniards. The conquistadors had colonized much of the Southwest, but they had failed here thanks to the efforts of the Comanches and the Apaches, foes more ferocious than even the conquistadors themselves. Forty some odd miles from here, the Maravillas would enter a canyon of the same name, and from there eventually feed the Rio Grande. The Maravillas watershed was poor and hardscrabble compared to the Blood. The Blood supported more ranches, bigger spreads, and fatter herds. Redrock on the Blood was the biggest town within a couple of hundred square miles. It had a big bank, too. The Blood River basin was the logical target for today's conquistadors.

Today was April 16.

It was late in the day when Slocum came to the ranch.

3

The sign was made from a piece of old board lashed by rawhide thongs to a crooked fence post. The legend, written in red paint, read,

> This is Ingram land.
> **KEEP OUT!**

"Friendly," Slocum said.

Ingram's spread was a mountain valley, a saddle between two ridges, with a stream winding through it. Slocum first saw the sign in mid-afternoon. Only an hour of daylight remained when he came in sight of the ranch house.

Cattle grazing near the banks of the stream stopped browsing and looked up as Slocum approached. He hoped that there weren't any ornery bulls minded to challenge the intruder, but he needn't have worried. They were disturbed by his presence, and moved fifty yards downstream.

"Can't say as I blame you, cows," Slocum said. "A walking man is something you don't see in Texas every day. It's downright unnatural!"

A rider crested a low hill and came into view in the

17

middle ground between Slocum and the ranch. He was herding in some strays and he didn't see Slocum at first. When he did, he reined to a stop and looked at him. They were too far apart for either of them to make out much detail on the other. Slocum waved. Abruptly the rider turned his horse and galloped to the ranch, vanishing behind a building.

The rider's horse had kicked up a lot of dust, but it had settled by the time Slocum reached the ranch.

The ranch house was a blocky one-storey structure made of stone and adobe, the most sensible way to build in this timber-poor region. The roof was flat and the door was solid. The windows were few, narrow, and protected by wooden shutters that closed from inside. They had narrow slots in them: gunports. A crude barn, not much more than a shed, stood on the opposite side of the yard, a stone's throw from the house. To the rear, a split-rail fence enclosed a modest corral with three horses in it. The horses sidled to the far side of the pen when their quivering nostrils caught Slocum's strange man-scent.

The dusty yard was empty; there was no one in sight. A blur of motion streaked around the corner of the barn and skidded to a halt ten feet away from Slocum. It was a dog, a dirty yellow mongrel that looked half-wolf.

"Whoa, boy," Slocum said. The dog barked at him. It barked and snarled and barked some more. Loudly and tirelessly. It would gather itself as if to lunge, then suddenly change its mind and back away growling, only to lunge forward again.

"Howdy," Slocum yelled. He had to yell to be heard over the dog. "Anybody home?"

Somebody was home; he was sure of that. Signs of life of a more homey variety showed themselves in the deep, rich, tantalizing aroma of a fresh-baked pie wafting from behind a shuttered window. Pecan pie, unless Slocum missed his guess, and he knew his victuals. The good food smell of it set his stomach to grumbling hungrily.

The ranch house door was open a crack, just wide enough to permit the muzzle of a double-barreled shotgun to peek through it. The door opened wider and the rest of the shotgun came through, followed by the man who was holding it pointed at Slocum. The weapon was held steadily in the work-hardened hands of a burly, scowling rancher.

He came into the yard, not stopping until he stood facing Slocum with only a few paces between them. Slocum tried not to think of what that shotgun could do to a body at point-blank range.

The rancher's entrance had emboldened the yellow dog to redouble its barkings and growlings. "Keep shut now," he told the animal, but the dog paid him no heed and barked still louder.

The rancher got red-faced and launched an angry kick at the dog. The dog jumped in time to escape most of the force of the blow, but it yipped in pain and darted a safe distance away.

"Keep shut, you goddam mangy cur!" the rancher shouted after him. The dog whined, lay down in the dust, and tucked its head down on its front paws.

"Hell!" the rancher said.

"Makes a big noise for a little feller, don't he?" Slocum said.

"What's it to you?"

"Nothing, mister. Just trying to be sociable, is all."

"Well, don't."

"You Ingram?"

"That's right. I'm Ingram, and you're on my land. Why?"

"I'm looking to buy a horse," Slocum said.

Ingram looked more stubbornly skeptical than ever. "You ain't got no horse," he said accusingly.

"That's why I'm fixing to buy one." Slocum's patience, never great, was kept from wearing thin by the other's shotgun. "Got any you want to sell?"

"Sell? To *you*?" Ingram sneered. "What're you going to use to pay for it? Lead? A bullet in the back, maybe?"

"How about dollars?"

"You don't look like you got much money, stranger. Hell, you ain't even got a horse!"

"I've got it," Slocum said. "Okay if I set down this saddle? It's a mite heavy."

"Go ahead. But don't try any tricks. Remember, I've got you covered. I could cut you in half before you can pull one of those Colts."

Slocum set the saddle down. "You're not the easiest man in the world to do business with."

"You don't like it, you can just get the hell out of here! Now, let's see the color of your money."

"I'm reaching for it now," Slocum said, "so don't go getting nervous with that scattergun."

"Nervous? Not me, stranger. Cautious, that's what I am."

Slocum had a few other ideas about what Ingram was, but he kept them to himself. He unbuttoned his shirt and reached inside, taking out a worn, flat wallet looped around his neck on a rawhide thong. Inside it was a thin billfold of greenbacks—too thin. Slocum showed it to Ingram.

"Satisfied?" Slocum said.

"I reckon we might be able to do some business."

"How about pointing that shotgun somewhere else?"

"All right," Ingram said at last, as he lowered the muzzle. "But no tricky business now." He eyed Slocum with new interest. "What happened to your horse, stranger?"

"Busted leg. Had to shoot him."

"Tough," Ingram said cheerfully. "You look like you've done some walking. You must want a horse pretty bad."

"It beats walking."

"Yeah, don't it?" Ingram laughed. "Man without a horse in these parts might as well have his legs cut off. Me, I only got a few horses and I need every one of them. Couldn't hardly get along without one. They're mighty dear to me."

"I bet."

"Still, I wouldn't feel right about sending you off again on foot. I wouldn't be doing my Christian duty. So, I'll tell you what I'm gonna do, cowboy—What's your name, anyhow?"

"Slocum."

"Tell you what I'm gonna do you for, Slocum. I'm gonna do you a favor and sell you one of these fine animals, even though it'll work a hardship on me. Providing we can come to terms, that is," Ingram added quickly. "What say we mosey over to the corral?"

"Sure."

"You go first. Not that I don't trust you, mind, but I'd just as soon not show my back to a stranger. There's been some funny things going on around here lately."

"Such as?"

"Too many strangers in the territory, for one thing," the rancher said pointedly.

There were three horses in the corral: a trim, smart little black cow pony, a big gray draught horse, and a skittish roan gelding. The cow pony was lathered with sweat from being run in by the range rider. And where was the rider? It hadn't been Ingram out there herding cows.

Ingram said, "It's a sacrifice, Lord knows, but I can let you have the roan."

"How much?" Slocum said without enthusiasm.

"Sixty dollars."

"Sixty dollars!" Slocum said. "That's a high price even for a good horse!"

"Well, now, cowboy, if you don't like it, why you can just trot on down the road to the next ranch and try your luck there. That's Melliker's place. You can't miss it, it's just another ten, twelve miles down the road," Ingram said.

"That's no sixty-dollar horse, mister."

"Depends on how bad you want it, cowboy. What's it worth to you not to walk?"

"I've only got fifty," Slocum said. "You can count it yourself."

Ingram was smug. "Sixty," he said.

"Fifty is twenty dollars too much for that nag."

"Sixty's my price," Ingram said. "Take it or leave it."

"I'm leaving it."

Slocum turned his back on the corral and Ingram, and walked away. He picked up his saddle and kept on walking, out of the yard and away from the ranch. When the yellow dog saw Slocum's back, it jumped up and started barking. Slocum kept walking, waiting for Ingram to break first and call him back. The dog barked, but Ingram stayed silent. Slocum finally turned around and walked back to the corral.

Ingram stood in the same place where he'd been standing when Slocum left. He shouted at the dog to be quiet, but it wouldn't shut up until he kicked a stone at it that hit it in its side. The dog yelped and ran back behind the barn.

"Stupidest animal on God's green earth. Well, I sure called your bluff," he said to Slocum, grinning. "Only you should've took my first offer, cowboy. Now it's seventy dollars."

When he saw the look on Slocum's face, he knew that he'd pushed too hard, shotgun or no shotgun. His grin vanished. "I was just joshing you," he said hastily. "The price's sixty dollars, same as before."

Slocum dug deep in his pants pockets and fished out some crumpled bills and a few coins, adding them to the money from his wallet. "Well, what do you know? You was able to scrape up the rest of that money after all."

"Fifty-seven dollars and change," Slocum said, "and that cleans me out, mister."

Ingram made a show of thinking it over before he took the money. "Well, that ain't quite sixty dollars, but I reckon it'll do. I'll let you slide for the rest."

"That's big of you," Slocum said.

"Yeah, ain't it?"

Ingram thought he'd skinned Slocum pretty good on the horse trading—and he had—but what he didn't know was that Slocum had a couple of hundred-dollar gold pieces sewn into a flap on the inside of his gun belt. But that was getaway money, not to be touched except in case of emergencies. Some paper money was hidden in his saddlebags, too.

"I figured you for a man who's had a bellyful of walking," Ingram said.

"You figured right."

The roan was filmy-eyed, bad-teethed, and sway-backed. It groaned and staggered when Slocum threw the saddle on it. "This nag's liable to give out before I reach Blood River," he said.

"That's your lookout," Ingram said, "he's your horse now. And I wouldn't waste no time in making tracks, cowboy. Night's coming on fast, and this is bad country to ride through in the dark. When it's light out, too, come to think of it."

"Okay if I fill my canteens from your well?"

"Help yourself. I won't even charge you for it," Ingram said.

The well had been dug in the middle of the yard, so the house dwellers wouldn't have to walk a hundred yards or so down to the stream to get their water. Slocum wasted no time in filling his canteens from the well's wooden bucket. Ingram didn't want him hanging around here any longer than it took to do the deal. The rancher held his shotgun pointed at the ground, but he was clearly getting impatient.

Slocum wasn't about to ride off without some proof of purchase that would prevent Ingram from claiming that the horse had been stolen. They *hanged* horse thieves. "I'll need a bill of sale," he said.

"You'll get it. I'll go inside and write one up. You know how to read?"

"Uh-huh," Slocum said, nodding.

"Oh." Ingram looked briefly disappointed. He started toward the house, saying, "Stay put. I'll be back with that bill of sale in two shakes."

"I'm not going anywhere," Slocum said.

One of the shutters that had been closed before was open now, revealing a girl standing inside, framed by the window. A ray of golden light from the setting sun shone on her, so that she seemed to glow against the brown dimness inside the house. Long blond hair, parted in the middle, hung down on both sides of her delicate oval face. A blue-and-white checked dress covered her slender form from the neck down.

It had been a long time since Slocum had seen a pretty girl, and the sight of her was as refreshing to his spirit as cool sweet water to a thirsty man.

"*Karen!* Dammit, girl, get out of that window!" Ingram shouted.

The girl, Karen, recoiled, stunned by the violence of his outburst. The shadowy hovering form of an older woman—Karen's mother?—hurried up behind her and drew her aside. The shutter banged closed.

Ingram, hard-jawed now and mean-faced, said to Slocum, "Our business is done. You got your horse, so git!"

"Not without that bill of sale," Slocum said. "Say, you're pointing that shotgun at me again."

"I'll do more than point. Get off my land, cowboy. If I see you again, I'll kill you."

Slocum had just about had a bellyful of Mr. High and Mighty Ingram. "You got a mean mouth, mister. Are you man enough to back it up with your fists, or are you just a big bag of wind without that shotgun? Put it down, if you're game, and I'll whomp you from Hell to Texas, boy."

"Sure, you'd like me to put down the gun. Then you could shoot me down nice and easy—you think," Ingram said.

Slocum shook his head in amazement. "Man, you are one contrary son of a—"

"Don't say it. I'd hate to have to clean up the mess it'd make of you if I cut loose with both barrels," Ingram said. Keeping his eyes on Slocum, not turning his head, he called, "Jase! *Jase!*"

"Right here, Pa," piped up a young voice. A youth in his early teens opened the back door of the shed and stepped out, leveling a rifle at Slocum's middle. This was the rider Slocum had seen earlier.

He said, "Want me to plug him, Pa?"

"Not yet, Jase," Ingram said. "You riding out, cowboy?"

"I'm riding," Slocum said.

"Don't shoot, Jase," Ingram said.

"Okay, Pa, if you say so."

"Well, damn it, boy, I do say so! I ain't just talking to hear myself talk! When I tell you to do something, do it; and when I tell you to don't do something, then don't do it!"

"Sorry, Pa."

Jase worried Slocum. Ingram, Senior, didn't want a shooting fight, he just wanted Slocum gone. He wouldn't fire without thinking of the consequences, but the youngster might. Kids are like that. They do things without thinking and pay the price afterward. Slocum knew that for a fact because he had been that way himself. When he thought about what a damn fool he had been at Jase's age, he realized that there was a pretty good chance the kid would pull the trigger if he thought his father was in danger. That would be a pity, because then Slocum would have to kill them both first, and he didn't want to kill a green kid and his hardheaded old man.

Slocum climbed into the saddle. The roan grunted, lurching slightly under his weight.

"Much obliged for the hospitality," Slocum said.

"Go on, git!"

Slocum got.

4

James Ingram wasn't a bad man, but bad luck had made him a hard man. His story was a catalogue of the perils of frontier life. His mother died in childbirth. His father was scalped by Comanches. Just when he and his brothers had built up a pretty good-sized herd, the War Between the States broke out. They all enlisted on the day Texas seceded from the Union. James Ingram was the sole surviving member of the family by war's end. When he returned home, his herd had been long since rustled and his ranch burned. He married Matilda Sanders from Mission Church and started raising cows and a family, in that order. For over fifteen years, he had eked out a marginal existence as a small rancher in West Texas. He'd been shot at by rustlers and shot back at them and even killed a few. He'd been harassed by Texas outlaws and Mexican *bandidos*, but more to be feared were the raiding parties of the Apaches. When Victorio led his Mescalero Apaches on their final raid last year, Ingram had sent his wife, daughter, and younger son to live with her relatives in nearby Mission Church until the danger had passed.

It was not the kind of life that instills much faith in the brotherhood of man, and James Ingram acted accordingly.

He and Jase stood watching Slocum ride east, away from the ranch.

"Think we've seen the last of him, Pa?"

"I reckon so, son."

When Slocum was a hundred yards distant, the dog took it on himself to chase him and took off after him. Yapping furiously, the dog tore across the fields, deaf to Ingram's callings to him to return.

"Damn fool dog," Ingram said.

The ranch house's stout wooden door was unbarred and opened, and the rest of the Ingrams came out into the yard, into the red light of the setting sun.

Matilda Ingram's plain face was weathered and her matronly body stooped from a lifetime of hard work and woes. A tiny plot in back of the house held three rugged wooden crosses marking the graves of three children she'd buried. An infant girl was stillborn, a baby boy died of a coughing disease at eighteen months, and a five-year-old daughter had been carried off by a fever. Not a day passed that she didn't say a few prayers over the graves.

Fifteen-year-old Karen Ingram was strong and straight and healthy, perhaps too much so, or so her worried mother thought. Karen was restless. She wanted to see more of the world than the family ranch and too-infrequent visits to Redrock and Mission Church.

Twelve-year-old Harry was the youngest member of the family, a towheaded lad, quiet, with a serious expression.

Matilda sighed heavily and wrung her hands until her husband said irritatedly, "What're you fretting about, woman?"

"He didn't seem like such a bad 'un, Jim," she said.

"Maybe, maybe not. Either way, I ain't taking no chances," Ingram said. He turned to Karen. "As for you, girl, sometimes you don't show no sense at all."

"I didn't do nothing, Pa," she said.

"The hell you didn't!"

"Don't go swearing in front of the children, James," Matilda said. On certain matters concerning what she thought of as "decent conduct," she was not to be cowed by her husband.

"All right, all right," he said. "But dammit, Karen, I told you time and time again, you keep out of sight when strangers come around!"

"James!"

"Sorry, Mattie. That last one slipped out," he said. Jase and Harry exchanged knowing glances but were careful not to laugh, or even smile.

Karen said, "I was just looking, Pa. That's all."

"Looking, hell, you was seen! A man like that, a drifter, you don't want to go putting ideas in his head by showing yourself."

"What kind of ideas?" asked Harry.

"Never you mind about that!" his mother said.

Color came into Karen's face. "You can't keep on hiding me away anytime a man comes by!"

"The hell I can't," Ingram said, chuckling.

"Anyhow, he didn't look like no outlaw."

"Not too many honest men ride alone in this country, girl. And he wasn't even riding!"

"Ma said he didn't look like a bad 'un."

"That's the most dangerous kind, 'cause they sneak up on you when you're not looking. And nobody sneaks up on Jim Ingram."

"You sure sneaked up on him, Pa, when you sold him the roan," Jase said.

"Your pa's an old horse trader from way back, son, but I never thought I'd unload that sorry nag for anything more than the cost of sending him to the glue factory!"

"How much did you get, Jim?" Matilda said.

"I got plenty, woman, so never you mind about that! We can celebrate tonight over some of that good pecan pie you've been baking," Ingram said.

"Land's sakes, I forgot all about it," Matilda said, hurrying into the house.

Harry said, "Gee, Pa, where's Sunny?"

"Da—er, derned if I know," Ingram said. "That mangy mutt's chasing after the cowboy. Probably chase him all the way to Redrock."

"Oh, no!" Karen said. "What if he gets lost? Or the cowboy shoots him?"

"That'll teach you not to trust strangers, then," Ingram said. But when he saw his youngsters' unhappy faces, he quickly added, "Sunny'll come back as soon as he gets hungry. Don't you worry about him. That dog's harder to get rid of than a poor relation."

Karen and Harry went to call the dog. "Don't go too far from the house," Ingram said.

Slocum and the dog were in the middle distance, where blue-gray shadows billowed across the fields. The dog circled Slocum's horse, careful to keep its distance, its frantic yips sounding faintly across the valley. If it heard its young masters' calls, it ignored them.

Jase went to the corral to tend the horses. Matilda set a hot fresh-baked pie out on the sill to cool. Karen and Harry shouted vainly for the dog to return. James Ingram savored the feeling of money in his pocket. "Not a bad day's work," he said.

Suddenly, the insects fell silent. Their humming and buzzing and clicking stopped all at once, without warning.

A tremendous blow came out of nowhere, smashing into Ingram with sledgehammer force, slamming him to the ground. He lay sprawled facedown in the dirt, alive, but unable to move or speak.

He'd been shot. More shots followed.

Montana Cates was a buffalo hunter who looked more like a buffalo than a hunter. He was a huge, shaggy man-mountain almost seven feet tall. He once strangled two men to death at the same time, one in each hand. He was a dead shot with a rifle. A buffalo hunter who'd run out of buffalo.

Somehow the fancy-eating set back east had cultivated a taste for buffalo tongue. That was the killing stroke that had finished off the fast-shrinking herds of bison that had roamed the plains in the hundreds of thousands within recent memory. Montana had been part of a shooting crew that made plenty of good money for a too-short while by slaughtering buffalo for their tongues. On some good days, he killed a couple hundred buffalo between sunup and sundown. All they took were the tongues. They left the meat and the hides to rot where they fell on the prairie. Next winter, the Plains Indians tribes, like the Sioux, the Cree, the Cheyennes, and all the others who depended on the buffalo herds for their food, would starve. As far as most of the white settlers were concerned, that was all to the good.

Montana Cates and his cohorts had done their work too well. With the buffalo gone, they were out of a job. The fad for buffalo tongue had died out back east, along with the species.

Montana was killing people now. He'd done it before, lots of times, for free, mostly, but this time he was getting paid big money for doing what comes naturally. It was easy, too. "A whole lot easier than shooting buffalo," he said to himself, "and they's just about the dumbest critters going."

He lay prone on top of a knoll a good distance behind the back of the Ingram ranch house, shooting his Winchester. He didn't need a scope. He just allowed for windage and elevation and took his shots as he found them, each one scoring. His part of the job was over and done with in less than half a minute. The rest was all gravy.

He wasn't alone. There were three others in his band. They had been hidden in a wash a couple of hundred yards away. They had put their spurs to their mounts as soon as Montana fired his first shot. They galloped up out of the wash and charged the ranch, not shooting. They didn't have to. Montana had done the shooting for them, and he never missed.

Montana picked himself up and jogged down the back of the knoll to where he'd hidden his horse. The animal was as outsized as its master, a huge quarter-horse that would have looked at home drawing a freight wagon. Its sides swelled and it staggered a few steps when Montana slung his freight into the saddle. He rode out from behind the knoll and charged the ranch house, too, not wanting to miss the fun.

The other three were already there. They reined to a halt in the yard, kicking up dust. Pete Keane was the leader of the band; the other two were Vin Stoddard and Wrecker Lutz.

Young Jase Ingram lay on his back near the corral with a hole in his middle that had been put there by Montana Cates. He was dead. His mother crouched in the dirt beside him, shaking him, screaming for him to wake up.

James Ingram crawled on his belly in the middle of the yard, trying to reach the shotgun that lay ten feet away. It might as well have been ten miles. Montana's long-range sniping hadn't killed him, but it had busted him up pretty bad inside. He wriggled around like a bug that's been squashed in the middle but whose legs are still moving.

Karen and Harry stood frozen at the edge of the yard.

Pete Keane was a Texas gun, from Waco. He had carroty hair and a rust-colored beard. He had a boyish face, but his shrewd eyes were deep-lined and his middle was thickening. He could outride and outshoot men half his age, though.

Vin Stoddard, Arizonan, was long, lean, and leathery. Desert sun had bleached all the emotion and most of the personality out of him. His hat was decorated with a snakeskin headband. The rest of him was gray.

Eric "Wrecker" Lutz looked as if he belonged on an iron horse, instead of a horse of the four-legged variety. He rode that way, too. He wore a railroader's cap and lace-up work boots instead of a Stetson and cowboy boots. Back in Cincinnati, Ohio, he'd helped derail a train as part of a robbery, causing the deaths of its crew and thirty-seven passengers.

Montana Cates rode up, completing the foursome.

Ingram kept crawling toward the shotgun with single-minded intentness. Breath hissed through his clenched teeth as he moved at a snail's pace, but at least the shotgun was no longer ten feet away. Now, it was nine-and-three-quarters feet away.

The outlaws watched his efforts for a moment. "That old boy's a diehard for sure," Stoddard said.

"Finish him," Pete Keane said. He sounded bored.

"Let's see how close he gets before he kicks the bucket."

"No time, Vin. We're in a hurry," Pete Keane said. He drew his gun and fired one shot, drilling Ingram through the back of the skull. Ingram flattened as if he'd been poleaxed, kicked, and died.

Matilda Ingram fainted.

Lutz's horse chose that moment to have some fun with its unsteady rider. It danced sideways, fighting the reins.

"Damn, Lutz, can't you control that animal?" Pete Keane said.

"I'm trying to!" Lutz bawled, as his horse rose up on its hind legs. He let go of the reins and threw his arms around the horse's neck, holding on tight to keep from falling off.

"That's one sorry sight," Stoddard said, wincing.

Lutz was half-on, half-off the saddle. He lost his grip and fell off his horse.

Twelve-year-old Harry, taking advantage of the distraction, raced to the shotgun and picked it up.

"Uh-oh," Stoddard said. His gun was already in his hand, but Lutz's horse moved between him and the kid, blocking his shot.

Harry braced the shotgun butt hard against his shoulder, just as he'd been taught, swung the barrels up, and squeezed the trigger.

Fired at point-blank range, the blast just about cut Stoddard in two. There was a scream, but it came from Lutz, cowering on the ground, not Stoddard. Stoddard was dead and blown out of the saddle, but his boot was caught fast in the stirrup and he hung head-down from it. His horse, stung by buckshot, put its head down and ran, dragging Stoddard's body. Lutz's horse ran, too.

The horses in the corral went wild with terror. They kicked down the rails of a section of fence and broke out of the corral.

Pete Keane and Montana fought their mounts under control. Harry Ingram was swinging the shotgun toward them, but Pete Keane fired first, putting a big slug in the small boy.

"Do I got to do everything around here?" he said.

Karen Ingram broke free from her spell of nightmarish paralysis. She fled toward the darkness blanketing the fields.

Lutz ran after her. "I'll get her!" he shouted back, over his shoulder. Now that he knew that he hadn't been hit, he was ashamed of his shriek of fear when the shotgun went off.

"Get the horses, Montana," Pete Keane said.

"Right. Don't go divvying up the spoils until I get back."

"Spoils?" Pete Keane laughed. "If you can find anything worth stealing in this shithole, you're welcome to it."

"I'll hold you to that, Pete."

Shrieks came out of the darkness, female shrieks. "Sounds like Lutz's getting his," Montana said.

"Get the horses. I'll take care of Lutz."

"Sure, Pete. Just save some for me. That's a little bitty gal and I misdoubt me that there's enough of her for all three of us," Montana said.

"There ain't even enough girl there for just you, Montana. She wouldn't be much good for anything else after you got through with her."

"That's no lie."

Moans came from Matilda Ingram as she started to come around from her fainting spell. She was befuddled, not in her right mind, which was a blessing. After a struggle, she managed to sit up.

Montana said, "What about her?"

"Too old," Pete Keane said.

Montana held the Winchester as easily as an average-sized man wields a walking stick. Holding it with one hand, he leveled it on Matilda Ingram and shot her through the chest. She fell back dead, stretched out beside her son, Jase.

"I should've known that things were going too smoothly for it to last," Pete Keane said.

He and his band had spent the better part of the day getting into position for the raid on Ingram's ranch. Their local contact man in Redrock had tipped them off about the girl, Karen. They were after females in general and pretty girls in particular, both of which were in damned short supply in this godforsaken piece of Texas. There'd be a whole lot less of them in these parts a few days from now.

The outlaws came out of the jagged rocks and ravines of the Santiago Breaks, which marked the western boundary of Ingram's spread. They came out of the hills and sneaked up as close as they could, taking their time, careful not to spook the cattle and thus alert Ingram that he was being stalked. An unexpected stroke of luck showed itself when the stranger appeared, walking out of nowhere. And it was unexpected. Watching from his hiding place, spying on the ranch, Pete Keane was so surprised by the newcomer's arrival that he could've been knocked over with a feather. Not by his presence, although that hadn't been planned for, but by the fact that he was walking.

Pete Keane had equipped himself with a pair of field glasses, but even with the help of their high-powered magnification, he couldn't make out the stranger's face. That was too bad, because there was something tantalizingly familiar about the tall man with the saddle slung over his shoulder. He was sure he knew him from somewhere, but he just couldn't place him. Maybe he was one of the gang of raiders. Pete Keane's bunch was just one of a number of similar bands that made up the gang. Perhaps he'd seen the stranger back at the hideout in Yellowsnake Canyon, back in the Breaks. He could've lost his horse and gotten separated from one of the other bands that even now were harrowing the countryside on this side of the Sawtooth Mountains.

Whoever he was, the stranger was a godsend for the outlaws, since they were able to sneak up close to the ranch while its occupants were distracted by the lone intruder. Even the dog's attention was focused on the stranger in the yard. Having the family clustered out in the open was a big help, too. Some of these ranch houses were built thick-walled and strong to resist raiding bandits, rustlers, and Indians. The defenses were tough to overcome when the family managed to barricade themselves inside. Then the only way to beat them was to burn them out, no easy task if the defenders kept up a steady stream of gunfire. That's why Pete Keane had Montana along, to use as a sniper to pick off the men before they got inside. Pete Keane was a pretty fair hand with a rifle himself, but the ex–buffalo hunter was a dead shot.

Pete was relieved when the stranger saddled up a horse from the corral and rode out, since it proved that he was what he appeared to be, a man looking to buy a mount, rather than the inscrutable agent of some unknown counterconspiracy.

The opening moves of the raid had gone off without a hitch, like clockwork. Montana was in position on the knoll, overlooking the ranch with a clear field of fire. Pete Keane, Stoddard, and Lutz were hidden at the bottom of a dusty draw. After the stranger rode east, with the dog chasing him, Pete Keane gave the signal to proceed by holding the binoculars so that the last rays of the setting sun bounced off the lenses. When Montana saw the glinting flashes, he opened fire, shooting down first Ingram and then Jase. He hadn't bothered to waste a bullet on Harry, deeming him too young to be any kind of a threat.

After that, though, things went sour. Who'd've expected a freckle-faced kid to cut loose with the shotgun, blowing Vin Stoddard's belly out his back? Not Stoddard, that's for sure. Too bad it hadn't been Lutz. Stoddard was a quiet, dependable gun, while Lutz was a blowhard who could barely ride a horse. In fact, if it hadn't been for Lutz's poor horsemanship, Stoddard might still be alive. On the other hand, though, there were a lot of good guns in the gang, but Lutz was the only one of them who knew anything about steam engines. That might come in handy later on. Besides, one less gun meant a bigger payday for everybody else.

Pete Keane decided he'd better go ride herd on Lutz and keep him out of further trouble. Ma Jones wanted Lutz alive.

He nodded grimly as his horse stepped past Harry Ingram's small, slumped form. Game kid. Smart, too. He'd used only one barrel of the shotgun on Stoddard, saving the other for another of the outlaws. He'd have tagged Montana or Pete Keane for sure if Pete Keane hadn't shot him first.

"You died game, kid," Pete Keane said. There were worse ways to go. He'd have died in any case, because he was young enough to testify in court, and the outlaws weren't leaving any witnesses alive.

Two forms were rolling around in the grass not far from the house: Lutz and the girl. Lutz was laughing; she was screaming and crying. She managed to break away from him and get her feet under her, but before she could run he grabbed her ankle and pulled her back down on the ground.

Lutz slithered on top of her. She tried to fight, but her small fists didn't make any headway and he brushed aside her efforts. He pinned her down, crushing the breath out of her. He held her with one hand and squeezed and rubbed her with the other. He grabbed a fistful of the top of her dress and tore it open.

He went wild when he caught a glimpse of her bare flesh, all pink and white. He ripped the top of her garment to shreds, the dress and the thin white cotton wrapper beneath, stripping her naked above the waist.

She clawed at his face. He grabbed her hands and held both her wrists in one hand, pinning them down behind her head. He rubbed his whiskery face against her bare breasts, slobbering, licking them. His free hand reached between her legs, grabbing her, pulling her dress up.

Lutz was so involved in what he was doing that he didn't take notice of Pete Keane riding up and halting nearby. Pete Keane climbed down from the saddle and walked over to Lutz. He drew his gun and laid its long barrel across the side of Lutz's head, hard.

There was a loud clonking sound. Lutz saw stars. He was still seeing double as he clawed for his own gun. He froze when an icy gun muzzle pressed hard against the underside of his chin.

"Don't even think of reaching for your gun," Pete Keane said, not angrily, but in a conversational tone of voice. "Orders are, don't sample the goods," he said. "Savvy?"

"Yeah—yeah, Pete, sure," Lutz said thickly. "I wasn't doing nothing, I was just having some fun with her, that's all."

"Well, don't. Get your ass back to the house and give Montana a hand with the horses."

"Sure, Pete, anything you say. I'm getting." Lutz rose shakily and started staggering toward the house, holding his head.

Pete Keane couldn't resist having a little joke. He called after him, "Lutz!"

Lutz stopped in his tracks, fearful of a bullet. "Y-Yeah, Pete?"

"Consider yourself lucky. As bad as you are with horses, this little filly would've throwed you, too, I reckon," Pete Keane said.

Lutz made his way to the house, not laughing. Pete Keane wasn't laughing either, when he turned to face Karen, who lay flat on her back where Lutz had left her, too terrified to even sob.

"You want to live, girl?" he said. "Well? Answer me when I ask you a question, girl. You want to live?"

"Yes," she said.

"Good. Do like I tell you and you'll come out of this alive. Cross me just once and you'll join the rest of your family, I promise you that. Savvy?"

"Yes."

Pete Keane holstered his gun. "Smart girl. Stay smart, and you'll stay alive."

When Montana returned, he found Pete Keane sitting on a horse, riding double with Karen Ingram sitting in front of him. She was covered up with an old shirt he'd found in the house and made her put on over her torn dress, not out of kindness, but because it was just too damned distracting to have all that smooth bare skin showing. There was no sense in putting temptation before Lutz and especially Montana, either.

He hadn't even bothered tying the girl's hands. She was tame, numbed by shock. She stared off into the distance, where she didn't have to see the corpses of her family.

Montana rode up with one horse in tow. "I see you got your hands full, Pete. Hey, there, missy," he said, leering at Karen. She didn't so much as look at him, she just kept staring somewhere off into space.

"Standoffish, ain't she?" Montana said. "I reckon she'll get cured of that directly."

"She don't even know you're here," Pete Keane said.

"I can fix that, and I wouldn't mind not even a little bit."

"Monroe Jones would. So would Ma and the rest of the clan. Ma says, you can't sell damaged goods."

Even Montana, formidable though he was, shied away from tangling with the Joneses, especially the terrible Monroe. "Well, she's a pretty little thing. I reckon those Mexes'll pay a high price for the likes of her," Montana said.

"I reckon so," Pete Keane agreed. "You only caught the one horse?"

"Yup. Stoddard's horse is so spooked, it won't stop running till it reaches the Rio Grande."

"We don't need it. We got enough horses now."

"What about Stoddard?" Montana asked.

"What about him?"

"His foot must've worked loose from the stirrup. I found him about a bowshot away from the house."

"Dead?"

"Deader'n hell, Pete."

"Then he won't be telling no tales. We got nothing to worry about."

Montana swung down from the saddle. His horse seemed to grow a few inches taller after the buffalo hunter dismounted. He stuck his boot under James Ingram's body and flipped it over on its back, then hunkered down beside it and rummaged through the dead man's pockets. "Haw!" he exclaimed when he found the money that Slocum had paid the rancher for the horse. He pocketed it and then crossed to where Matilda Ingram lay.

A gold locket on a chain hung around her neck. He tore it off with such violence that he left marks on her flesh.

"Montana, you'd steal the gold teeth out of your mammy's head," Pete Keane said.

"Momma didn't have no gold teeth. She didn't hardly have no teeth at all, and them she had was rotten."

He tugged at the dead woman's gold wedding band, but it was on so tight that it couldn't come off. He reached for his knife. Pete Keane turned his horse so the girl couldn't see what was coming next. Shock had left her manageable, and he didn't want her jarred into a screaming fit by the sight of fresh horrors.

Montana's skinning knife would have looked like a short sword in normal-sized hands, but in his hands it looked like a dinner knife. He cut off the woman's ring finger, pulled off the ring, pocketed it, threw away the finger, and wiped the blade clean on his pants leg.

"T'ain't much, but every little bit helps," he said, grinning. "Say, where's Lutz?"

"Setting fire to the house," Pete Keane said.

"What?" Montana hurried across the yard, reaching the front door of the house just as Lutz emerged from it, trailed by thin scrolls and streamers of smoke. Lutz's eyes were tearing and he coughed.

More smoke drifted outside. Red and yellow light, firelight, flickered within, brightening steadily as the blaze grew.

"Hell, Pete, what'd you go and do that for?" Montana said. "I wanted to search the place before you put it to the torch!"

"Forget it. We got the only thing worth getting on this spread—the girl."

"Hell, these honkers always got a few dollars salted away somewhere, and I mean to find 'em!"

"We're leaving now," Pete Keane said.

Pausing at the threshold, Montana said over his shoulder, "You go ahead, I'll catch up with you later."

"We're leaving now, all of us. That means you, too, Montana."

Montana turned, facing him. Outlined by the lurid red glow pouring out the open doorway, he looked like some primordial man-beast from the dawn of time.

He said, "When I hired on to this outfit, they told me it was pay plus found. I'm fixing to get me some of that found. Any objections?"

He was ready, willing, and able to push it all the way. Pete Keane wasn't ready to push it to a showdown, especially not with Lutz waiting in the wings, hanging on every word, waiting to see which way things would jump. Lutz was a backshooter if ever he saw one.

"Suit yourself. I'm heading back to camp."

"I know the way," Montana said. "I'll catch up to you."

"Watch out you don't get burned," Pete Keane said, but Montana was already entering the smoky house.

Pete rode off, holding Karen Ingram with one arm circling her slender waist. Lutz followed, holding the saddle horn to keep from falling off. They vanished into the breaks west of the ranch.

Five had died, including one of their own, so that the outlaws could steal one fresh blond virgin. Not a bad day's work, for Pete Keane and company.

5

Slocum pointed his horse toward the trail to Redrock. The roan had a peculiar, slippery gait; not lame, but favoring one leg. He figured that if he didn't push the animal any faster than a canter, it just might make it all the way to town. Maybe. If he dismounted and walked the horse through the steeper parts of Notch Pass in the Sawtooth Mountains.

Daylight was closing fast; the sun was almost hidden below the horizon. A hush fell over the dusky landscape, but not over the yellow dog, which was still barking as it followed Slocum east across Ingram's land. It kept its distance, staying a stone's throw away. It yapped on, seemingly inexhaustible. The noise irritated Slocum more than it did the horse. The horse was used to it.

"Get on home, you! Go on, git!" Slocum shouted. The dog ignored him, except to bark at him. "Lucky for you I like dogs or I'd shut your yapping with a bullet!"

The dog stopped barking.

"Huh! Well, I'll be damned!"

The dog stopped moving, too. The horse kept on going, plodding along. Slocum turned in his saddle, looking back at the dog. The dog now faced the ranch house. It didn't start back for home, but stood frozen in place, on point: silent, intent, quivering with alertness.

Slocum, nagged by a sense of unease, turned the horse toward the ranch, too. The house was a smudge outlined against the darkening distance.

For a moment, nothing happened. The dog stayed motionless; that was all. The horse's tail swished lazily, shooing away a fly buzzing around its hindquarters.

Slocum was ready to say the hell with it and ride on. Then he heard the shots.

They came from far off, sounding like little pop-pop-pops. Gunshots. Slocum knew gunfire when he heard it.

After the first volley, the dog took off like a bolt, tearing across the fields toward the ranch.

It was too far and too dark for Slocum to see what was happening at the ranch, but he knew what the shooting meant: trouble.

Not his trouble, though. No, sir. Whatever it was, he was out of it. Well out of it. A man shouldn't mix in other folks' troubles, not when he has more than enough troubles of his own.

Ingram's no kin of mine, he thought. I don't owe him anything but the back of my hand, for skinning me on that horse trade. Besides, he looked like he could take care of himself.

But what if he couldn't?

That's his lookout. If a man can't take care of himself, he don't belong out here.

But an ordinary rancher would be hard-pressed to handle the likes of a cutthroat like Bill Rigdon and his equally vicious sidemen. Chances were pretty good that it *was* Bill and his boys bedeviling the ranch, and not some local desperadoes. That's what Slocum was here for, wasn't it, to track down Bill? Track down Bill and his partners and kill them? Sure, he thought, but when I go up against those three, it'll be at a time and place of my choosing, with the deck stacked in my favor.

And what about the girl? Whatever happened at the ranch would happen to her, too.

Oh, hell.

He was disgusted with himself for wasting the time arguing with himself when all the time he had known how the argument was going to come out, and it wasn't on the side of good sense, either. Disgusted, because there'd never been any question of what he was going to do.

Cursing himself for a damned fool, he urged the horse forward, toward the ranch. The way his luck was running, he'd probably get shot by Ingram, the very man he was riding to help.

He couldn't ride at full gallop, for fear of the horse's giving out long before he reached his destination. He pushed the animal as hard as he dared, but that wasn't very fast.

He was a little more than halfway to his goal when the ranch house roof burst into flames.

The dog stood beside Ingram's body, panting. It whined puzzledly, then licked its master's hand. Suddenly, its spine stiffened and the hair rose at the back of its neck. Ears pinned back, fangs bared, it bellied low to the ground, snarling at the figure emerging from within the fiery, smoky chaos of the burning house.

Montana lurched out of the open doorway as part of the roof fell in. He had to duck his head to keep from knocking his hat off against the top of the tall door frame. Behind him, flaming rafters and planks crashed to the hard-packed dirt floor, sending up a cloud of embers thick as a horde of fireflies. Black smoke poured out the door, the windows, and the massive hole in the roof.

Pete Keane was right—there wasn't anything worth stealing in the house—but Montana didn't count it as a total loss. He'd found Matilda Ingram's fresh-baked pecan pie and wolfed it down, all but one last wedge, which he held in the hand that wasn't holding his rifle.

His eyes teared from the smoke. He wiped them on his sleeve. He saw the dog; then a rift opened up in the swirling smoke clouds and he saw Slocum.

Slocum stood in the yard, near the well. Montana stared stupidly at him for a minute, chewing a mouthful of pie.

"Who're you?" Montana said at last. "I don't know you."

He started swinging the rifle up, but Slocum's gun was already in his hand. Slocum got him first, right between the eyes.

Montana fell backward, making a big noise when he hit the ground.

"Now you do," Slocum said.

6

The man he'd killed was a stranger to Slocum. But the world of Western outlaws, lawmen, and the gunfighters who straddled both sides of the fence was a close-knit one. Maybe he could figure out who the dead man was.

The corpse's bulging eyes were crossed, as if staring at the raw red bullet hole between them. He was a big man, even in Texas. But he wasn't a Texan. He wore a pinch-crowned hat, the kind worn on the North Range, in mountain country. That was a buffalo skinner's knife strapped to his side. He'd helped massacre a family, killing a woman and a child. That kind of savagery was uncommon, even among the badmen of the West.

Those attributes could fit damned few men—only one, that Slocum could think of—and that was Montana Cates. Sure, it all added up. It had to be him.

He was a long way south of his usual stomping grounds in the northern high country. Why? Because today was April 16? Was Montana part of the same outfit as Bill Rigdon? All the Ingrams but one had been wiped out—all but the girl, who'd been carried away. Was that part of the April 16 deal, too?

Slocum wasn't standing still while he was thinking. He was doing. He took Montana's horse. The big man wouldn't be needing it, but Slocum would. It was a damned sight better mount than the roan. He'd have liked to switch saddles, but there wasn't enough time for that, not if he wanted to give chase while the trail was still fresh. He transferred his rifle to Montana's saddle scabbard and hung his saddle bags on the other's horse.

Firelight from the burning house showed which way the outlaws had come from and which way they had gone. They'd fled into the Santiago Breaks, of course, the same place where Bill Rigdon and his cohorts had disappeared. Were they part of the same bunch that had massacred the Ingrams? How many outlaws were in this, anyway?

Slocum was a good tracker, but it would take a superb one to follow the outlaws' trail at night. Luckily, he had an expert to rely on: the Ingrams' dog.

Some tattered scraps of fabric littered the yard. Slocum picked one up, a strip of blue-and-white checked cloth. It had been torn off the girl's dress. An ugly piece of evidence, but a useful one.

The dog was squatting on its haunches by Ingram's side, yowling. It quieted down and showed intelligent interest when Slocum held the tattered scrap of dress in front of its snout.

"I hope you're part bloodhound, boy," Slocum said. "Where's the girl? You can find her, dog, sure you can. Come on, boy! Get up and find her, take me to her. Come on, boy!"

He went on in that vein for a few minutes, relying not so much on his words as the emotion that lay behind them to get the idea across to the dog. Just when he was beginning to despair, the dog got interested. Its black nostrils crinkled as it lifted its snout and sniffed. It stood up on all fours.

"Attaboy," Slocum said. "Attaboy, now you got it!"

Holding the scrap of cloth in front of the dog's face, close to the ground, Slocum guided it to where the outlaws' horse tracks started leading away from the house.

"She's out there, boy. Where is she, boy? Take me to her. Come on, boy, you can do it!"

For an instant, his spirits lifted when he thought that he was actually getting across to the dog. But instead of getting on the trail, the dog started running around in circles.

That was too much for Slocum. "You damn fool mutt! What the hell are you good for, then?"

The dog lunged at him. Slocum stepped back quickly, but the dog wasn't actually trying for him. Its fangs snapped shut, not on his hand, but on the piece of cloth he was holding. It tore the scrap loose from his grip, clamped it tightly in its jaws, and took off running in the direction the outlaws had taken.

"Good dog! Hey, wait for me!"

The dog wasn't waiting for anybody. It streaked away from the ranch, racing west.

Slocum swung aboard Montana's gray stallion and raced after the dog. The gray wouldn't win any prizes for elegance, but it was strong, swift, and surefooted.

He rode out of the flickering zone of firelight and into the shadowland of oncoming night. Way up ahead, the dog was a pale smudge skimming the dark fields.

Slocum could only hope that the dog would lead him to the girl and not over the edge of a cliff. Day or night, he didn't fancy riding alone into the Breaks, not when there was a gang of killers hidden somewhere within its recesses. "Oh, well," he told himself, "hung for a penny, hung for a pound."

He passed the knoll on his right, the place from which Montana had done his bushwhacking. It whisked by. He pulled his hat down tight on his head to keep it from flying off. Leaning far forward in the saddle, he strained to keep the dog in sight. It would be easier to see him if the moon was up, but then it would be easier for the outlaws to see him, too.

The ground dipped, tilting downward. Slocum galloped into the sudden hollow of a dusty draw—and into trouble.

A line of mounted men loomed up all around him, in front and on the sides, too, surrounding him. They'd been hidden from his sight in the hollow, and he hadn't known they were there until he was right in their midst. It looked like there were ten of them, maybe more.

At least they weren't shooting. Even as Slocum completed the thought, a gun went off.

It was a warning shot. There were too many men for him to try shooting his way clear. He was trapped all right, but good.

So much for playing good Samaritan. When would he learn to leave well enough alone?

"Hold it right there, stranger!"

Slocum didn't recognize the voice, but the authority behind it was unmistakable. It was the voice of the Law, accustomed to obedience. The next shot wouldn't be a warning shot, either.

Slocum reined in hard, the bit cutting deep into the gray's jaws, pulling it up to a short stop that kicked up plenty of dirt. The horse took it in stride, being used to a steady diet of far more brutal treatment from Montana.

These men weren't outlaws. The outlaws would have cut him down as soon as they saw he wasn't Montana. Big though he was, there was no mistaking Slocum for that hulking giant, not even at night.

These men were on the side of the law, but that didn't mean that they couldn't kill him as dead as any outlaw could.

They were a posse, as Slocum was to learn later. They came from Redrock. Their leader was Frank Pitts, the

county sheriff, who alternated between his offices in
Redrock and Mission Church. He'd been in Redrock
earlier today, when the hue and cry was first raised.
Gene Cardenas, a veteran hand at Abe Melliker's ranch,
had ridden into town, more dead than alive. He was badly
shot up, and had lost so much blood that it was a miracle
he had hung on long enough to tell his tale. He told
it in the middle of Main Street, where he'd fallen off
his horse and couldn't get up again. A crowd gathered
around him, but he wouldn't let them move him until
he'd had his say.

A gang of killers had descended on Melliker's ranch
in a predawn raid. A savage, irresistible attack. They
slaughtered the hands in the bunkhouse and the boss's
family in the ranch house, and then they put the buildings to the torch. Gene had been sleeping off a drunk
in the hayloft of the barn; when he realized what was
happening, he threw himself on a bareback horse and
tried to escape. The outlaws had put a couple of slugs
in him, but he hung on to the horse's neck tightly and
kept going. Somehow he'd managed to elude the killers
in the confusion and make his way to town.

He told his story, and when they lifted him to try to
move him inside, he coughed up a mouthful of blood
and died.

The sheriff put together a posse, fast. With him were
his two deputies, Glen Mayfield and Charlie Bowen,
and a force of ten men, divided about equally between
townsmen and cowboys. The posse would have been
two, three times as large if Pitts had been willing to
wait long enough to gather a group of that size, but he
was eager to get on the trail while it was hot.

When the posse reached Melliker's ranch, they found
burned buildings and dead bodies. Gene Cardenas hadn't
exaggerated. What they didn't find were the bodies of
Abe's young second wife, or his two grown daughters,
or the wife's personal maid, or the cook's daughter. They

were still alive, undoubtedly, but gone—taken.

The massacre had been so fast, furious, and over-whelming, that Gene had thought a small army was responsible for the devastation. But when the posse's trackers examined the sign, they discovered that there had only been five outlaws. Their terribleness had mul-tiplied their numbers in Gene Cardenas's mind.

They had carried away their stolen women on stolen horses. That was a break for the posse. The women slowed down the outlaws' getaway. What's more, they left a trail that a child could follow. It didn't occur to anyone on the posse that the trail had been left deliber-ately, so they would follow it.

The trail led right into the Breaks, surprising no one, since those rugged badlands had long been the haunt of bandits and bushwhackers. It should have been cleaned up a long time ago; then maybe this brutal raid might never have happened. If the posse moved fast enough, they could overtake the raiders before they disappeared into the maze of canyons with their tender prey.

They rode hard—right into an ambush near the mouth of Yellowsnake Canyon. A few sharpshooters hidden in that mass of jagged splintered rock could have held off an army, and there were more than a few of them planted there and waiting for the posse to ride into the trap. The opening volley killed Deputy Charlie Bowen and two others. Only the broken ground with its abundant cover saved the posse's losses from being much greater. A handful of outlaws with rifles was able to keep them pinned down just outside the canyon throughout the long hot day.

The outlaws stopped shooting about an hour or so before sundown, when purple shadows began filling up the canyons. The posse had had enough. They were glad enough for the chance to call it quits when the deadly accurate rifle fire finally eased up. They tied up their wounds and tied their dead facedown across their saddles and rode toward the open country as if the Furies were on their heels. They didn't want to be in those badlands after dark.

They reached the safety of the open range at the dying of the light, emerging at a point not far from Ingram's ranch. They headed toward it, a welcome refuge where they would find food, water, and rest. But there was no sanctuary to be found at Ingram's place, which was already blazing like a bonfire as they neared it.

And then Slocum rode right into their midst.

The posse was formed up in a loose semicircle, surrounding Slocum. Most of its members had their guns out and pointing at him. Only the fact that he was a lone rider saved him from instant annihilation. They thought he might be one of their neighbors, running for his life from the outlaws. His chances lessened when they realized he was a stranger. Strangers weren't too popular in the Blood River basin.

Sheriff Frank Pitts stepped his horse a few lengths ahead of the rest of the line to confront Slocum. He was burly, slope-shouldered. He was dressed like a businessman, in a tan hat, dark suit, and button-down shirt, but he wore a badge and a gun. The badge was on the inside of his lapel now. He'd unpinned it during those awful early moments of the ambush in Yellowsnake Canyon, when he realized that the shiny tin star made a fine target for a bushwhacker's bullet. He'd pinned it to the inside of his jacket for safekeeping and had forgotten about it until now, when he flashed his badge at Slocum.

The sheriff said, "You're sure going somewhere in an all-fired hurry, mister."

"I'm chasing some killers. They just wiped out Ingram and his family."

The posse members bristled, not liking the news. They were in an ugly mood, itching to take it out on somebody.

"Wiped 'em out, huh?" the sheriff said, his voice flat, neutral.

"All but the girl. They took her,"

"It's them women-stealers again!" a posse man said.

"Again?" echoed Slocum. "You mean there's been more like this?"

"I'll ask the questions here," the sheriff said. "Who're you, mister?"

"The name's Slocum. John Slocum."

"Never heard of you."

"Probably an alias," somebody said.

"I know every voter in this county, and you're not one of them, Mr., uh, Slocum." The sheriff put just enough hesitation on Slocum's name to imply that it was doubtful that it was his real name.

"Where do you hail from?"

"Big Spring. Look, why don't we save the how-de-dos for later? They've got the girl but they don't have much of a head start. We might be able to catch them if we hurry."

The sheriff scratched himself. "Well, to tell you the truth, Mr. Slocum, we've already been in a hurry today. Hurrying got three good men killed, including my deputy, Charlie Bowen, as fine a peace officer as ever was. I'm the one that's got to tell his wife, but she's got the real hard job. She's got to tell their kids."

"I'm sorry about that, Sheriff. But those men are dead while the girl's still alive. She's still got a chance, if they haven't killed her already."

"They're not killing the women, friend," a voice said. "Not the pretty ones, anyhow. They've got better uses for them."

"Shut up, Wilmot," another posse member said.

"Why should I, Rex? It's true, isn't it?"

"Just keep your filthy trap shut or I'll shut it for you!"

"Since you're so full of fight, why don't you take some of it to the outlaws?" Slocum suggested.

"You shut up, too!" Rex said. "I'll bust you wide open, mister."

A large, sloppy man whose hat brim was curling up at the edges said, "Me, I've had my bellyful of chasing outlaws today. I'd just as soon chase my ass back to Redrock."

"Bah! You lost your guts back at Yellowsnake Canyon, Brock," an angry voice accused.

"I didn't see you staying behind when we pulled out, Carruthers," Brock said.

"I would have, if anybody else did."

"Please, men, please!" said an impassioned, slightly nasal voice. "We're not doing any good by tearing ourselves apart like this!"

"Save the preaching for Sunday, Cantwell," Wilmot said.

"Don't you go bad-mouthing the reverend or I'll put a fist in your eye," Rex said, starting another round.

Slocum kept his mouth shut and eyed the ones in the posse who did likewise. They were the ones to watch, the silent, guarded ones. They were the ones who mattered. There were a few of them: the sheriff, for one, and his surviving deputy, Glen Mayfield, and one or two of the others.

"I'm starting to get the drift of things," Slocum said. "You boys won't get out after those hombres tonight come hell or high water."

"Where do you come into this, Mr. Slocum?" the sheriff said.

"I was just passing through and I thought I'd lend a hand."

"Tackling those killers all by yourself? That's mighty brave of you."

"Any man'd do the same," Slocum said blandly.

"Could be that you're not afraid to ride after them because you're one of them."

"Could be, Sheriff—but I'm not."

"You'll pardon me if I don't take you at your word, Mr. Slocum, but I'm not the trusting soul I used to be. Not after today," the sheriff said. "Glen, get his guns."

Deputy Glen Mayfield had a smooth chiseled face, broad shoulders, lean hips. He sat his horse well, cutting a fine heroic figure in the saddle. Despite the day's fatigues, his back remained ramrod-straight. His badge was pinned to his chest, in the same place he had worn it throughout the long hot hours of even hotter gunfire in the canyon. Now, the untarnished badge was red-lit from the fire glow in the night sky.

His gun glowed with firelight, too, as he pointed it at Slocum. Slocum was relieved of his two sideguns, his rifle, even his knife. It was too much hardware for Mayfield to handle all at once; he had to hand some off to the sheriff.

"This fellow's loaded for bear!" Mayfield said.

"I'd say it's just about right for these parts," Slocum said. "Maybe even a little under-gunned."

Frank Pitts sniffed the barrel of one of Slocum's guns. "This one's been fired recently," he announced.

"One shot," Slocum said. "You'll find it in a dead outlaw back at the ranch."

"So you're a killer, too, and by your own admission."

"Self-defense, Sheriff. But if there's any reward money outstanding on him, I'll be glad to collect it."

"You'll be lucky to get out of this without getting your neck stretched, friend," Wilmot observed.

Slocum was inclined to agree with him, but Sheriff Frank Pitts said seriously, "That's enough of that kind of talk. This man's my prisoner and he won't be harmed while he's under my custody."

"Prisoner?" Slocum said. "What's the charge?"

"I'm arresting you on suspicion."

"Suspicion? Of what?"

"Suspicion of murder, robbery, arson, and abduction, for starters."

"You can only hang him once," Wilmot said.

"That's enough of that hanging talk. I won't have it. I'm warning you men, there won't be any lynching while I'm the sheriff of this county."

Slocum couldn't help thinking that the sheriff was doing more to stir up lynch fever by putting the idea in the posse's head while outwardly he was so vigorously opposing it.

"Amen to that, Sheriff," Reverend Cantwell said. "For all we know, this man's story could be true, as unlikely as it seems."

"It is true," Slocum said, "and I can prove it, if you'll give me the chance."

"You'll get it," Frank Pitts said.

"*Then* we'll hang you," Carruthers said. He was one of the wealthiest ranchers in the district.

The sheriff didn't contradict him.

7

Everything made of wood in the ranch house had gone up like kindling—roof beams and planks, furniture, window shutters, and the big front door. Scorch marks and soot smears blackened the gutted shell of the adobe walls. Sparks and flying embers from the blaze had touched off the shedlike barn, too, burning it to the ground, where it lay smoldering in a heap of charred poles, planks, and still-smoking ashes.

The posse dismounted to take a look around. Howie Dixon, Brock's sidekick, was the first to find Montana's corpse. "Whoo-whee," he marveled, "he sure was a big old boy!"

"Some of you men move him out into the yard, away from the house," the sheriff said.

Four men each took hold of one of Montana's limbs and dragged him away from where he had fallen. "Looky here," a flat-faced man named Mooney exclaimed, "he's been shot right between the horns!"

"This the man you claimed you killed, Mr. Slocum?" the sheriff asked.

"That's right,"

"Pretty fair piece of shooting."

Deputy Glen Mayfield was examining Slocum's guns.

"There's only been one bullet fired from this Colt; all the other rounds are chambered. And the other gun and the rifle haven't been fired, not recently, anyhow. Looks like he was telling the truth about that, at least."

"How do we know he didn't reload it before we caught him?" Carruthers said. "And even if he fired only one shot, there's no telling where that bullet went. Could've gone into an Ingram, as likely as not."

"You're in an all-fired hurry to get this man hung, Carruthers," Wilmot said.

"You'll find another one of the gang lying on the other side of this rise," Slocum said, pointing toward where Stoddard's body lay.

"I suppose you killed him, too," the sheriff said.

"Not me. He was shotgunned. One of the Ingrams must have done for him."

"I don't see him," the sheriff said, peering into the darkness.

"He's there."

"Somebody go down there and have a look-see."

"I'll go," Mooney said. "It's a darned sight better than having to see those poor pitiful Ingrams."

Mooney got on his horse and rode down the rise to search for Stoddard's body. "That Mooney—always volunteering," Brock said.

"Not you, eh, Brock?" Dixon said.

"Hell, no. I don't volunteer for nothing. That's a good way to get yourself killed."

"You should've thought of that before you had us join up with this posse, Brock."

"Howie, old buddy, if I'd knowed how this was gonna be, I'd'a kept my butt planted safely in Redrock, and that's a fact. Wish I was back there now,"

The four dead Ingrams—James Ingram, his wife Matilda, Jase, and young Harry—were laid out together side by side near the corral.

"Dirty murdering bastards!" Rex spat.

"I don't understand," Cantwell said. "Why must they murder innocent women and children?"

"Because they've got no use for them, Reverend," Wilmot said, "and dead folks tell no tales."

"It's an outrage! This is worse than the Apaches!"

"Well, no, Reverend, not quite." The speaker was Ralph Yerkes, who'd kept quiet up to now. "I saw what Victorio's bucks did to some Mex soldiers they caught on the road to Chihuahua last year. It made this look as tame as a church social, begging your pardon, Reverend."

"If you ask me, hanging's too good for whoever done this!" Carruthers opined.

"Damned straight," Rex said. His small ranch adjoined Carruthers's much larger one, so he generally towed his powerful neighbor's line.

"What're we waiting for?" Carruthers said. "We got one of the gang right here! Let's put his feet to the fire and find out what he knows before anyone else gets killed!"

"Now, Tom, you don't know for sure that the stranger's one of them," Cantwell said.

"I'm just talking sense, that's all. Who is this man?" he said, stabbing an accusing finger at Slocum. "A stranger, a drifter, a gunman by the looks of him. What're the odds on his just happening along by chance right when Ingram's getting massacred, huh?"

Frank Pitts said, "I've got a feeling that you know more than you're telling, Mr. Slocum. If you've got something else to say, now's a good time to say it."

"While you still can," Rex said.

The sheriff was right. Slocum knew a lot more than he was telling. But this was a situation where he wouldn't be doing himself much good by telling the whole truth and nothing but. If he identified Montana or mentioned Bill Rigdon, he'd only feed the posse's suspicions that he, too, was part of the gang—else, how would he know so much about them? And he couldn't be sure that some members of the posse weren't secretly in league with the gang. It wouldn't be the first time that outlaws had benefited from having an inside man or two planted in advance at the scene of the crime.

He decided that he'd be served best by giving the posse a few half-truths for now.

"All right," he said, "I'm a bounty hunter."

"That's more like it," the sheriff said. "I knew you weren't an ordinary cowboy, not with those fancy shooting irons of yours."

"Bounty killers ain't much different from the scum they hunt."

"Shut up, Rex," the sheriff said. "Keep talking, Mr. Slocum."

"I came down here because that's where the outlaws are. Figured I could flush a few of them out of the Breaks. I didn't know there'd be a whole gang of marauders here, though. About fifty, sixty miles back on the trail my horse broke a leg. Ingram's was the first ranch I came by. He sold me a horse and I was starting on my way when I heard shots."

"So he sold you a horse, did he?" Rex said with an air of triumph. "Well, mister, that's a goddam lie! I knew Ingram, and that gray stallion never belonged to him! You sure as hell didn't get it from his corral!"

"I didn't say I did. The gray belonged to the outlaw I killed," Slocum said, meaning Montana. "Ingram sold me a roan."

"Then where is it?!"

"It must've wandered off. And not far, is my guess. Judging from the condition that nag was in, it couldn't have gone too far without collapsing."

"Ingram did have a busted-down roan," Yerkes said.

"So what?" Rex said. "And here's something else: if Ingram sold him a horse, like he claims, then where's the money? Ingram didn't have a dime on him when we found him!"

"His pockets were turned inside-out, too. One of the outlaws must've stolen the money. Maybe him," Slocum said, pointing at Montana.

"Maybe you," Brock said.

"If you can find a nickel on me, you're welcome to it. Maybe the outlaw's got it on him. Why not search him?"

"Because we don't believe your story," Rex said.

"Tracks and sign don't lie. They'll prove my story is true."

"We can't check on that until daylight," the sheriff said. "That's a long way off from now."

"I'm not going anywhere."

"I'll say you're not."

Carruthers gave a great shout. All heads turned in his direction. He stood next to the gray horse, holding aloft a leather pouch. "Look what I just found!" he roared.

He hurried over to display his find. Opening the top of the pouch, he reached inside and pulled out a fist-ful of glittering baubles. They glinted goldenly in the light of banked fires.

"Look here! Loot! Stolen loot—stolen from the dead, no doubt. Jewelry, lockets, rings, necklaces—and what's this?" Carruthers plucked the object in question from the pile and held it to the light to examine it.

Suddenly, he recoiled. "My God, it's a tooth! A gold tooth—a fresh one! It must've been torn right out of some poor devil's head. Gah!"

He threw away the grisly trophy as if it had scorched his fingers. "And you know where I found it?" he went on. "Tied to the gray horse's saddle! Let's see you smooth-talk your way out of that, stranger!"

"I told you: that's not my horse. I borrowed it for the chase," Slocum said.

"Now I'll tell you something: I think you're a liar.

I think you're a liar and a woman-stealing baby-killer. What you got to say about that?"

"You're breathing in my face, mister."

"I'll do more than that." Carruthers lifted a big hard-knuckled fist.

The sight of the bloody gold tooth was one more horror heaped high atop the pile of all the other horrors they'd seen today. The posse men weren't thinking straight and in no mood to try. The circle of them closed tighter around Slocum, a wall of hard unforgiving faces and harder fists.

"What'd you do to that girl? Where'd your partners take her? Where's the hideout? Talk!" Carruthers said.

"You're barking up the wrong tree," Slocum said.

"Yeah? Maybe you'll be hanging from it!"

"This is getting out of hand, Sheriff," Mayfield said.

Frank Pitts shrugged. "Seems to me like Tom is doing pretty good so far."

"What're we wasting time for?" Rex wanted to know. "Make him talk! Beat the truth out of him!"

"Maybe he's innocent," Wilmot said.

"Who the hell asked you?" Carruthers said, pushing his face in front of Wilmot's, forcing the other to back off.

Rex sidled up near Slocum, then rushed in, grabbing him from behind. A crushing bear hug pinned Slocum's arms to his sides.

"I got him!" Rex yelled. "Give him what-for, Tom!"

"It'll be a pleasure," Carruthers said, starting forward with ominous slowness. He made a show of pulling on a pair of leather gloves, fitting his fingers into them, flexing them.

Glen Mayfield moved to intervene. "Wait a minute—"

Sheriff Pitts stopped him by putting a hand on Mayfield's chest. "No, you wait, Deputy. What's the rush?"

"He's in our custody—"

"He's in *my* custody," the sheriff corrected him. "You let me worry about it."

"You've got to stop this, Sheriff," Reverend Cantwell said.

"Don't worry, Reverend, I'll put a stop to it if it goes too far. But a good shellacking just might shake some of the truth out of that fellow."

"Come on, Tom, give it to him good!" urged Rex.

"He'll spill his guts before I'm through with him," Carruthers said.

"Don't get carried away, Tom," the sheriff said.

"He's the one they'll be carrying away!"

Carruthers came in low, in a wide stance, feet planted far apart to give him plenty of grounding when he threw his haymaker. He wound up, cocking his fist way back to deliver a roundhouse right that would have felled an ox if it had connected.

It never came near the target. While Carruthers was still winding up, Slocum kicked him between the legs, hard. Some of the onlookers winced or grunted in sympathy.

Carruthers didn't have enough breath left even to grunt. His mouth gaped wide but not a sound came out of it. He grabbed himself with both hands and dropped to his knees. He seemed to shrivel up, bowing his head so low that his hat fell off and landed bottom-up on the ground.

Rex, outraged by what he considered to be Slocum's lack of fair play, said, "Why, you dirty—"

Slocum silenced him by shoving the back of his head hard into Rex's face, butting him. There was a wet crunching sound, like a melon being thrown against a wall. Slocum could feel Rex's nose pulping against the back of his skull.

Rex's strangled outcry was a mixture of pain and rage, but he gamely hung on. Slocum head-butted him again, only harder. Rex shrieked, his arms flying open.

Slocum was loose. If he only had a gun, or even his knife—!

Some of the others rushed him. Slocum had built up a whole lot of mad and welcomed the opportunity to do something about it.

A tangle of bodies, arms, and fists hemmed him in. He lashed out with a hard right to the nearest face in reach. It landed square on the button, connecting with a satisfying thud on the point of Yerkes's chin. He fell backward, stretching his length on the ground, knocked out cold.

Fennel, Baylor, and Stewart were three cowboys who'd been sleeping off a drunk in Redrock when the hue and cry was first raised. They weren't afraid of trouble and liked a fight. They piled on Slocum, bowling him over by sheer weight of numbers. Howie Dixon jumped in, too, when he was sure they had Slocum pinned to the ground.

Brock was smarter. While everybody else was occupied with the fight, he faded back to Montana's corpse and went through his pockets. He found the money, took it, and eased his way back among the others with nobody the wiser.

The melee worked somewhat to Slocum's advantage. The ones trying to hold him down kept getting in the way of those who were trying to hit him, and vice versa.

With one eye blackened and his nose bloodied, Howie Dixon shouted, "Don't just stand there, give us some help! He fights like a wildcat—oof!"

Slocum's booted foot dug deep into Dixon's middle, doubling him up and sending him flying.

"I'll stomp him a new lung," Stewart said and proceeded to try to do just that. His boot heel hammered against unprotected flesh—but not Slocum's.

"You damned fool! That's me you're stomping, not him!" Baylor cried out.

"Sorry."

Fennel clubbed Slocum with a massive fist. Slocum saw stars.

"Get him, Fen! Whup him good!" Stewart said.

"I will, if you'll just hold him down—"

Gunfire blasted nearby, two shots, stopping the fight.

The posse men looked around to see who had fired the shots. It hadn't been the sheriff, or his deputy. They were as surprised as everybody else.

A pair of shadowy figures hovered at the edge of the yard, then stepped into view. Tough-looking characters, covered with dust from much hard riding.

One was a few paces ahead of his partner, ahead and to the side, so as to not get in the way of his line of fire. The man in the lead had dark eyes and a thick, drooping mustache. He was the one who'd fired; the gun was still in his hand, only instead of pointing into the air as it had been when he'd fired the warning shots, it was leveled in the general direction of his partner.

His partner looked to be about ten years younger than the grizzled older man, but he shared the same leathery toughness. He held the reins of both their horses, whose heads hung low to the ground in fatigue. His gun was in its holster. His attention seemed to be focused elsewhere than on the posse; he kept glancing over his shoulder, looking back the way he had come, his eyes searching the darkness, seeking—what?

The older man spoke first, addressing his remarks to the posse at large. "You boys are the luckiest pack of fools I ever did see," he said, without rancor, merely stating what he held to be a fact.

"Who in the hell are you?" Frank Pitts said, after suddenly remembering that he was supposed to be in charge.

"I'm Bowman. *Ranger* Bowman," the older man said, moving closer so they could see the five-pointed star pinned to his chest—the badge of the Texas Rangers. His partner wore a star, too.

"This here's Terry Lee," Bowman said, identifying his companion. "He's a Ranger, too. Who're you?"

"I'm Frank Pitts, the sheriff of this county."

"Is that so? Where's your badge?"

Pitts glanced down at his chest, frowned, then remembered where he'd put his badge. Moving his hand carefully—*very* carefully, since he'd heard of Bowman, as had most Texans—he flipped back his jacket, revealing the sheriff's badge fastened to the inside of his lapel.

"What're you hiding it for? Ashamed of it?"

"Of course not!" Pitts said, flustered. "Glad to know you, Ranger. I've heard a lot about you."

"I've heard of you, too, Pitts." Bowman kept a poker face, but the tone of his voice indicated that what he'd heard about Pitts was far from complimentary. "In fact, I've been fixing to go to Redrock for some time now, to see if what I heard is true. Ain't that so, Terry Lee?"

"That's so, Ben," the other ranger said.

Frank Pitts frowned but he didn't dare take offense, for fear that Bowman would call him on it. He'd rather ride back alone into Yellowsnake Canyon than try to buck Ben Bowman. Bowman looked more like a veteran trailhand, who'd spent most of his adult life working for wages, than what he really was: one of the most feared manhunters in all of Texas—in the West.

"We sure can use your help, Ranger," Glen Mayfield said, a touch of what sounded like awe at meeting the celebrated lawman coloring his voice. Frank Pitts didn't like hearing that respectful note in his deputy's voice, especially since it had never been there when Mayfield addressed him.

"A gang of outlaws has been raiding the ranches on this side of the mountains, stealing the women and killing everybody else," Mayfield said.

Slocum sat up on the ground, shaking his head to clear it. He felt his jaw. It wasn't broken, but he groaned anyway, because it was sore as hell. He still had all his teeth and they weren't even loose, as far as he could tell, so he counted himself lucky.

"Who's he?" asked Bowman.

"That man's my prisoner," Pitts said. "I was just questioning him when you came along."

"Yah. I saw how you were 'questioning' him," Bowman said.

Terry Lee spoke up. "What's that rascal supposed to have done?"

"He's suspected of murder," Pitts snapped.

"Bad hombre, huh?"

"You can see what he did for yourself," Pitts said, gesturing toward the posse men who'd come out the worse for tangling with Slocum.

Carruthers was still hunched over on his knees, holding himself, white with pain. Rex lay curled on his side, hands cupped protectively over his smashed nose, as he breathed heavily through his gasping mouth. Howie Dixon sat on the ground, hugging his middle. Baylor was rubbing his side, where Stewart had booted him by mistake. And Yerkes lay flat on his back where he'd fallen, still out cold.

"Lucky you didn't question him no harder, or he'd have ruined the rest of you, too, most likely," Ben Bowman said. "But then, you boys are fools for luck. Otherwise, the Apaches would've carved you up but good while you all were having your little go-around."

"You're mistaken there, Ranger," Sheriff Pitts said with a superior air. "It wasn't Apaches did this, it was outlaws."

"Then you can call off your posse, 'cause the outlaws ain't gonna trouble you no more."

"Why not?"

" 'Cause the Apaches'll take care of them, too. And you, too, if you ain't a damned sight more careful than you've been up to now."

"Apaches?" the sheriff echoed. "What Apaches?"

"Sombra's bunch," Ben Bowman said.

The posse reacted to his statement as if he'd just dropped a live stick of dynamite into their midst.

Sombra was more dangerous than dynamite. He was an Apache war chief, a Mescalero who'd gone out on raids with Victorio as often as he'd feuded with him. Spanish-speaking people on both sides of the border had named him "Sombra del Muerte"—"Death Shadow"—for his many killings and phantomlike elusiveness. The Anglos just called him "Sombra." By any name, he was feared as much as the dreaded Geronimo. His constant companion was his older half-brother, Many Kills, a redoubtable warrior who lacked Sombra's devilish cunning.

"Sombra! I thought he was killed in Mexico along with the rest of Victorio's bunch," the sheriff said.

"You thought wrong," Bowman said. "Sombra's too smart to make a last stand, like Victorio did. Him and Many Kills and a couple of the others slipped off the night before the final battle. They must've been hiding out in the mountains of Coahuila since then. We got word that they came out of the hills sometime last week. They raided a couple of pueblos, wiped out a gang of smugglers camped out on the river, and crossed the river into Texas at September Crossing."

September Crossing was a shallow fording place across the Rio Grande, located about midway between Dos Rios, at the head of the Blood, and the mouth of Maravillas Canyon. It was a favorite ford of Comanche war parties during their yearly raids into Mexico during the month of September. It was well known to the Apaches, too.

Deputy Mayfield gave a bit of a start. "September Crossing, did you say?"

"Yah," Ben Bowman said, eyeing him. "That mean something to you, Deputy?"

"I'll say it does! It means that Sombra could be anywhere in this county right at this very moment!"

"You're getting the idea."

The other posse men got the idea, too. They were glancing over their shoulders, peering into the dark, trying to see everywhere at once. More than a few hands tightened around gun butts.

"I thought the danger was over when we pulled out of Yellowsnake Canyon," Wilmot said, "but instead we went from the frying pan into the fire!"

"Are you sure it's 'Paches? Couldn't it be more of the outlaws?"

"I don't know nothing about no outlaws, but it wasn't them who burned out the Overland stage station northeast of here and massacred everybody in it," Bowman said.

Fennel stopped wiping a trickle of blood from the corner of a split lip to say, "You don't mean old Dusty Tate's station?"

"He a friend of yours?"

"He was the first man to hire me on for a job when I came into this country ten years ago!"

"Sorry," Bowman said. "Dusty was a good old boy; I liked him, too."

"How—How'd he get it, Ranger?"

"You don't want to know that."

"But how do you know Sombra did it?" Frank Pitts asked.

"He was seen. A couple of sheep herders were up in the hills when Sombra hit the station. They saw the whole thing. The Apaches didn't see them, naturally, or they'd've been killed, too. They're even luckier than you boys," Bowman said.

"Then you're not chasing the outlaws? You're chasing Sombra?"

"Not hardly," Ben Bowman said, chuckling. It sounded like a cough. "We've been doing our damnedest to keep from getting chased by him. He's got close to twenty braves in that war party of his."

"Twenty?"

"Good Lord!" Cantwell gasped.

"We could use His help," Bowman said, "and it wouldn't hurt if you was to post some guards around here. 'Course, that's just a suggestion, since this ain't my show. But we seen the fire from a long way off, and anybody else could, too."

"We snuck up on you, and we ain't even Apaches," Terry Lee added.

"Say, where's Mooney?" asked Wilmot.

Sheriff Pitts and his deputy did what they could to shape up the posse into an effective fighting force. It wasn't easy. Slocum had messed up more than a few of them. A bucket of well water splashed in Yerkes's face finally succeeded in bringing him around to consciousness. Rex held a wet bandana under his smashed nose to catch the blood still trickling from it. He breathed through his mouth, cursing.

Brock hooked his meaty hands under tiny Howie Dixon's arms and hauled him to his feet. "That'll teach you not to volunteer," he said.

Carruthers was a big man, so it took two men to help him up. He stood shakily, hunched almost double, sobbing for breath. Abruptly he shook off the helping hands and clawed for his gun. "Let me at him," he wheezed, "I'll shoot his heart out!"

"Save your bullets for the Apaches, mister," Ben Bowman said. "Save one for yourself, too, if they hit us in force."

"Like hell! No man kicks me and lives!"

"I'd've hit you but your pal was holding my arms," Slocum said.

Bowman stepped in front of Slocum even as Carruthers's gun was clearing its holster. Bowman's hands dangled empty at his sides.

"Get out of the way," Carruthers said.

"Mister, I ain't funning with you."

People moved away from Carruthers fast. "Easy, Tom, that's *Ben Bowman*, for God's sake!" Frank Pitts said.

The name sank in. Carruthers's eyes came into focus, and he blinked a few times, as if awakening. His face showed comprehension first, then fear. "Christ!" he whispered huskily. "Don't shoot, Ranger! I'm putting the gun away. Don't shoot."

He eased down the hammer, holstered his gun, and moved his hand far away from it. "Sorry, Ranger. I wasn't thinking. Lost my head for a minute there."

"You'll lose your scalp if you ain't careful, and that goes for the rest of you, too. There's no second chances with Apaches, and no first ones with Sombra."

Bowman turned his restless gaze elsewhere. Carruthers took his cue, and slunk off to one side, trailed by Rex and the cowboy trio of Fennel, Stewart, and Baylor. Baylor wasn't too spry himself, on account of having had his ribs tenderized by Dixon's boot during the earlier free-for-all.

"Did you see that?" Dixon said in a loud whisper.

"Ain't many men who could buffalo Tom Carruthers like that," Brock said. "Seeing him crawl almost makes this whole trip worthwhile."

Brock and Dixon hadn't seen what Slocum had: throughout the confrontation between the big rancher and the ranger, Bowman's partner Terry Lee had been standing behind Carruthers with his gun drawn, covering him from the start. It had been a nice piece of teamwork, thought Slocum.

"Thanks," Slocum said.

"I didn't do it for you, I did it to stop him from becoming a murderer," Bowman said. "Murder's against the law."

"Thanks anyway. Maybe someday I can return the favor."

"I hope not."

Sheriff Frank Pitts came up, a rifle in his hands. "Mooney's gone," he said. "His horse, too. Not a sign of either of them!"

"What in the hell was he doing, going off by himself like that?" Bowman asked.

"Looking for a dead outlaw. *He* said there was one down there," Frank Pitts said, pointing at Slocum.

"Is there?"

"I don't know. I'm not going out there to find out, and have the Apaches get me, too!"

"You're learning, Sheriff," Bowman said.

"You—you reckon they'll hit us tonight?"

"It all depends. Apaches don't like to fight at night. That doesn't mean they won't if they have to, but they'd just as soon not, given their druthers. A lot of it depends on Sombra. If it's him, and he's got his whole war party with him, chances are they'll hit us at dawn. Generally, though, that's not how he works. He likes to split his force into a couple of smaller bands to throw off pursuit. Each band raids for a few days, striking all over to muddy their trails. Then they come together at a meeting place, ride a hundred miles or so, and start it all over again."

"What do you suppose they'll do? To us, I mean."

"We'll find out tomorrow, one way or the other," Bowman said. He turned away, ending the conversation.

8

It was a long night. The posse men camped in a circle, facing out, taking advantage of the cover provided by the ranch house's still upright adobe walls. The horses were picketed right beside them, still saddled in case they were needed for a quick getaway. They and the camp were well guarded. Sentries were posted, each of them standing two hours' watch. Few of the posse slept that night.

The moon rose, flooding the mountain valley with silver light. "I don't see nothing out there," Fennel said, while standing watch.

"There could be a hundred Apaches on the plain," Terry Lee said, "and you wouldn't see a one of them until they wanted to show themselves."

Fennel continued to stare at the nightscape until his eyes seemed ready to pop from their sockets.

"What do you suppose they done to Mooney?" the cowboy asked.

"If Sombra got him, the kindest thing they could've done to him is kill him," the young ranger said.

"Hell! Don't talk like that. You give me the shivers!"

Terry Lee shrugged, but Fennel didn't see it.

When the moon was directly overhead, shining its light down squarely into the campsite, Ben Bowman went down on one knee beside Montana, studying his face. Bowman was too trail-wise to risk lighting a match or a fire and making himself a target for snipers.

Slocum went over to him, making a fair amount of noise so Bowman wouldn't think he was trying to sneak up on him. He hunkered down on the opposite side of the corpse, facing Bowman.

"Know him?" Slocum asked, low-voiced.

"No. Do you?" Shadows from his hat brim hid his face; his voice was equally unreadable.

"I can make a pretty good guess."

"So?"

"Montana Cates."

"Hmm," Bowman said. After a moment of silence, he said, "Could be. Friend of yours?"

"He didn't think so when I killed him."

"Wouldn't be the first time thieves fell out."

Slocum rocked back on his heels to take some of the strain off his tensed thighs. "I've got something to tell you, Ranger."

"This a confession?"

"Not that kind."

"Have your say."

"To start with, I'm not here by accident."

"Now, why don't that surprise me?"

"Up until a few days ago, I was up in Big Spring, working for the railroad. I was a kind of troubleshooter."

"When you find trouble, you shoot it, huh?"

"Yes."

"Mister, I tagged you for a gunman the first time I laid eyes on you."

"I was working for Sam Ely, the foreman in charge of getting the line built."

"I know him. Good man."

"Check with him, and he'll tell you my story is true."

"I ain't heard your story yet."

"You know the kind that hangs around the railroad camps: grifters, tinhorns, backshooters. A gang of them followed the railhead cheating, robbing, and killing the workers. Sam hired me to clean up on them, and he wasn't too particular about how I got the job done. The worst of the bunch was a fellow named Bill Rigdon."

"I know him, too. So Billy Boy's back in Texas, eh?"

"Closer than you think, but I'll get to that. A few days ago, I got a tip that Bill and his gang were going to hold up the railroad payroll. It made sense. He hadn't been hanging around Big Spring for a month just to gun down railroad men for the few dollars in their pockets, although he did plenty of that, too, while he was waiting. The railroad was paying a bonus for finishing the section of track ahead of time, so this was going to be the biggest payroll yet.

"I was ready for him. I had as neat a trap planned for him and his pals as you ever did see, but I never got a chance to spring it. They cleared out before payday without so much as trying for the cash."

Intrigued despite himself, Bowman decided to play along. "That's easy to figure," he said. "They knew you was waiting and decided not to ride into an ambush."

"I made sure they wouldn't find out. I was the only one who knew about the trap."

"What about the others in it with you?"

"There weren't any," Slocum said. "I planned on going it alone. So you see, they couldn't have been warned off. I was the only one who knew."

"Interesting—if true."

"It bothered me. Bill'd put in a lot of time, waiting and working toward the big holdup, yet on the night before payday, he and his partners suddenly cleared out of Big Spring without so much as a by your leave. Why? What was so important that he walked away from the payroll job right on the eve of it, after spending all that time and effort setting it up?"

"You're telling it."

"I wanted to find out, so I did some digging. I thought it was a trick, at first. I was expecting him to double back and hit hard from some unexpected direction. But he didn't. He was gone, plumb gone, and I wanted to know why. A whore that Bill had been keeping pretty steady company with gave me part of the answer.

"She said that on the day before the robbery, a man came looking for Bill. She didn't know him from Adam, but Bill did, and he seemed mighty glad to see him. They were thick as thieves, talking and drinking for hours. They were careful not to talk in front of her, but she'd seen enough outlaws planning jobs to know that's what they were doing. One thing she did manage to overhear, though: the words 'April sixteenth.' "

"April sixteen," Bowman said. "That's today."

"Yesterday. It's after midnight."

"True."

"April sixteenth, that's what she heard. And that's all she heard, because she was eavesdropping and if Bill had caught her he'd have put a bullet in her. After passing the word, the stranger rode out. Bill rounded up his two boys and they all cleared out within the hour.

"It was obvious that something big was planned for April 16," Slocum continued. "Big enough to make the planned payroll job look like peanuts. What could it be?"

"What?"

"I decided to find out. The trail was hot and I jumped on it fast. That's when I got a lucky break, right at the start of my search. Before they left Big Spring, the boys stopped in at the general store to lay in some provisions for the trip. They stocked up on food and ammo—plenty of ammo. The storekeep wasn't liable to forget those three in a hurry. He was scared to death that they were going to hold him up, but they paid him off in good cash money. That surprised me, too. Bill hates to part with a dollar, and Choey Bravo, who rides with him, would just as soon steal as breathe."

"Bravo," Bowman said. "He any kin to them Bravos that run Mextown in Laredo?"

"The same."

"Bad bunch."

"He's worse," Slocum said. "And Whiteface Ames rounds out the trio."

Bowman made a dry coughing sound that Slocum realized was laughter. "So ol' Whiteface finally graduated from stealing cows and hoorahing Kansas towns, did he?" Bowman said, almost fondly. "I arrested him back when he was mavericking his first steers."

"He's a wicked gun. He planted four men in Boot Hill the month he was in Big Spring. Killed each one in a fair fight."

"He always could shoot. But Billy Boy's a regular wizard with the plow handles."

"He's fast. As for Choey Bravo, now, well, he's not much with a gun. Knives are his specialty. Throwing *and* cutting."

"I'll keep that in mind."

"If those three killers didn't rob the general store and kill the owner, they must've had a pretty good reason for not doing it. Hell, they were leaving town anyway, without the loot from the big payroll job, so why not leave with a little something jingling in their pockets? Because they didn't want the law on their trail, not with April 16 coming up.

"Don't forget, they didn't know I was dogging them. If they had, they'd've killed the storekeep for sure and damn the consequences. They should have, because he'd heard something important. He'd heard Choey and Ames arguing over what was the best way to Blood River.

"April 16, and Blood River. That's all I had to go on, but it was enough. Or at least it was, until my horse busted a leg. Things haven't been going so well for me since."

Slocum quickly sketched out a brief history of his misadventures since the accident. Ranger Bowman was silent for a time, mulling it over. Finally he said, "That's a mighty big whopper. You expect me to swallow all that?"

"Yes."

Bowman was silent then for an even longer stretch of time. "How come you didn't tell this to Pitts?"

"Because he's a horse's ass."

"No argument there."

"He and the others didn't want to hear anything I had to say."

"I noticed that."

"Lucky for me you happened along when you did."

"For you, sure. But is it lucky for me?"

"What I can't figure is the Apaches horning in. It's stretching it mighty far to believe that Sombra just happened to raid these parts at the same time that a gang of outlaws goes on the rampage. If I didn't know better, I'd think that they were in it together."

"Forget it," Bowman said. "Apaches don't side with outlaws, because they hate all whites, and Sombra's an Apache's Apache, one of the last of the wild ones. Hell, he don't even get along with his own kind. He's been on the wrong side of every tribal feud in the last twenty years. His band's mostly renegades and outcasts. He wouldn't team up with a white man for any longer than it'd take to cut his throat—which is what he'll do to your outlaws if and when he finds them."

"That's one way to get rid of them," Slocum said, "but it's awful hard on the captives that way."

" . . . Yah."

"Still, it's got to be more than coincidence, outlaws and Apaches hitting Blood River at the same time."

"Maybe so, maybe so. I'm not saying I believe your story, but I don't disbelieve it, either."

"I can prove it."

"If we live that long."

"Well, yes, there's that."

"I'll tell you something, Slocum. There's outlaws on one side, and Apaches on the other side, and this piss-poor excuse for a posse in the middle, but as far as I can see it, you're the joker in this deck."

"Maybe so."

"I ain't quite sure how to play you in this deal, not yet."

"Play me to win and bet your shirt on it," Slocum said.

9

The posse had a good night. They didn't lose anybody.

Ben Bowman and Terry Lee made plans in the predawn light. They were off by themselves where no one else could hear them, but it could plainly be seen that they talked much and in earnest. "Now what do you suppose that's all about?" wondered Deputy Glen Mayfield.

"Damned if I know. Probably something too important for us mere mortals," said Sheriff Frank Pitts. He was careful to say it softly so the rangers couldn't hear him.

A pale moon still hung in the sky when the sun made its welcome appearance. The posse men threw off their blankets, rose, stretched. They were careful to avoid stretching too high for fear of presenting too tall a target to unseen snipers.

"You sleep any, Brock?"

"It's hard to sleep when you're worrying about some murdering devil creeping up on you and cutting your throat, Howie."

They slunk around camp with their shoulders hunched and muscles tensed, as if expecting to catch a bullet at any second. They weren't the only ones.

The rangers finished their talk. Bowman crossed to where Slocum lay stretched on his back, hat over his face, his folded jacket serving for a pillow. Bowman lifted his foot to nudge Slocum awake with a boot toe in the side, but before he could do it, Slocum sat up and said, "Morning, Ranger."

"Tricky cuss, ain't you?"

"Just a wakeful one. I heard you coming," Slocum said.

"You wouldn't have heard me if I was an Apache."

"I was counting on you to hear them."

Bowman snorted. "Trusting fellow."

"Not really."

"Me, neither."

The old set of guards went off watch and a new set came on duty. The coming of daylight only intensified the men's watchfulness. Weapons were checked and rechecked.

"You fought the Apaches, Yerkes," Fennel began.

"Not fought—chased," Yerkes said. "Never did catch up with Victorio and his bunch. It was the Mexes did for him. I saw enough to lose my stomach for tangling with Apaches, though."

He was silent for a moment, then said, "I never would have come out on this posse if I'd knowed there was 'Paches in the stew. I thought it was just outlaws."

"Maybe they'll do for the outlaws."

"Maybe they'll do for us."

"Think they'll attack soon?"

Yerkes shrugged. "Your guess is as good as mine, cowboy."

Baylor, after much squinting into the steadily lightening landscape, said, "I don't see nothing. Maybe they ain't even there!"

"You wouldn't see them if they *were* there," Yerkes said. A mournful look came over his face. "I used up my luck on the hunt for Victorio. This time . . ."

"You're talking loco," Fennel said, forcing a laugh. But later, when he was alone with Baylor and Stewart, he said, "A man knows when his luck's run out. Stay away from Yerkes. He's bad medicine."

Slocum was wary, silent, self-contained. He was under arrest but not under restraint. He wasn't tied up. "Hell, where's he gonna run to—the Apaches?" was Frank Pitts's opinion on the subject.

Carruthers was able to walk around this morning without too much difficulty. He ignored Slocum. Rex's smashed nose was a raw red lump in the middle of his face. "What the hell you looking at?" he said.

"Nothing much," Slocum said.

Rex's face flushed as red as his nose. His hand darted toward his gun.

"Back off," Ranger Terry Lee told him.

Rex's hand moved away from his gun. "What're you sticking up for *him* for?"

"I don't need you to fight my fights, Ranger. I'll fight them myself," Slocum said. "Just give me a gun."

"Can't do that. You ain't my prisoner."

Rex, backing off, said to Slocum, "You and me ain't finished yet."

"I already busted your nose. Maybe you'd like to try for a couple of black eyes, too?"

"We ain't done yet. Just you remember that," Rex said, sidling off.

"You talk funny. Must be that busted nose," Slocum called after him.

Rex glared but said nothing.

"You've got a real way of making friends, Slocum," Terry Lee said, shaking his head.

"I've got a lot of friends like Rex on the posse."

"Yeah. That's what's worrying Ben."

"Why? Does he have a soft spot for an innocent man?"

"He says he don't know if you're lying, and he don't know if you're not lying. That's what worries him."

"And you? What do you think, Ranger?"

"I ain't formed an opinion in the case yet. But I know this: there's some dirty business going down in Blood River."

"That's no lie."

The men wolfed down a cold and meager breakfast of day-old bread, jerked beef, and water. "Don't I get some?" Slocum said. "I'm hungry, too."

"Looks like we're plumb out of food. Sorry," Frank Pitts said.

"What do you call that?" Slocum said, pointing to an open pack loaded with plenty of supplies.

The sheriff didn't bother to look where he was pointing. "Me? I don't call it nothing at all."

"Give him some food," Terry Lee said.

"Why?"

"Because I said so."

"You rangers sure take a lot on yourselves, don't you?"

"Yes," Terry Lee said.

Pitts looked away and mumbled to Slocum, "You want some, take it. I'll be damned if I'm going to serve it to you, though."

"Thanks," Slocum said, helping himself to some food.

"Choke on it."

"Never thought I'd see the day that a ranger would side with a backshooting baby-killer," Rex said.

"I didn't hear that. 'Cause if I had, I'd have to take offense at that remark," Terry Lee said.

Rex's sneer dissolved and he looked down at his feet and didn't look up. "You know what, Rex? You still talk funny," Slocum said. "That must be why the ranger couldn't make out what you said."

Rex twitched and his neck swelled up and got red, but he didn't look up.

"That's enough out of you," Terry Lee said. "Don't make it any harder to keep you alive, Slocum."

Stewart, Fennel, and Baylor joined the group but remained standing. Fennel said, "What are you going to do about them, Sheriff?"

"Them who?"

"Them Ingrams."

"Nothing to do about them, cowboy. They're dead." Pitts chewed off another chunk of stale bread.

"Can't just leave them out in the open like that. The animals will get them."

"Animals already got them, cowboy."

Fennel set his jaw and squared his shoulders. He could be stubborn when he knew he was right. "It ain't fitting to leave them like that, without a proper burial."

"You'd better start worrying about your own neck, cowboy," Wilmot said. "They might be burying all of us before this day is out."

"There's a woman and a kid there. You can't leave them for the buzzards and the coyotes."

"You want to bury 'em so bad, go ahead," Brock said. "I don't see nobody stopping you."

"All right, I will," Fennel said. He turned and walked away, with Stewart and Baylor following. Rummaging around the burned barn and the corral, they managed to find a pick and shovel. They trooped off into the tiny graveyard behind the house and started digging, taking turns with the tools.

"Me, I don't volunteer for nothing," Brock said smugly.

"Me, neither," Dixon chimed in.

"You make me sick, the both of you," Carruthers said, glaring. He got up and went to help with the digging. Rex trailed after him, once he saw which way the wind was blowing. Cantwell was already there, and Terry Lee, too.

"They're going to wish they'd saved their strength, later," Pitts said, watching the diggers.

" 'Scuse me, Frank, but I believe I'll go join them," Mayfield said, rising.

"Suit yourself," Pitts said.

With many hands ready to replace those that grew tired, the digging was soon done. A shallow hole was gouged out of the hard earth. The mound of dirt heaped by the graveside was dark and moist compared to the sun-baked surface soil.

"That's deep enough, men," Mayfield said.

Gently the bodies of the Ingrams were lowered to the bottom of the grave. The grave wasn't wide enough for them all to be laid out side by side, but the sun was rising and the men were eager to be gone so they crowded the bodies until they fit.

"Maybe you could say a few words over them, Reverend?"

"Yes, I can, Deputy."

"A *few* words," Ben Bowman said. "We've got to be moving."

Some men stood guard, keeping watch during the brief service. The others bowed their heads while Cantwell commended the souls of the dead to the mercy of the Lord. He recited the Twenty-Third Psalm from memory and got most of it right. He let a handful of dirt slip through his fingers to fall on the blanket-shrouded bodies. The grave was filled in and a number of large stones placed on top of it to prevent animals from digging there.

Cantwell, troubled, asked what was to be done with Montana's body. "Leave him for the buzzards," Fennel said.

"If they'll have him," Stewart added.

The red ball of the sun cleared the horizon. The men were eager to be gone. "What do we do now?" Frank Pitts said.

"I don't know what you're going to do, but I'm going to Mission Church," Bowman said, "or at least, I'm going to try."

"I thought you were going back to Redrock with us."

"Mission Church is where I've been headed all along. Just stopped here for the night. Would have been loco to try and make it in the dark."

"Why Mission Church?"

"There's a Ranger company camped on the flats outside of town. They're just waiting for word of where Sombra is so's they can get after him. I can telegraph from there to Fort Stockton for reinforcements from the U.S. Cavalry, too. Between the Apaches and the outlaws, we're going to need all the help we can get," Bowman explained.

"Those are mighty long odds against the two of you making it through," Glen Mayfield said.

"Just one," Bowman corrected. "Me. Terry Lee's going to string along with you boys to Redrock."

"Mission Church is a hard ride for a lone man."

"I've taken them before. The way I figure it, both Sombra and the Apaches are working their way south and east, toward Blood River. Mission Church is northeast of here, so there's a pretty good chance that they've already passed through the way I'll be heading. You boys are the ones more likely to ride into trouble."

"I don't like it," Pitts said. "If that's the way things are, we might need every gun to get through."

"That's why Terry Lee is going along with you."

Bowman went to tend to his horse, ending the discussion. "I don't like it," Pitts said, shaking his head.

"What don't you like?" asked Terry Lee. "Ben leaving, or me tagging along?"

"Him leaving, of course! We can't spare a single gun!"

"Oh, I reckon we'll get through somehow." He walked off without waiting to see if the sheriff had anything else to say.

After witnessing the exchange, Fennel said to his partners, "Sounds like the sheriff is losing his nerve."

"I heard that!" Pitts said. "You better just remember who I am and show some respect for this badge!"

"I got me a feeling that somebody else will be wearing it, come Election Day," Fennel said, taking a step forward. Baylor and Stewart threw their hard-eyed glares at Pitts, too.

Pitts gave ground, saying, "Hell, none of you cowpokes are voters anyhow."

"We know plenty of 'em, though," Fennel said.

"Yeah, and we ain't shy about speaking to them, neither," Stewart seconded.

"I think we're riding with the wrong outfit, fellows," Baylor said.

"You see that, Brock?" Howie Dixon pointed at a dark shape at the bottom of the eastern slope of the rise on which the ranch house was located.

"Yeah, I see it."

"Reckon that's Mooney?"

"I don't know. Why don't you go down and see for yourself?"

"I ain't that curious."

"You might find out anyhow. Looks like we're getting ready to move out."

"We can't get out of here fast enough to suit me," Dixon said, trying to stifle a shudder and not succeeding.

They joined the others, who were already by the horses.

Slocum said to Cantwell, "Mind if I ask you a question, Reverend?"

"No, go ahead."

"I couldn't help notice that you're wearing a gun. You must have a mighty ornery congregation."

"Remember what it says in the Good Book, Mr. Slocum: 'I bring not peace, but a sword,' the Lord said."

"But you're not the Lord," Wilmot pointed out.

"No, Carruthers is," Brock said.

"You better plan on clearing out of the Basin permanently, Brock," Carruthers said.

"I'll do that," Brock said, laughing, "if we get there."

Fennel, Stewart, and Baylor went over to Bowman. "Can we talk to you for a minute, Ranger?" Fennel said.

"What's on your mind, men?"

"Well, we been talking it over, and we decided that we'd be right proud if you'd let us ride along with you to Mission Church."

"A man alone ain't got much chance, but with four guns, we might be able to shoot our way through where one man couldn't," Baylor said.

"Ups and odds that one of us will get through to get help, too," Stewart said.

"You must like trouble," Bowman said.

"We ain't afraid of it," Fennel said. "Anyhow, we soured on this bunch yesterday when they crawfished and broke off the fight at Yellowsnake Canyon."

"Well, I don't know how good chances are of getting through, but if you're of a mind to risk your scalps, I'll be glad to have you along."

"Here, now, what's all this?" blustered Frank Pitts as he rushed over. "You can't quit this posse!"

"The hell we can't," Baylor said.

"It stopped being a posse when you backed off from the outlaws," Stewart said.

"Anyhow, what do you care, Sheriff? Like you said, we ain't voters," Fennel said.

"Stop them," Pitts said to Bowman. "I can't afford to lose three more men. We're already under-gunned as it is!"

"Then you'd best not waste any more time getting to Redrock," Bowman said, swinging into the saddle.

Slocum was aboard Montana's steeldust gray stallion. It was a high-strung animal for one so big, but spur scars and whip marks on its sides and flanks showed it had been frequently abused in the past. Slocum gentled it some by talking to it and patting its neck.

"That horse big enough for you?" Terry Lee asked as he came alongside Slocum. "Man, that's a Texas-sized horse, all right."

"Had to be, to carry its former owner. He's strong, but not fast."

"That's all right. You're a fighter, not a runner, ain't you, Slocum?"

"Not without my guns."

"You'll get them back if you need them."

"Last time I saw them, the deputy had them. Two Colts and a Winchester. They're good guns; I'd hate to lose them."

"I'll see about them directly."

"My knife, too. Don't want to lose that, either," Slocum said.

The swollen sun was only a hand's span above the horizon, but the winds it sent sighing across the plains were already warm, without a trace of coolness or moisture.

"Going to be a hot one today," Terry Lee said. "A scorcher."

The plan was for the group to stay together until they reached the main road east of Ingram's spread. They mounted up and moved out, riding one by one in a long file. Slocum rode somewhere in the middle. "Run and I'll put a bullet in you," the sheriff told him.

"What if everybody's running?" Slocum asked, but Pitts didn't answer. Ignoring Slocum, he rode back up the line. Not too far up the line. He didn't want to ride point.

They had barely gotten started when they stopped to investigate the corpse at the bottom of the eastern rise. "I don't know who it is, but it ain't Mooney," Fennel said.

They didn't know it was the body of the Arizonan, Stoddard, who'd been shotgunned by young Harry Ingram and dragged by his horse. The scavengers had been at him during the night. His hat with the snakeskin headband, boots, and guns were missing. His bare feet looked chalk-white against the grass.

"Mooney was here," Yerkes said, kneeling down beside a patch of ground about fifty feet away from Stoddard. There were hoofprints, torn up turf, and dried bloodstains on trampled grass.

Yerkes interpreted the sign. He was a good tracker. "Mooney came this way," he said. "The other was on foot, hiding behind the rock, waiting for him. He jumped Mooney. Knifed him, most likely, since there's blood and we didn't hear a shot. Then he threw Mooney across the horse and walked it down to the creek. The horse tracks lead down there. You can see that they're deep enough for the weight of one man but not of two. You can see his footprints from where he walked, leading the horse. They ain't booted feet, neither. Not Western boots. They're mocassins."

"Apaches!" Dixon said. "The Apaches got him!"

"Looks like," Yerkes said.

"I don't understand," Cantwell said. "Why take the body? Why didn't he leave it here, instead of going to all the trouble of carrying it away?"

"Maybe it was a live body," Yerkes suggested. " 'Paches like to take prisoners, sometimes."

Color drained from Cantwell's face as the implication sank in. "Dear God! But the blood—I thought he was dead!"

"Reckon not."

Cantwell turned to Frank Pitts. "Isn't there anything we can do, Sheriff?"

"I'm afraid not, Reverend. Those tracks go into the creek. That's an old trick to lose a trail. We couldn't follow it."

"He's right, Reverend," Yerkes said.

"I will pray for the poor soul."

"Let's vamoose before the same thing happens to us!" Brock urged.

They moved on. They breathed easier and their skin crawled a little less when they had finally left Ingram's ranch behind. Slocum turned in his saddle for a last look behind before it dropped out of sight. A blackened chimney rose from a pile of rubble to stand outlined against the sky.

Things could have been better, but at least this time he wasn't walking. He remembered how he had arrived at Ingram's ranch on foot, not much more than twelve, thirteen hours ago. It seemed much longer because so much had happened since then. Yesterday, he'd been a man without a horse. Today, he was a prisoner who faced a possible death by hanging, if he was lucky enough to survive attacks by outlaws and Apaches. And luck was something that had been in short supply ever since he left Big Spring.

He wished he'd put his own saddle on the gray before giving chase to the outlaws who stole Karen Ingram. Then he wouldn't be stuck riding Montana's saddle. He hated to ride another man's leather, one that wasn't broken in to his own special fit. Besides, this saddle smelled of Montana. It stank.

They reached the road after an hour and a half. They rode steadily, deliberately, at a pace not much past a quick walk, saving the horses in case of attack, at which they'd need every ounce of speed and endurance they could muster.

The dirt road crossed the plateau in a wide curve running from northwest to southeast. Bowman and the three cowboys would ride north for a dozen miles or so, then pick up the trail that ran northeast to Mission Church. The others would ride south, to Blood River.

"Here's where we part company," Bowman told Terry Lee.

"I'll buy you a drink in Redrock, the next time I see you."

"Make it a bottle."

"Done."

"I'll be there," Bowman said. He turned his horse toward the three cowboys, Fennel, Baylor, and Stewart. "Ready?"

They all nodded, and Baylor said, "Yes, sir!"

"You all are Texans, ain't you?"

"Yes, sir."

"Then call me Ben, long as we're riding together."

They pointed their horses north and rode. "I don't like it," Frank Pitts said with a long face as he watched them go.

"Me, neither," Mayfield said. "Well, no point in letting the dust settle. Let's ride."

The rest of the posse pointed south and moved out. The road loosely followed the line of the Santiago Mountains as they stretched across the county. Santiago Peak towered over all other features of the rugged landscape. Somewhere in the southern distance, the road climbed Notch Pass, the gap between Redsaw Mountain and Blacksaw Mountain, which together made up the Sawtooth Range.

"Taking this road is asking for trouble," Yerkes said. "We're sure to run into the outlaws or Apaches somewhere along the way."

"What choice do we have? There's no other way into Redrock that wouldn't take us a hundred miles out of our way," Pitts said.

"There might be a way: the old miner's trail through Blacksaw Gap. I never tried it myself, but I heard it could be done."

"Not a chance," Mayfield said, shaking his head emphatically. "It can't be done. Not on a horse, anyway.

On foot in a day or two, maybe, but otherwise, no."

"I'm not so sure of that, Deputy," the sheriff said. "Seems to me I recollect a couple of prospectors came through there last winter."

"You're a little mixed up, Sheriff. I remember them. They didn't come through the pass; they entered on the basin side, went halfway into the gap, and came back out,"

"We're safe once we reach Notch Pass," Carruthers said. "Spinell and some men from town sealed it off after we rode out."

Duff Spinell was the town marshal of Redrock. The town council paid his salary, and they didn't like it when he strayed too far from Redrock. The most generous interpretation of his jurisdiction conceded that his authority only encompassed the limits of Blood River basin. Beyond it was the domain of county sheriff Frank Pitts, whose estimate of the marshal's authority took in considerably less territory.

"It's mostly open country between here and the foot of the pass," Yerkes said. "Makes it a little harder for bushwhackers to surprise us."

"Sure, and Spinell's crowd can cover the whole northern slope from the top of the pass. All we have to do is reach them," Mayfield said.

"Old Duff couldn't cover a vegetable patch with manure," Brock said.

"Even Brock's right once in a while," the sheriff said, "and this is one of those times."

"Our only real hope of making it is Notch Pass," Mayfield insisted.

"That's my feeling," Carruthers said.

It was decided that they would head for Notch Pass. As the group broke up to form back into line, Slocum drifted his horse alongside Yerkes. "Your idea didn't sound so bad to me," he said. "Where is Blacksaw Gap, anyway?"

"Five miles west of Steeple Peak, in a gulch on the far side of Baldhead Knob."

"Deputy Mayfield sounded mighty definite that we couldn't get through."

"I wouldn't know. Never had reason to try it, not when I could breeze right through Notch Pass. Nobody goes through Blacksaw Gap without a reason, and the only ones with a reason are prospectors. I've heard of one or two of those who got a pack horse or mule through, though," Yerkes said.

Sheriff Pitts rode up. "Thinking of making a run for the gap, Slocum? I'd like that. Then I could put a bullet in you."

"Ben wouldn't like that," Terry Lee said. "He told me he wanted him safe and sound in Redrock jail, and I mean to see that he gets there."

"Don't tell me, tell him," Pitts said, pointing to Slocum.

"If things go wrong, we might all have to run," Slocum said. "Only then it would be a little late for me to start asking directions."

"Don't you worry, Mr. Slocum, we'll get you to Redrock in one piece. You've got a date there with a rope and a hangman's knot."

"You're a comfort, Sheriff."

Pitts replied by silently riding on ahead, catching up with Mayfield, who was eager to ride near the point.

"I got your guns back from the deputy, Slocum," Terry Lee said. "If there's trouble, I'll give them back to you."

"I'm already in trouble."

"This ain't the kind of trouble I meant."

"Oh, you mean if *you* get in trouble!"

"You better hope I don't, because if I do, you're going to be in a world of hurt. This posse wants to see you dangle and they just might try to hurry you along."

10

Saddle leather creaked, hoofs clip-clopped as the posse wound its way through the rising ground far below Notch Pass. They rode in file, maintaining regular lengths between them, not bunching up, so as to present a harder target to ambush. Yerkes rode point for most of the trip, sometimes scouting a good distance ahead of the rest of the line. Occasionally he was spelled by Mayfield and once or twice by Carruthers, but neither of them rode as far ahead as he did. Flankers were sent out to scout on both sides of the line, but they were afraid to venture too far from the others, which reduced their effectiveness.

After crossing Turok Run and Andar Creek, they climbed out of the watershed that drained into Maravillas Creek. It was early morning. It was hot in the sun and cool in the shade. The ground sloped steadily upward, the road following the contours of the land. The trees grew smaller, their shade shrinking like water evaporating in the sun.

Then there were no trees, just bushes. The line crested a ridge, emerging on a flat tableland a thousand feet above the Maravillas country. Level, open country stretched long miles to the Sawtooth Mountains. On the other side of them lay Blood River. Notch Pass was still too far away to be seen, but its neighboring landmark of Steeple Peak was visible even across the distance, a narrow rock needle soaring into the sky.

The tension lessened somewhat after the riders reached the stony plain. But the seemingly level terrain had its rises and hollows where enemies could hide. The heat of the ever-mounting sun made the far mountains look cool and inviting.

They crossed the halfway point at noon, the hottest time of the day. The sun hung directly overhead, a white-hot hammer pounding the yellow sky. Heat waves shimmered over sun-blasted ground.

The road detoured two miles to the right to avoid a narrow, steep-sided gully. A thin stream at the bottom of it looked like a strand of molten gold. The dirt road rounded the far end of it, cutting across the other side of the plain at a diagonal. It ran straight for a half mile, jogged right to skirt three low hills, then ran straight again to the mountains.

The three hills were a few hundred yards to the left of the road. At one point, the bulk of the nearest hill turned the path into a blind curve. Yerkes and Mayfield were at the head of the line.

The line of riders rounded the curve on the hill. An unexciting vista of table land opened before them, little different from that which they had already crossed except for one detail: an object lay in the road a hundred yards further south.

The column halted. The object was too far away to be identified. It lay sprawled on the ground. Apart from it, the landscape seemed utterly empty.

"Dead animal, maybe," Frank Pitts said.

"Dead something," Yerkes said.

"I'll go see what it is," offered Mayfield.

"We'll both go," Yerkes said.

"Probably it's nothing, but it won't hurt to take a look," Pitts called after them.

Further down the line, Dixon said, "Looks like the deputy is bucking for the sheriff's job."

"He can have it," Brock said, "and this whole stinking county, too. I've had a bellyful of it."

"Wonder why we stopped," Dixon said, leaning forward in the saddle, peering, trying to see what Yerkes and Mayfield were doing now that they had neared the unknown object. "What is that thing?" he asked.

"More damned foolishness. We should keep pushing on, we'll be at the Notch soon. Look around you," Brock said, making a sweeping gesture to indicate the wide-open spaces on all sides of them. "Any fool can see that there ain't a soul in sight except us."

Terry Lee, frowning, swiftly but calmly opened the top of his saddlebags and pulled out a bundle of two holstered guns wrapped in their gun belt. "You might need these," he said, riding toward Slocum.

A shout came from one of the scouts—then came gunfire. But it didn't come from down the road, where Mayfield and Yerkes were. It came from both sides of the road at point-blank range, a withering blast of gunfire that came crashing down on the posse like a thunderbolt.

There were three of them there, dug into the dirt on both sides of the road less than a dozen yards after it rounded the blind curve. They were known as Two Guns, Raven, and Octavio. These were not the names they were born with, these were names they had taken along the route from childhood to the full-blown pride of manhood. These names perhaps more accurately characterized them than their true names, which were secret and rarely if ever revealed even to their intimates among The People. The People is what they called themselves. All others called them "Apache"—"enemy."

Two Guns, Raven, and Octavio were part of Sombra's raiding party. The band had broken up into smaller groups and scattered after encountering a cavalry patrol from Peña Colorada on the plain between the creek and the Del Norte mountains. The subgroups would raid separately for a while until the pursuers were thoroughly confused, then reunite later at a given time and place. A certain subgroup consisted of Two Guns, Raven, Octavio, and one other, Quarrels.

The four Apaches had been striking south along the line of the Santiago Breaks when shots and fire drew them to Ingram's ranch. Hidden beyond the revealing circle of firelight, they watched the posse arrive and make camp. Raven crept up from the creek, but before he could strip Stoddard's body of its weapons, Mooney came along.

Any of the other three braves would have silently knifed Mooney, robbed him, and made off with his horse, leaving none of the posse the wiser. But Raven was more subtle. Dragging Mooney from his horse, he used the hilt of his knife rather than the blade, knocking Mooney out instead of cutting his throat. Blood from Mooney's head wound stained the grass at the scene of the swift, fierce struggle. Then Raven slung the unconscious man facedown across his own horse and walked the horse down into the creek bed, covered by its earthen banks and shielded by its fast-running stream that erased all tracks.

The others were not surprised that Raven had brought Mooney to the night camp they had made some distance from the ranch. Live prisoners are always welcome. They roused Mooney to wakefulness by building a small fire on his crotch. They amused themselves by torturing him for most of the night. They didn't torture him just for the fun of it. They wanted to discover what kind of a man he was, to test his strength and power. But it was fun, too.

They were careful not to kill him. Raven's plan would work better if they used live bait. They had seen the posse come from the general direction of Blood River on the previous day. Eventually they would have to return there. When they did, the Apache foursome would be there waiting for them. In the meantime, other prey might venture forth along the road. The Apache raiders knew the lay of the land as well as any settlers and better than most. They broke camp early and rode hard for the heights, speeded by extra horses they had stolen earlier. They took Mooney with them. There wasn't much left of him, but he was still alive.

They raced to the three hills south of the gully, getting there hours ahead of the posse. They didn't care if they killed some horses in their haste, because they could always steal more.

Then there was nothing for them to do but wait. They cut out Mooney's tongue so he couldn't scream a warning, then idled away an hour or two by working on him some more. When they were done there was even less of him left than before, yet he lived on. They staked him out in the middle of the road and left him there.

Here was where the true subtlety of Raven's plan emerged. He tethered Mooney to a place where mounted men would see him almost as soon as they rounded the curve of the hill, but far enough back so that they wouldn't quite be able to make out what he was. What would the riders do? They would halt and send a few scouts to investigate.

Which is exactly what the posse from Redrock did.

Raven's stroke of genius was to set his ambush not where Mooney was staked out, but where he calculated the posse would stop when they caught sight of him.

Raven and Two Guns were hidden on the same side of the road as the three hills; Octavio was hidden on the opposite side. Raven and Octavio had repeating rifles, while Two Guns was armed with the six-shooters that had given him his name. Quarrels, also armed with a rifle, was hidden behind the three hills, where he held all their horses.

Yerkes and Mayfield had to get up close to the thing on the ground before they recognized it for the horror it was. They didn't know it was Mooney; they just knew that the raw red thing that lay flat in the middle of the road had once been a man.

Mayfield shouted, not a warning, but an unthinking cry of fear and terror.

That set off the shooting. The three Apaches took his outcry as their cue to open fire.

They lay prone, buried in the loose gray dirt, every square inch of them covered with fine sandy soil from head to toe. Only the small round holes of their gun muzzles protruded from the sand, and those would have been hard to find even if you knew they were there. Blending into the landscape, the ambushers lay utterly motionless until the moment of truth, when they struck.

Flames lanced from gun muzzles as the Apaches opened fire. Shifting sands formed into ghostly gray figures that rose up and pumped slugs into the posse in a blistering crossfire at close range.

All was chaos. There were shots, shouts, the screams of horses and men. Bullets thudded deep into flesh.

Sheriff Pitts was blown out of his saddle. A bullet tore off Rex's nose along with the rest of his face. Wilmot threw up both his arms when he was shot and flipped over backward like a tin target in a shooting gallery.

Terry Lee was reaching out to hand Slocum his guns when Raven's rifle bullet ripped through him, boring through his back and bursting through in a red blossom on his chest. He rocked in the saddle; his face went slack. He knew he couldn't reach Slocum and tried to toss the guns to him, but he died before completing the throw. Slocum leaned out, straining to catch it, but the gun belt fell inches short of his fingertips, to the road.

Slocum figured it would be a good idea to follow his guns, so he kept on going and dove out of the saddle headfirst. A bullet whizzed through the space he had occupied a split second earlier.

He belly flopped on the ground, barely noticing the impact. Panicked horses kicked up clouds of dust, helping to hide him from the ambushers' bullets, but also making it hard for him to see his guns. Iron-shod hoofs pounded the ground inches from his head; he rolled to one side to keep from being trampled.

Two Guns rose up and came on in a crouch with a Colt blasting in each hand, pouring shots into Dixon and Brock, cutting them down.

Carruthers's gun was in his hand, but there were Apaches on both sides of him and he didn't know which to shoot first. Octavio, free from such doubts, rose on one knee and levered his rifle, working it in rapid-fire succession. Bullet holes clustered in a target group no bigger than the palm of a man's hand on Carruthers's left breast, as Octavio's bullets shot the heart out of him.

The big rancher was too tough and ornery to know that he was dead. He sent bullets crashing into Octavio's middle. Octavio raised his rifle and held it in front of him as if it could ward off bullets, but Carruthers's next shot killed him.

It was his last shot. His gun was empty, and Carruthers realized that he was dead, and died.

Horses bucked and reared, maddened by gunshots, smoke, blood, and death.

Slocum slithered across the road like a snake on a hot rock, hands frantically threshing the ground, feeling for his guns, which were hidden by masses of gray, choking dust. One of his hands hit a gun butt, knocking the weapon away.

Cantwell fell off his horse and stood up dazedly. Two Guns shot him. Cantwell sat down. Two Guns shot him again, laughing, exulting in his power.

Shooting came from much farther up the road, where Yerkes and Mayfield—and Mooney—had been, but Slocum had more immediate problems to occupy his attention.

Raven glimpsed Slocum through a rift in the dust clouds and fired a shot at him. It missed, drilling into the ground twelve inches from his head, so close that his teeth rang from the impact.

The rising dust revealed Slocum's guns lying on the ground nearby, just within reach. Raven swung his rifle around, searching for a clear shot.

Slocum reached out, stretching his arm, curling his fingers around the gun belt. He grabbed it and pulled it to him, dragging the twin holstered guns through the dirt.

Still sitting in the road with the life gushing out of him, Cantwell remembered his gun, drew it, and shot Two Guns in the back. The Apache groaned, staggered, then spun around to face Cantwell. Cantwell's next shot hit him while he was still turning. Two Guns opened fire, both guns blazing as he riddled the fire. Cantwell kept shooting, emptying his gun into the Apache. Both men fell.

Slocum didn't waste time drawing. He lifted his guns and fired while they were still in their holsters.

The bullets dropped Raven to his knees. Slocum gave him some more. Raven fell backward and lay there, not moving.

The dust settled; Slocum rose. His guns were out of their holsters now and in his hands.

The immediate area was carpeted with bodies. The horses had fled, some not far. They grazed on greasy grass in the middle distance, waiting.

Slocum wasn't the only human survivor. In the far distance, Mayfield galloped south, riding toward Notch Pass. The fast-dwindling figure was already too far away to be clearly seen, but Slocum knew it was Mayfield because Yerkes lay dead considerably closer to him. A fourth Apache who had not been part of the ambusher's crossfire sprawled near Yerkes.

After a while, unseen insects began to buzz, hum, and click. The bodies remained motionless. A shiver ran down Slocum's spine. Shivering in the noonday sun, he thought. If that don't beat all!

He was covered with sweat—cold sweat. Apart from a few minor cuts and bruises he'd gotten when he hit the dirt, there wasn't a mark on him. Maybe my luck's taken a turn for the better, he thought.

From where he stood, he could see all three Apaches. Raven was nearest. A half-dozen of Slocum's bullets had shattered his chest. He looked dead, but why take chances? Slocum walked toward him and when he was ten feet away shot him in the head. The body jerked from the impact, but that was all.

Slocum started toward the other two, carefully picking his way through the tangled corpses of the posse. Two Guns lay facedown in the road, and Octavio sprawled on the ground to the right of it.

Two Guns rolled over on his back to face Slocum, but before he could fire either of his guns, Slocum shot him first. Two Guns flattened as if he'd been nailed to the ground with a railroad spike. Slocum shot him again, just to be on the safe side.

Cantwell stirred, groaned. Slocum ignored him and delivered the coup de grace to Octavio, shooting him in the head. If he was dead, it wouldn't make any difference; but if he wasn't, it would.

Cantwell's limbs thrashed as if he were swimming on dry land. More groans escaped him. Slocum kept on ignoring him.

The fourth Apache, the one who'd fought with Yerkes, was too far away for a handgun to do much damage to him, if it even hit him. Slocum used Octavio's rifle to hammer a few slugs into the distant inert form. They'd take care of him if he was playing possum.

Slocum felt a bit more comfortable now. He was a man who liked to dot the *i*'s and cross the *t*'s.

Cantwell stopped moving and his groans weakened. Slocum went to him, surprised that the preacher wasn't dead. With all the bullet holes in him, he should have been.

Slocum went down on one knee beside him. There was nothing he could do. On the verge of dying, Cantwell's eyes opened and focused on Slocum. Recognition flickered in those dying orbs. His mouth opened and his lips moved, as if he was trying to say something.

Slocum moved his ear closer to hear better.

"Not peace . . . but a sword," Cantwell murmured, then fell back dead.

"You done good, Reverend."

He emptied the spent brass from his Colts and reloaded. It felt good to be wearing guns again, especially his own. They were good guns and he'd have hated to lose them.

He was certain that Terry Lee was dead, but he checked him over anyway. Someday Ben Bowman would demand an accounting of how his partner had died, and Slocum intended to be able to look the ranger in the eye and tell him he'd made damned sure that not a spark of life flickered in Terry Lee when he'd left him. That is, assuming that the Apaches or the outlaws hadn't killed Bowman.

They might get Slocum, too, if he didn't get moving.

He had Octavio's rifle and a bandolier filled with cartridges for it that he'd taken from the Apache's body. He reloaded the rifle, threw the bandolier over one shoulder, and started down the road.

Here I am, without a horse again, he thought. Damn!

He came to Yerkes, the fourth Apache, and the thing staked out in the road. The thing was Mooney, but his own mother wouldn't have known him. He was spread-eagled naked on his back, each limb secured by rawhide thongs tied to wooden pegs driven into the ground. He was minus his eyelids, his tongue, and a number of other essentials of his anatomy. If he hadn't been dead Slocum would have finished him off for mercy's sake. But agony, shock, and exposure had finally combined to stop Mooney's heart.

The fourth Apache was Quarrels, although Slocum would never know his name. Slocum liked his being there. There was a logic and symmetry to it. There had to be a fourth man to cover up the tracks made by the other three when they concealed themselves for the ambush. He could guard their horses and make sure that no one escaped the trap.

By Slocum's calculations, the fourth Apache must have been hidden nearby. The only place where he could have hidden with the horses was behind the three hills. When the shooting started, he rode out and charged Yerkes and Mayfield. He and Yerkes killed each other, and Mayfield escaped. Quarrels's horse wandered the stony gray plain with the posse's horses.

Slocum didn't fancy the idea of trying to catch one of those horses on foot. Besides, he had a better idea. He guessed that the Apaches' horses were hidden somewhere on the far side of the three hills.

He guessed right. He found the Apache horses picketed in a shrub-screened hollow between the hills. For a mount he chose a black-maned brown stallion, a tough little surefooted cow pony that must have been stolen from Ingram's ranch. There were no saddles, but he found some blankets hung in the crotch of a dwarfed tree. He threw a blanket across the horse's back, unhitched it from the bush to which it was tethered and on whose fresh green shoots it had been contentedly munching. Holding the reins, he gentled the animal by patting its strong neck and speaking to it in an easy voice. It didn't fight him when he swung aboard its back. Riding bareback was nothing new to Slocum. He rode out of the three hills and into the open.

He was eager to be gone, but there were still things to do that would increase his chances of staying alive. A couple of fast horses held in reserve could save his life in case he was chased by outlaws or Apaches. It would be easy to round them up now that he was on horseback.

Within the hour he was back in the saddle, riding Terry Lee's horse, the best in the bunch. Two more horses were strung out behind him on a lead rope, Wilmot's swift sorrel and the brown cow pony, whose surefootedness might come in handy later. Slocum had also retrieved his saddlebags and rifle and knife, along with plenty of ammunition.

High overhead, the vultures were already gathering. Slocum silently counted the toll: Sheriff Pitts, Reverend Cantwell, Ranger Terry Lee, Carruthers, Rex, Wilmot, Brock, Dixon, and Yerkes. All of them snuffed out in less than sixty seconds of shooting by four Apaches. Four! Bowman had said that Sombra's war party originally numbered about twenty braves. Where were Sombra and the rest of them? Slocum hoped he wouldn't find out.

All this shooting and killing, he thought, and I ain't even made a nickel out of it yet.

He urged his horse forward, toward Blood River.

11

"Thank God those civilians had sense enough to hold Notch Pass!" Captain Butler said. He had a neatly clipped gray mustache and sat his horse with a spine held ramrod-straight after long hours spent in the saddle on the chase.

"The outlaws could raise hell up and down the basin if they got through the pass, but why would they want to?" asked Lieutenant Osborne, second in command. "All we have to do is close up the pass and they'd be bottled up like flies. Trapped with no way out. It would only be a matter of time before they were hunted down."

"Not if they go by boat. They could follow the Blood all the way down to Dos Rios and beyond."

"Luckily it looks like we won't have to worry about that, Captain. The marshal seems to have the situation well in hand."

"I hope you're right, Lieutenant."

They commanded a thirty-soldier cavalry force out of Camp Peña Colorada. Survivors of an outlaw raid had reached the fort and raised the alarm. Captain Butler's mission was to secure the pass, protect the town of Redrock and the farmers and ranchers scattered across the basin, and prevent the outlaws from escaping by water. News of Sombra's raid had not yet reached the fort when Butler set out on his mission; consequently he was unaware of the Apache threat.

Notch Pass was a U-shaped natural gap between the eastern slopes of Blacksaw Mountain and the western slopes of Redsaw Mountain. Each "mountain" was an extensive range made up of many hundreds of peaks, knobs, and ridges. The mountains curved from west to east. Every drop of water that fell on the northern slopes drained into Maravillas Creek. Every drop that fell on the southern slopes drained into Blood River.

A road switchbacked up the middle heights to the north entrance of the pass. Shelfspring Station sat on a ledge a little below and off to the right of the gap. It had been a military post during the War Between the States and in the lawless years after, but had been taken over by the stagecoach company when the Army abandoned it after the threat of Comanche war parties had ended.

A natural spring bubbled up from a cleft in the rock on the ledge, the "shelfspring" from which the station took its name. A thick stone wall, chest-high to a standing man, circled a long, low adobe blockhouse, stables, and corral. Old Glory hung on a flagpole in the center of the yard, snapping in the winds blowing down through the gap.

The gate in the stone wall fronted the road on its last turning before entering the pass. Marshal Duff Spinell stood in the open entryway, braced by a pair of tough-looking deputies. A few other men were posted along the wall as sentries. Spinell waved to the head of the ascending cavalry column.

The horse soldiers came in a column of twos. They were hot, dusty, and tired after their long ride, but their bright bannered guidons were held high. As they neared the civilians from Redrock, the troopers squared their

shoulders, sat up straighter, and assumed a more sol-
dierly demeanor, as if to suggest that a breakneck race
through some of the ruggedest country in the state was
a mere nothing, the sort of thing one did for exercise
before breakfast.

"There's water enough here for horses and men. We'll
rest here for a short while, then push on straight to
Redrock," Captain Butler said.

"Yes, sir," said Sergeant Evans, a burly red-bearded
veteran noncom.

The column slowed, halted. The cessation of move-
ment brought a sudden silence in which the wind could
be heard whistling-through the pass. The billowing flag
snapped and popped like a carriage whip.

Duff Spinell called out to the officers, beckoning to
them. His other hand held a rifle point downward. Butler,
Osborne, and Evans rode to meet them.

Duff Spinell had been a tough town tamer once, but
that was a long time ago. He'd lost his stomach for a
peacekeeper's life years earlier but he didn't want to
starve, and being a lawman was all he knew. He'd
jumped at the town council's offer of a job as marshal of Redrock. Up to now he'd never encountered
any problem that couldn't be handled by laying the
long barrel of a six-gun against somebody's hardheaded
skull or showing troublemakers the business end of a
double-barreled shotgun.

"He looks terrible," Lieutenant Osborne said, low-
voiced.

"Duff is getting too old for this sort of work," Butler
said, his lips compressing to a thin straight line. He was
five years older than the middle-aged marshal, but he
was *Army*.

Spinell was heavyset with a suety face that was wider
than it was long. He fidgeted, looking sick. He was
flanked by two rugged individuals with stars pinned
to their chests—not the star of the county sheriff

or the Texas Rangers, but Redrock deputy marshal's badges. Strands of long straw-colored hair hung down from under one unshaven deputy's hat, but his bright blue-eyed gaze was shrewd, sharp. The other deputy, blue-jowled and lantern-jawed, stood leaning against a stone wall, smoking a cigar, thumbs hooked into the top of his gun belt.

"Tough-looking deputies," Lieutenant Osborne said, then was surprised when Sergeant Evans failed to acknowledge his remark. Glancing at Evans, he saw that the noncom was straight-out staring at the deputies, openly subjecting them to the keenest scrutiny.

They were aware of it. The shrewd-eyed blondish deputy nodded pleasantly in the sergeant's direction. Evans then stared solely at him. The blue-jowled deputy spat out his cigar, unhooked his thumbs, and stood up straight.

Captain Butler's back was to Evans and the lieutenant, so he didn't catch the byplay. He was looking at Spinell. The marshal's face was swollen and bruised, with a mouse over one eye and a split lip. His skin was waxy under the bruises; his expression was cheerless.

"Glad to find you here, Marshal," Butler said heartily. "Occupying the pass before the outlaws got here was fast work."

"Yeah." Spinell fidgeted, uneasily shifting his weight from foot to foot, staring down at the tops of his boots.

The bright-eyed deputy spoke up. "You seen any sign of them bad hombres, Cap'n?" he said, smiling, showing a mouthful of teeth that gleamed extra-whitely in contrast to his begrimed, bearded face.

Sergeant Evans started at the sound of the other's voice, unable to fathom his audacity in calling further attention to himself. Accusations fought to burst free from him, and he restrained himself from saying them only by a supreme effort of will.

"No, we didn't come across any of them, worse luck, but we saw plenty of places where they'd been. Too many," Butler said. He had answered reflexively, without thinking, but his military sense of fitness was offended by the casual, almost insolent attitude of the blue-eyed deputy. And the other deputy, the blue-jowled one, looked more like a crook than a lawman.

"I don't believe I know your deputies, Duff," Butler said.

"I do," Sergeant Evans said.

"Know what this here piece of machinery is, Pete?" Pink Jones had said earlier that day. He still wore the undertaker's black stovepipe hat.

"Sure. It's a Gatling gun," Pete Keane said, bored.

"No."

"The hell you say." Pete Keane chewed on a piece of straw for a while, then said, "Well, you sure could have fooled me. I'd have sworn that's a Gatling gun."

"Sure, it's a Gatling gun, but it's much more than that. It's the shape of the future."

"That's too deep for me."

" 'Cause you ain't paying attention. Listen: with a knife you can kill one man. With a gun, six. With a shotgun you can stop a mob, maybe. But with Mr. Gatling's gun here, you can stop an army. Stop it and kill it."

"Small army, maybe."

"No maybe about it!" Pink said with some heat. "That's progress. Science! You know what your trouble is, Pete?"

"No, but I'm sure you're going to tell me."

"You got no science. That's what's holding you back, Pete. You ain't scientific. Not moving ahead with the times. But progress don't stand still, Pete. And a man with a six-shooter can't stand against a Gatling gun. That's just a plain fact."

"Maybe, but you can't tote it around in a holster."

A high-sided freight wagon stood sideways in the middle of Notch Pass. Sandbags were stacked in the wagon bed, partially shielding a tripod-mounted Gatling gun. The brake was on and stone blocks were wedged under the wheels to keep it from rolling. The wagon was loaded with plenty of ammunition.

Pink Jones sat astraddle of a sandbag barricade, one leg dangling off the side of the wagon as he buffed the weapon with a polishing cloth. Pete Keane stretched out nearby in a patch of shade with his back propped up against a rock, loafing. "You fuss over that thing like it was a wife," he said.

"It's sharp-tongued enough for a wife," Pink said.

Sentries were posted high up on the rocks on both sides of the gap. One of them took off his hat and waved it, signaling. The other shouted, "Here they come!"

The pass and Springshelf Station suddenly came alive with activity as a dozen well-armed outlaws stopped whatever it was they were doing and scrambled to their posts.

Pink Jones hopped down from the gun wagon, and he and Pete Keane rushed out of the pass and into the open down on the ledge. Somebody handed Pink a telescoping spyglass after he clambered atop a five-foot-tall flat-topped boulder. He unfolded the spyglass and focused it on a column of dust rising far below the stony gray plain.

The dust was being raised by the distant approach of a column of blue-coated cavalry.

"Huh!" he said, surprised.

"What is it, Pink?" Pete Keane said.

"Blue-bellies!"

"Ahead of schedule, ain't they?"

Pink lowered the spyglass, accordioning it closed. "They're early, but it don't matter. We'll be ready for 'em by the time they get here."

"You'll be able to try out that overgrown sausage grinder of yours sooner than you thought, Pink."

"I'm looking forward to it."

Pink called his henchmen to him and gave them their orders: "Lowery, get our rifles in position along the wall and if any man of them sticks his head up before I give the signal, I'll shoot it off! Cas, you and Ridley and Duncan take some rifles and hide up in the rocks above the other side of the road! Folsom, go and get out 'guest.' I've got a use for the marshal."

"Right," said Folsom, the blue-jowled tough.

"McBane, take some strongbacks and move the wagon out of sight. Take damned good care of the gun. I'll shoot the man who puts a scratch on the finish. No, wait! I'll go with you and take care of it myself!"

That was good news to McBane, since no one could handle Pink's new toy carefully enough to satisfy him. He and Pink and a crew of five strong men hurried to the gun wagon in the gap. Pink hopped in the wagon and held the Gatling gun steady, hugging it to him, anchoring it. The others took up positions around the wagon. The hand brake was released and the stone blocks moved out from under the wheels. The crew rolled the wagon into a fissure in the rocks of the east wall of the pass, a hole in the cliff big enough to hide a house in.

Pink didn't want to abandon his precious gun, not even for a second, so Pete Keane oversaw the final deployment of the men. Half of them were able to remain out in the open, posing as the marshal's men from Redrock. The others were hidden behind the station's stone walls or up in the rocks overlooking the pass.

Folsom got the marshal from the blockhouse and hustled him over to Pete Keane. "Hey, Duff. Some friends of yours are on the way. Thought you'd like to say hello to them," Pete Keane said.

"You scum—" Spinell began, but his words were choked off when Folsom grabbed him by the throat and lifted him off the ground.

"Watch your mouth, lawman," he said.

"Easy, Folsom. Duff's got to be able to talk."

"Okay, Pete." Folsom gave Spinell a good shaking before setting him down.

Spinell sucked air, red-faced and pop-eyed, wheezing and choking. "Kill me. You will anyway."

"Don't sass me, Duff, or I'll have that pretty little yellow-haired niece of yours up here to entertain the boys. All of them. Before I kill her."

"Don't—Don't . . ."

"I won't, if you do like I tell you. Savvy?"

Spinell nodded yes. He couldn't talk; he was so full of emotion. Pete Keane patted him on the cheek in what could have been taken for an affectionate gesture by anyone who didn't know the two men. "Ah, old Duff here ain't such a bad sort," Pete Keane said.

"I don't like him," Folsom said.

"You'd like his niece, though. Pretty little thing."

"Them Mexes will like her."

"If she lives that long."

"You said Suzanne wouldn't be harmed if I cooperate!" Spinell said.

"She'll live, if you play your part right, Marshal. Which reminds me . . ." Pete Keane's words trailed off as he reached into his shirt pocket and took out two badges. He pinned one on himself and gave the other to Folsom. "Don't forget your badge, Deputy," he said.

"Okay, Pete."

"You know, Folsom, this takes me back. I used to be a lawman myself, once."

"You don't tell me! I can't figure you for a lawman, Pete. What was it like?"

"Man, wearing that badge was like having a license to steal."

"I bet! Why'd you quit it?"

"I got caught. Keep an eye on Duff for a second while I take care of this last business."

The cavalry column had cut the distance by half, but they were still far away. Pete Keane stood in the road facing the pass to give final orders to his troops. "Those of you who are supposed to be hiding, get under cover now and stay hid until the shooting starts. I'll kill anyone who starts shooting before I do. When the fight starts, try to herd them soldier boys up the pass to the gun wagon. But whatever you do, kill 'em and keep on killing 'em until they're dead."

"Guess I told them," he said when he'd rejoined Folsom in the entryway of the stone wall. "Nothing to do now but wait."

Folsom lit a long, fat black cigar. When it was smoked three-quarters of the way down, the van of the cavalry column had climbed to the middle heights of the road.

"Won't be long now," Pete Keane said. He started unloading a rifle.

"What're you doing that for?"

"Duff's got to have a weapon. He's supposed to be heading this outfit."

"Yeah, right. Smart."

"Here go, Duff. Go on, take it. It won't bite," Pete Keane said, handing the rifle to Spinell. "I took all the bullets out so you won't hurt yourself. Now pull yourself together and start looking like you're ramrodding this deal or I'll shove a ramrod up your ass."

The cavalry came on. Folsom leaned back, trying to look casual, but his cigar butt went out and he didn't even notice it, he just stood there with a dead cigar butt chomped in the corner of his mouth.

Marshal Spinell grew tenser as the horse soldiers neared. He trembled, white-knuckled fingers clutching the empty rifle like a club. He tried to make like he wasn't eyeing Pete Keane and measuring his chances, but he did a bad job of hiding it.

"What's the name of that niece of yours, Duff? Suzanne, ain't it?"

"What does it matter? You'll kill her, too."

"You know better than that, Duff. A dead gal's no good to me, I can't make no money off her. I got to have a reason to kill a female. Don't give me one."

"I won't." After a pause, he blurted out, "This is crazy! You can't buck the Army! They'll kill us all!"

"You know better than that, too, Duff. Now, put a big smile on your face for your bluecoat friends, like you're glad to see them. Wave to them. Attaboy, Duff, you're doing fine. Keep up the good work and I just might let you live."

The column halted. Two officers and a noncom detached themselves from the line and started toward the station on the rock shelf.

"Who's that, Duff?"

"Captain Butler from Camp Peña Colorada."

"They're almost here. This will be over before you know it, Duff. I—Uh-oh," Pete Keane said.

Spinell glanced sharply at him.

"Don't get yourself in an uproar, Duff. There's no change in plans. It's just that I know one of them fellows. Nothing for you to concern yourself with."

Captain Butler, Lieutenant Osborne, and Sergeant Evans rode to meet Spinell. Evans eyed Pete Keane and Folsom as if they smelled bad. They did smell bad, but he wasn't close enough to notice it yet. He just plain didn't like the looks of them.

Captain Butler said, "Glad to find you here, Marshal. Occupying the pass before the outlaws got here was fast work."

"Yeah."

"You seen any sign of them bad hombres, Cap'n?" Pete Keane said.

"No, we didn't come across any of them, worse luck, but we saw plenty of places where they'd been. Too many. . . . I don't believe I know your deputies, Duff."

"I do," Sergeant Evans said.

The officers were surprised to hear him speak, and turned to look at him.

"I know that man," Evans said, pointing. "He's no deputy. His name is Pete Keane and he's wanted for killing three troopers at Fort Laramie."

"You should have stayed there," Pete Keane said, and drew.

Evans was already pulling his gun when Pete Keane's hand moved, a blur of motion. He was dead with Pete Keane's bullet in him before his own gun had cleared the holster.

Lieutenant Osborne shouted; Captain Butler sputtered in rage. That was all they had time to do before Pete Keane shot them dead, too. He didn't fan the gun, he simply put one bullet into Osborne and then another into Butler. Each shot was a killing shot—always—for Pete Keane.

"Jeez, Pete!" Folsom said, openmouthed. He'd expected action but not that fast.

Pete Keane whipped the gun barrel hard against Spinell's head. Spinell dropped.

The cavalry troops were stunned by the eruption of swift savagery. Pete Keane and Folsom ducked behind the stone wall before the soldiers thought to fire. A few seconds later, they overcame their shock and unleashed a furious fusillade. Bullets ripped through the air, smashed against the stone wall, ricocheted.

"Charge!" a quick-witted cavalryman shouted. The troopers put their spurs to the horses, charging up the road and onto the ledge, toward the station. Hoofs thundered; gunfire roared.

Wheels rumbled as the gun wagon was rolled out of its hiding place in the cleft in the rocks and put into position at the top of the pass. The brake was thrown and the wheels blocked, immobilizing the gun platform. The strong-armed crew of handlers dodged for cover, grabbed their weapons, and started shooting.

Pink Jones manned the Gatling gun. Three riflemen crouched behind the sandbagged sides, covering him. The weapon was mounted on a tripod, so Pink had to stand to operate it properly. From the top of the pass he commanded a clear field of fire encompassing the road and the rocky ledge.

He cranked the handle. The ten-barreled mechanism turned on its axis, flame rimming the muzzles with each shot. It turned so fast that its snout seemed rimmed with a dancing circle of fire. Over eight shots a second, five hundred shots a minute.

Suddenly the cavalry charge fell apart into a mass of boiling chaos as the Gatling gun wreaked havoc. The soldiers were mowed down by a scythe of hot lead.

Pink turned the crank and swung the barrel back and forth, knocking the troopers out of their saddles. He tried not to hit the horses. Not that he gave a damn for the dumb brutes; it was only that he hated to waste good ammunition killing horses instead of men.

Raking fire clawed blue-coated troopers. The reports came so fast, in such rapid-fire succession, that the Gatling gun seemed to rattle with one long continuous burst.

Pink was having the time of his life. This wasn't shooting, it was sausage grinding! He cranked the handle and turned more men into meat.

The outlaws hidden up in the rocks and behind the stone wall were taking a toll, too, but basically they were just mopping up the leavings from the Gatling gun.

The charge broke and turned into a rout, and then it was every cavalryman for himself; only there weren't many of them left alive and more were dying every second. If they tried to run or take cover, they found that there was no escape from the hail of Gatling gunfire that sought them out and sieved them.

Some of them lived long enough to kill their attackers. A soldier's bullet drilled one of the riflemen in the gun wagon. Pink swiveled the barrel in the direction the shot had come from and cranked out a stream of lead. No more shots came from that quarter.

Pink blotted them out in groups of twos and threes until there were no more such groups, only lone fugitives. They weren't worth the effort; the riflemen could have them.

Besides, the Gatling gun barrels were hot as blazes. Pink touched one, then pulled back his fingers, cursing. The metal was hot enough to scorch skin. He wouldn't risk damaging the mechanism by overheating it. Spare parts would be hard to come by. And the weapon was much needed—here, now, and later in Mexico.

A cloud of gunsmoke, stinking of cordite, fogged the pass.

Three soldiers who'd been at the tail of the column and thus survived the slaughter turned their horses and fled down the slope. A lookout on a high ledge shot at one of them and missed.

Pete Keane took a rifle to the edge of the shelf, pointed it at one of the fugitives, and fired, knocking him from the saddle. His horse kept running. Another shot scored on the second man in line, unhorsing him. But the next shot missed the last man, and so did the shot after that, and he was getting farther away with each passing second.

"Soley! Dirk! Go get him!" Pete Keane said.

The two outlaws named jumped on their horses and took off after the last living trooper.

Pink Jones swaggered into view, drunk with slaughter. "What'd I tell you, Pete? Ain't that Gatling a world beater?" He was shouting because his ears still rang from the gunfire. "Did you see the feathers fly when I cut loose? There's an army's worth of firepower in that gun, Pete. It makes me a one-man army!"

"Yeah, well, the Army's got 'em, too."

"You'll have to speak up, Pete. I can't hear you so good."

"The Army's got 'em, too!"

"I know. Who'd you think I stole this one from? But we'll be long gone before they get here in force."

Pink was surprised to see Duff Spinell raise himself to his hands and knees. He was hatless and blood trickled from a big lump on his head. He was coming out of his stupor.

"He ain't dead?"

"I thought we might need him later, Pink," Pete Keane said.

"Not hardly. We don't need nobody, long as we got that Gatling gun."

Pink drew his revolver and fired some shots into Spinell. He could have killed him from the first, but he wanted to play with him a bit. The last bullet in the gun delivered the killing stroke.

"Of course, there's a lot to be said for the personal touch, too," he said.

12

Slocum went looking for Blacksaw Gap. It was hard to find. It was even hard to find a place to start looking.

Two formations made up the Sawtooth range: Blacksaw Mountain and Redsaw Mountain. They both looked brown to Slocum. Blacksaw Mountain was the one on the west. The towering rock needle of Steeple Peak jutted from one end of it, marking the location of Notch Pass.

Slocum originally started toward the pass, moving cautiously. The pass was the gateway to the entire Blood River basin, the logical target of outlaws and Apaches alike.

He stuck to cover as much as possible, avoiding open ground whenever he could and racing across it when he couldn't. In this manner he worked his way toward the pass, but was still a fair distance away when the cavalry rode into ambush.

Shots popped and cracked in the heights. Each burst from the Gatling gun sounded like a string of firecrackers going off. A fog of gunsmoke filled the pass. The shooting trailed off, ended. The gunsmoke blew clear of the pass and drifted off the mountain and hung in the sky, a dirty gray cloud.

"So much for Notch Pass," Slocum said.

He didn't think that he had been seen. He'd been careful to make his approach out of the sightlines of whoever was holding the pass. He rode west, putting the bulk of a mammoth stone buttress between him and Notch Pass.

Hugging the baseline of the mountain, where spurs and fans and fallen rocks provided plenty of cover, Slocum traveled roughly five miles, as near as he could guess, before beginning his search for Blacksaw Gap in earnest. It was hard to find because there were so many crevices and chasms and ravines among the broken rocks.

But if there was a route through the mountains there was sure to be a trail leading to it, no matter how infrequently it was used. And there were trails among the rocks, many of them, game trails that had been taken by riders often enough to wear paths in the ground. The trouble was that there were too many trails, a maze of them.

Slocum followed a likely looking trail that zigzagged deep into the cliffs. Bloodstains dappled the dusty path. They were fresh. Slocum drew his rifle from the saddle scabbard and held it in one hand, with the reins in another. His two extra horses were strung along behind him.

The rock walls rushed away from each other and the ravine opened into a box canyon whose oval floor was little larger than a bullring. The yellowish brown mud floor was baked hard and dry and was cracked like the surface of the moon. It had a resounding quality, like a drum head, and echoed to the ring of the hoofbeats of Slocum's horses.

There was a brown horse in the middle of the box canyon. A blue-coated cavalry trooper lay on the ground not far from it. The bloodstains led to him.

Slocum hitched his horses to some scrub brush sprouting from the rocks at the rim of the oval floor, then crossed to the inert trooper.

He lay facedown with his hands on either side of his head, his left leg bent at the knee, and his right leg extended. He'd been shot in the right side of his upper back, near the shoulder. His hat lay bottom-up a dozen paces away from him.

Slocum had already tangled today with a man who seemed dead but wasn't. From what he could see of it, the soldier's wound didn't look mortal, unless there were other, fatal wounds hidden on the underside of him.

Slocum's boot heels rang out on the hard-packed ground. The trooper didn't so much as twitch. Corporal's stripes were sewn onto his sleeve. A sidearm showed inside a button-down holster.

Slocum kept him covered with the rifle. He stuck the toe of his boot under the soldier and rolled him over. He was alive. He groaned, eyes fluttering open, focusing on the rifle muzzle held not far from his face.

"Be damned," he said, his voice weak.

"Probably, but not for this," Slocum said. "You're safe, Corporal. I'm not one of them. They're after me, too."

"Massacre . . . slaughtered all the others. I . . . got away."

"Sure. You can tell me about it later. First let me see what I can do about fixing you up."

"No time!" The soldier's left hand shot up, grabbing the front of Slocum's shirt. "Two of them followed me . . . shot me. I got away but they're close behind—"

The cow pony's ears pricked up and a heartbeat later so did those of the other horses. They turned their heads toward the mouth of the canyon, listening.

Slocum listened, too. The trooper froze, still clutching Slocum's shirtfront, hardly daring to breathe.

After a moment they heard hoofbeats, approaching at a walk.

"They're coming," the soldier said. The effort had exhausted him. He let go of Slocum's shirt and slumped back on the ground, breathing hard.

Slocum rose, turned, and raised the rifle hip high, hand on the lever.

The confrontation came suddenly. All at once, two riders rounded a corner and entered the box canyon. They were Dirk and Soley, under orders from Pink Jones to find the sole surviving soldier and kill him. They expected to find him in the box canyon at the end of a trail of bloodstains. They anticipated no threat; they came openly, so unconcerned that they didn't even bother to draw their guns.

They were surprised to discover Slocum standing there waiting for them. As soon as he came into their sight, he levered a round into the chamber of his Winchester. That stopped Dirk and Soley in their tracks.

Even then, they were unsure about the extent of the threat. They didn't know who Slocum was, but he looked more like a gunman than he did a local rancher or farmer. They thought he might have been one of the gang that they didn't know.

"Looks like you got here before we did," Soley called out to him.

"Looks like," Slocum said. "But you boys will be leaving first."

Soley and Dirk exchanged glances. "That's tall talk, stranger. I reckon you think that rifle makes you a pretty big man," Soley said.

"Yup."

"Slow down, mister," Dirk said, worried. "You're pushing too fast."

"I'm in a hurry today, boys."

"Easy, friend, we got no fight with you—"

"Who said anything about fighting?" Slocum said, then squeezed the trigger, putting a bullet in Soley's middle that knocked him off his horse.

Dirk's gun cleared the holster just as Slocum's bullet ripped through him. Levering the rifle, Slocum hammered slugs into him like driving nails. Dirk's corpse joined Soley's on the hard yellow-brown ground.

It wasn't a fight; it was a killing. All it would take was a few dozen more like it to clean up Blood River's outlaw problem. "Sure, that's all it takes," Slocum said, smiling to himself. It was easy to prescribe but hard to administer the medicine.

And then there was Sombra and his Apache band—more dangerous by far than the outlaws.

Slocum carried the soldier out of the harsh sunlight and into the shade. The trooper wasn't gutshot so there was no problem in giving him the water he craved, though not all of it. It would be dangerous for him to drink too much too fast.

The corporal had lost a lot of blood, but the wound had stopped bleeding. The bullet was still in him, in too deep for Slocum to risk trying to cut it out. That was a job for a doctor. The soldier would be better off if it were left in him until he reached qualified medical help. The bullet had shattered bones and smashed tendons, leaving the right arm paralyzed from the shoulder down. The trooper's yellow kerchief served as a sling, supporting the dead arm.

Through pain-gritted teeth he told Slocum of the massacre as his wounds were being tended. "A Gatling gun!" Slocum said when the trooper reached that part of the story.

"We never had a chance. It cut us to ribbons."

"A Gatling gun!" Slocum repeated. The presence of such an awesome weapon, with its devastating firepower, was a key factor in determining the final outcome of events in Blood River—perhaps the decisive factor.

The corporal thought he might be able to find the entrance to Blacksaw Gap. He'd glimpsed it while on routine patrols in the area, but had never entered it. He'd heard that it could be passed, all the way through to the other side of the mountain, but he didn't know anyone who'd done it.

It was time for them to be moving on. Past time, with a trail of bloodstains capable of leading other trackers into the box canyon, which had no other way out.

The corporal could ride. He needed to be helped into the saddle of his horse, but once he was on it, he was able to stay on by himself. All he needed to overcome the weakness from his wounds was to hear that Sombra was leading a war party in the area. The news left him even paler than his loss of blood. There wasn't a cavalryman in the Southwest who didn't know and dread the name of Sombra.

"I'd rather give myself up to the outlaws than be taken alive by that devil," the corporal said.

They rode out of the box canyon and went west, threading the arroyos at the foot of Blacksaw Mountain. The jumbled rocks that could hide bushwhackers also hid them. They had to proceed at a deliberate pace, to avoid worsening the corporal's wounds, but that wasn't so bad since it kept them from kicking up telltale traces of dust that could be seen by enemies.

From time to time, Slocum dismounted and climbed to a higher vantage point to scout for signs of trouble. He saw none. That didn't mean that there was none; all it meant was that if trouble was brewing out on the stony northern flat under the mountain, he didn't see it.

Twice the corporal thought he'd found the entrance to the gap, and both times he'd been wrong. Slocum was doubtful the first time, but he went along and followed a twisty ravine as it grew ever-narrower before playing out into solid rock walls after a half mile's ride. They

retraced their way out and resumed the search. The
second ravine seemed a more likely prospect, with a
well-worn trail indicating that it was frequently traveled. Two miles into it, the ravine opened into a sink
with a natural spring at the bottom of it. The water
hole explained why the trail had been frequently used.
Slocum watered the horses, then got out of there fast.
The place unnerved him. It was just the sort of locale
favored by raiding Apaches, a watering place off the
beaten path, alone and lonely. He'd bet that Sombra
knew about it, too.

"Sorry. I was sure that this was it," the corporal said
as they started back.

Slocum grunted.

They rode out of the ravine and prepared to start
searching again. "I know it's around here somewhere,"
the corporal insisted. He looked around at the cliffs,
craning his neck, his pain-dulled gaze probing.

"We're too close," he said. "The last time I saw it, I
was riding about a quarter mile farther out from here.
Things look different when you see them from a distance. I might be able to spot it better from out there."

"Better chance of us being spotted, too," Slocum said.

"We'll have to take that chance."

"That's okay by me. I'm not the one who was shot.
You can't take much hard riding and we might get
chased."

"Not take much hard riding? You're talking to a member of the U.S. Cavalry, mister!"

"I like your grit, Corporal. Well, let's give it a go.
I'm game for it if you are."

The way was clear as they rode out of the mountain's
shadow for a quarter mile, then turned left and rode west.
"I think I can find it now," the soldier said, after they'd
gone a mile.

A mile more, and he said, "This looks familiar. The
gap's got to be around here somewhere!"

But another mile passed, and another, and still no sign of Blacksaw Gap. "I thought the gap was supposed to be about five miles west of Steeple Peak. We must be eight miles west, maybe more. Think we could have passed it? Could it have come *before* the box canyon where I found you, instead of after?"

"No," the corporal said, but then added less definitely, "I don't think so. Let's keep going a little while longer."

"You're looking a mite unsteady. Are you sure you can make it?"

"Don't worry about me."

Three-quarters of a mile farther on, they came to a massive rock spur that thrust out like the prow of a ship. "I know that," the corporal said.

They rounded it. The mountain looked different on the other side of the spur. The brown rocks were flecked with tiny black flecks, darkening the cliffs, making them more forbidding.

"We're on the right track now," the corporal said.

A patch of brightness showed five hundred yards ahead. "That's it!" the soldier said, spurring his horse forward into a run, followed by Slocum and the string of horses.

The brightness was caused by sunlight and air pouring through a slitted gap in the cliffs, one that reached from the foot of the mountain to the topmost ridge. At its base, the gulch was barely wide enough for four horsemen to ride through abreast, narrowing greatly after it reached the fifty-foot-tall mark, though it ran for hundreds of feet above that.

The gallop had been too much for the weakened corporal. Doubled over, he clutched the saddle horn with his good hand to keep from falling off. "I'll be all right," he said. After ten minutes he was better, but far from "all right."

"I told you I could find Blacksaw Gap," he said to Slocum.

"That you did."

"But I've never been in it. I'm not even sure you can get all the way through it."

"If I can't, I'll just come back out and try something else."

"Wish I was going with you."

"You'd never make it, if that trail is as rough as they say. Besides, you've got an important job to do. If anybody could make it through to Mission Church, it's Ben Bowman. And if he did, he's going to be heading for Notch Pass with a company of rangers and the cavalry, too. You've got to warn them about that Gatling gun to stop them from being slaughtered. To do it, you've got to stay alive, and that's no picnic, either."

"I'll make it. But even if you get through to the basin, what can you do alone against all those outlaws?"

"I've got a few ideas on the subject. There's only one way out of the basin and that's by water. They could never get the women out overland on wagons in time to escape the law. I reckon even a lone man might be able to sink their boat, or burn it. That should throw a hitch in their plans, and buy some time, too."

There were six horses: Slocum's three, the corporal's mount, and the two that had belonged to Dirk and Soley. Slocum planned to keep Terry Lee's stallion and the cow pony, and leave the others behind.

"They won't do me any good if I'm chased," the corporal said. "I can't switch horses, not with this bad arm of mine."

"Keep them anyway. You might be able to use them as a diversion to make your getaway."

He unsaddled the stallion and put the saddle on the cow pony. The stallion was faster on the straightaway, but the smaller, nimbler horse would be more surefooted on the rugged mountain trails.

He shook hands with the corporal. "Good luck," the corporal said.

"I'm due for some. Overdue," Slocum said.

The time had come for them to go their separate ways. The corporal, with three horses in tow, went off in search of a hiding place that could shelter him until the forces of law and order arrived. *If* they arrived—if Bowman had gotten through. Then the corporal remembered that his cavalry had been part of the forces of law and order, and look what happened to them. The future was uncertain, ominous.

Slocum rode into Blacksaw Gap.

County sheriff's deputy Glen Mayfield rode into Spring-shelf Station just below Notch Pass. He'd been ahead of Slocum, but not that far ahead, when the Gatling gun massacre began. He'd taken cover in the rocks far below the Notch at the first sounds of shooting, and stayed there until long after the last shots had been fired.

Then he rode out of the rocks and up the road. As soon as he began the climb, he took off his hat and waved it frantically at the men clambering around on the heights. It must have worked since none of them shot at him.

Dead horses and men were strewn all over the road and the ledge in front of the station. The outlaws hadn't bothered to clean up their mess yet. They were too busy cleaning and reloading their weapons in preparation for the next round.

He was just coming up to the place where the road leveled and met the ledge when one of the lookouts fired at him. It wasn't a warning shot. The sentry meant to kill him but missed. Mayfield, ducking, hugged his horse's neck and turned sharply to ride on the ledge toward the station.

"Hey, Pink, look who's here," Folsom said.

"Why, it's the little deppity. Leave him be!" Pink shouted to the sentry before he could take another shot.

The sentry held his fire. "But I'd've got him this time sure," he said to himself.

Mayfield looked around frantically until he saw Pink and then set his horse toward the outlaw chief. As he neared him, he reined in hard, so hard that the horse's iron-shod hoofs struck sparks from the rocks. The beast whinnied in protest at such rough handling. Mayfield flung himself from the saddle and hurried toward Pink, figuring that no one would dare risk a shot when he was in close proximity to the chief.

Mayfield was excited by his close call. "That damned fool almost killed me!"

"Must be that badge you're wearing. The boys, they don't like badges," Pink said.

Mayfield tore the badge off his chest with such violence that it ripped a hole in his shirt. He threw it at the ground. It hit a rock and bounced away.

Pink drew his gun, not fast, smiling. Mayfield started, raising his hands, backing away. "What are you doing?" he cried.

"I don't need you no more, ex-lawman," Pink said, then fired a shot into Mayfield.

Mayfield, staggering, held out his hands in front of him as if they could stop Pink's bullets. They couldn't. Slugs pierced him, spun him, knocked him down, killed him.

"If there's one thing I hate more than a lawman, it's a crooked lawman. You can't hardly trust the bastards," Pink said.

After looking around to make sure that none but his inner circle was within earshot, he added, "We already got enough mouths to feed around here as it is."

"Too many, if you ask me," Pete Keane said.

"Listen, Pete. I want you to ride back to town. Tell Ma what happened here. Tell her how good the Gatling gun worked. Tell her that the hound dogs are getting on our trail. We took care of this bunch, but there'll be more.

We can take care of them, too, but there ain't no sense in taking on the whole danged Army. They'll be coming for us, too, after this.

"Tell her I say we got to clear out no later than first light tomorrow morning. Not out of the pass, I mean clear out of Redrock."

"I'm on the way, Pink," Pete Keane said, and was.

They didn't know about Sombra. Mayfield had died before telling about the onslaught of Apache raiders.

And Sombra was near.

13

"When the preacher said the words about the Valley of the Shadow, he must have meant Blacksaw Gap," Slocum said.

He was talking to the cow pony more than to himself, hoping that the sound of a soft-spoken human voice would help gentle the beast. He didn't want it getting any spookier than it already was, not on a mountain trail that was only a few feet wide in some spots, with a five-hundred-foot drop yawning on one side.

The mountain had been thrust up from the earth in the form of molten volcanic rock. As it cooled rapidly, it cracked, with large sections breaking apart from each other. Blacksaw Gap was such a crack, a narrow, steep-sided gorge that wormed its way through the mountain. The trail began a few hundred yards inside it, starting up a slide at the bottom of the eastern wall. Hugging the cliffside wall, it climbed steadily as the gorge opened into a series of sculpted curves that twisted like a snake. It narrowed dramatically by half when it reached the hundred-foot mark, but kept on climbing, ever higher.

That's where Terry Lee's horse started balking. The

stallion trailed behind the cow pony on a lead rope. The trail ahead didn't look any less narrow, as far as Slocum could see, so he decided to fix the problem before the horse got any worse. He dismounted and walked back to the stallion. He loosened his knife in the sheath so he could get at it quickly. If the horse should rear and slip and start to go over, he'd try to cut the rope to keep it from dragging the cow pony along with it.

He tied his bandana over the horse's eyes, blindfolding it. That calmed it some. Its fear lessened when it couldn't see the dangers of the trail. It was still far from happy, but at least it would proceed now.

Slocum glanced over the edge as he returned to the cow pony. Only a hundred feet or so. That didn't seem too bad. It seemed worse when he was back in the saddle. He urged the animal forward and resumed the trek.

He rode as close to the cliff as he could, so close that sometimes his shoulder brushed the rock wall. The trail continued winding up and up and up, but the ledge it was on widened and its overhang prevented Slocum from seeing how high he had climbed. The opposite wall drew closer as the gorge pinched tighter. High overhead, the rock walls arched toward each other, blocking off all but a thin ribbon of sky.

The cow pony plodded along unconcerned. Then they came to a place where part of the ledge had fallen away and there wasn't much trail left. Slocum knew he should have dismounted and walked the horse through the difficult passage, but he hadn't seen it until it was too late. He couldn't climb down and he couldn't back up. The only thing to do was go forward.

He drew his knife and held the blade close to the lead rope to cut it at the first warning sign that the black horse had fatally lost its balance. He was also poised to throw himself off the saddle if the cow pony should start to go over.

The cow pony, no longer unconcerned, picked its way forward carefully. The tense crossing was so engrossing that Slocum had to remind himself to breathe. He was afraid to draw too loud a breath for fear of disrupting the cow pony's concentration.

At one point the pony stepped down hard on a small stone and sent it skittering over the edge. Slocum made the mistake of watching its fall. The effect was dizzying. The bottom of the gorge seemed to plunge away from him. He looked away fast.

"Maybe I should put the blinders on myself," he said.

The sound of his voice seemed to steady the cow pony so Slocum kept talking as it stepped across the broken ledge part of the trail. The gorge continued to unroll in a series of S-curves. Quicksilver Creek looked like a silver thread laid out across the distant ravine floor. Scallops of froth boiled in the catch pools, and there were lacey patches of white water rapids.

The broken ledge area ended at the midpoint of a horseshoe curve. Just when the cow pony's four hoofs were firmly planted on solid ground, the stallion, with only a few feet to go before reaching relative safety, started balking and sidling.

Slocum had had enough. He drew his knife and his gun and turned in the saddle and told the horse, "Quit acting up or I'll cut you loose and shoot you."

The message must have gotten through, for the stallion stopped its nervous sidling and advanced past the danger zone.

Slocum set the cow pony forward, along the horseshoe curve, up to the top of the far end. The trail vanished around the bend, presumably following another fluted curve, and another.

Slocum paused to wipe the sweat from his brow. He couldn't use his bandana because that was blindfolding the stallion, so he used his sleeve instead. After a few sips from his canteen, he was ready to continue.

"Looks like we're past the worst of it, horse," he said.

A flicker of motion glimpsed in the corner of one eye caused him to casually glance back along the way he had come. A rider came into full view at the top of the opposite end of the horseshoe curve.

He was an Apache. Other Apaches were on the trail behind him.

"Uh-oh," Slocum said as he got his horse moving.

The Apache and Slocum had seen each other at the same instant. Slocum got his horse moving even as the Apache was raising his rifle to his shoulder.

He fired but missed because Slocum was already around the next corner.

The chase was on.

Sombra's true name, in the language of his people, translated into something like "Darkness in the Daytime." A rare, terrifying solar eclipse had frightened his mother into giving birth to him prematurely. As an adult male in his prime, he was of medium height for an Apache, lithe, pantherish. The left corner of his mouth twisted upward in what was not a smile but a scar. He'd gotten it from the saber of a drunken cavalryman in a fight at age fourteen. The great regret of his life was that he'd never met up with that cavalryman again. But he'd revenged the injury a hundredfold on the U.S. Cavalry and a thousandfold on the settlers and citizens of the Southwest above and below the border.

For a time after the initial wounding, when he was still but a youth, and an unseasoned one at that, some of the older braves scornfully called him "Hole in the Face." Such name-calling ceased as he soon began to establish himself as a cunning and terrible raider. It had been many years since anyone had called him the hated name "Hole in the Face" to his face—and lived.

He was a relentless fighter, a master of desert and

mountain warfare, and a horse thief supreme. Adding to
his terribleness was his inseparable comrade in arms, his
older half-brother Many Kills. Many Kills was a mag-
nificent physical specimen, one of the strongest men in
the whole Apache nation. He was a warrior, not a think-
er, but he had the sense to defer to his cunning younger
sibling. Death Shadow's Shadow, some called him.

Sombra was respected as a war chief, the leader of
a small but potent faction of extremists. Young, wild
braves competed to join him on raids, but older and
wiser veterans noted that while Sombra's raids always
had more than their share of killing and burning, the
casualties were high, too, and the booty was low. Still,
he might have risen high in the tribal councils if not for
a lifelong feud with Cochise.

He and Cochise had hated each other since boyhood days, when they'd been rivals from contending
clans. Cochise hated the Mexicans but was occasionally
friendly with some of the English-speaking whites, the
"white eyes" as the Apaches called them. Sombra hated
Mexicans, too, but it was one of the white eyes accursed
horse soldiers who had given him the scar. This and
other reasons, both great and petty, locked the two of
them into deadly enmity that lasted for decades. In the
long run Sombra got the worst of it, since Cochise was
not only a great chief—one of the greatest—but he also
had many repeating rifles, which had been given to him
by his friends among the whites. But not even Cochise,
great as he was, dared to risk all by engaging Sombra
in open battle to settle their long feud once and for all.
Sombra shared a similar lack of enthusiasm for such a
final duel.

Cochise saw the shape of the future and changed
his ways to keep up with the times. Sombra sensed
the future, too, but preferred not to change. The white
eyes were overwhelming through sheer force and weight
of numbers. The Apache nation had lost an empire's

worth of ground since his boyhood days. The time of
the warrior, fierce and wild and free, was almost done.
His generation would be the last. Since his kind was
about to perish from the face of the earth, he must be
the most terrible of all, so the world would never forget
what it had been like when the Apache warriors rode
and raided in all their dreaded power and glory.

He hadn't been there when Victorio and his braves
and their families had jumped the reservation and begun
their epic odyssey. He hadn't been there because he'd
never gone into the reservation in the first place. He
and a small band of followers had been out raiding at
the time of the break. They joined up with Victorio's
group later, for the crossing into Mexico.

It had been a good raid until Mexican troops trapped
them in a high mountain valley. The braves might have
slipped the cordon and escaped, but not the elders and
women and children. They chose to remain and die with
their families. At the end, many of them had stepped
off the cliffs into space rather than be taken alive by
the enemy. Sombra and his band had witnessed the
finish from a safe distance away, since they had deserted
Victorio's camp the night before the battle.

There was no stigma attached to this. Apaches were
not slaves. A warrior joined a chief's band of his own
free will and reserved the right to leave it any time. The
war chief's authority was acknowledged during the raid
and in battle, but was sharply restricted outside it. Braves
flock to a chief who's winning and fly from him when
he loses once too often. Sombra didn't want to sing his
death song along with Victorio so he abandoned him
before the finish, taking his own personal following of
a dozen or so with him.

Victorio's band had been exterminated almost a year
ago. Since that time, Sombra had crisscrossed the prov-
inces of Sonora, Chihuahua, and Coahuila, raiding the
pueblos and hiding in the mountains, following a wide

course that roughly paralleled the Rio Bravo del Norte—
also known as the Rio Grande above the border.

Even when his face was blank of all emotions (which
was often), the scar on the left side of his mouth made
it look as if he were half-smiling, half-sneering. Once
in a very great while, however, the right corner of his
mouth would quirk upward to express what might well
be amusement. When that happened, he was usually
smiling at something that most men would be more
likely to consider terrible and frightening.

Such a smile touched his features a month ago, when
three border-hopping gunrunners fell into his hands.
They had sold many stolen U.S. Army weapons to Pepe
Morales, one of the bandit chiefs who ruled the border.
The gunrunners were part of the Jones Gang, operating
in Texas and the Louisiana coast. Sombra always needed
more guns and questioned the smugglers with an eye
toward stealing some. They weren't too talkative at first,
until one of them had his belly sliced open and a live
Gila monster sewed up inside it.

After that the others talked readily enough. Among the
tales they told was one that interested Sombra greatly.
It seemed that a major venture was in the works, a
combined operation by outlaws on both sides of the
border. The Jones Gang was going to lead a band of
marauders on a woman-stealing raid in the Blood River
region. When they'd gathered a hundred female captives
or more, they'd run them down the river by boat, around
the point at Dos Rios and into the Rio Grande. They'd
run the boat aground in the shallows at September Crossing on the other side of the border, where Pepe Morales
and his gang would be waiting with gold to pay for the
girls and wagons with which to transport them deeper
into the interior for later resale.

When Sombra had fully considered the implications
of the plan, he smiled.

Pepe Morales and his vaqueros took up positions at

September Crossing a few days before the date of the rendezvous. Morales planned treachery, of course, and expected no less from his erstwhile allies, the Jones Gang. He would take the women and kill the outlaw gringos and keep all the money. He and his men watched the water around the clock, never dreaming that they would be attacked and destroyed from a force that struck from behind, on their landward side.

Which is what Sombra did. He had a band of twenty followers, all of them well-armed thanks to the weapons and ammunition they'd captured along with the three gunrunners. They were all on fast horses, too. They struck like lightning, their stolen repeating rifles wreaking havoc on the *bandidos*. The rifles had originally been intended for delivery to Pepe Morales; now they came home to him with a vengeance. A handful of his vaqueros escaped. All the rest of them littered the riverbank, with their burned wagons for a funeral pyre. Sombra lost three men. He stuck the head of Pepe Morales on a pole with his face turned north toward the river and Texas beyond it.

That's where Sombra took his band, into Texas. Other war chiefs would have been delighted by such an out-standing victory against the *bandidos*, but Sombra was made of sterner stuff. Armed with stores of weapons and ammunition and horses they had taken from the bandits, Sombra's band forded the river at September Crossing to carry their conquests into the Lone Star state.

Sombra's brand of hell thrived on chaos, which the Jones Gang's woman-stealing raid would supply in abundance. So much the better. He would raid the raiders and the settlers. The outlaws would have many guns, horses, and women. He would kill them and take their goods. He would select a small manageable number of the strongest females, the ones most likely to survive the arduous trip, and take them down the Chihuahua trail into Mexico to sell them. The other women he would leave behind, alive, not out of mercy but because his pursuers would be slowed down by having to take care of them.

Such a bold exploit would spread his fame and lure many young braves off the reservation to join him. There would be horses and rifles to tempt them. He'd forge a fighting force of his own and ally with Geronimo, and together they'd have a hard-hitting mobile army that would carve out, in the heart of the desert Southwest, a no-man's-land that would be the domain of the Apache.

Such was his grand design.

The band had just finished raiding in the grassy plateau north of the Sawtooth Mountains, but that was only a diversion, a feint to mislead the cavalry. The town of Redrock in Drowned Canyon was Sombra's ultimate goal, the ripest fruit to be plucked. That was where the outlaws would be with the women. Sombra knew they had taken over the town, even though he hadn't yet set foot in the Blood River basin. Hadn't he seen them slaughter the crew manning Springshelf Station, closing off Notch Pass? A small number of fugitives fled the carnage in Blood River, only to be shot down like dogs when they reached the pass. All but the women. They were sent back to town on the wagons ferrying captive females to Redrock.

Sombra was not unduly concerned that the outlaws held the pass. He and his men were Apache. If they had to, they could take the pass by stealth, but he thought he had a better way. They would take Blacksaw Gap, a difficult passage to be sure, but one that could be done. They would emerge on the other side of the mountain, in the basin, and not far from the south end of Notch Pass, either.

The arrival of the cavalry force from Camp Peña Colorada today had somewhat surprised Sombra. The clumsy outlaws must have somehow blundered and put the bluecoats on their trail. Sombra's plans did not include a battle in the open with a well-armed force equal in firepower and superior in numbers. He and his band fled miles to the west, far beyond Blacksaw Gap, only to discover that the cavalry wasn't chasing them.

As a result, however, Sombra failed to discover that the outlaws had a Gatling gun.

He and his band returned to Blacksaw Gap some hours later, missing by only a few minutes the chance of catching the wounded corporal out in the open. Spying their dust from a long way off, he had taken himself and his horses to cover before the Apaches came close enough to see him.

They rode into Blacksaw Gap. Stealth and surprise were all-important. They would enter Notch Pass and smash into the outlaws from the direction they least expected an attack, just as they had done so successfully with Pepe Morales.

That was the plan. It was vital that they strike with the element of surprise. Sombra was greatly displeased when the warrior riding point at the head of the band saw and was seen by a lone-riding white eyes. He was even more upset when the warrior shot at the white eyes and missed.

The rider must be killed before he could give warning that the Apaches were in the basin.

"Dig dirt, horse! If those Apaches catch us, we'll both be buzzard bait!"

The cow pony may not have understood Slocum's words, but it was game for a run. It lowered its head and pushed forward, its legs a blur of motion.

Slocum had a good head start, but it might not be enough. Apache bullets didn't have to hit him; if they hit his horse, he would be just as dead—provided the horse didn't misstep and send them both plunging into the void. His margin of safety lay in keeping far enough ahead of the Apaches to put the projecting buttresses and blind corners of the gorge's S-curves between him and the braves' bullets.

Terry Lee's horse wasn't minded to run. Its balky weight was a dead anchor on the lead rope, slowing down Slocum. The knife blade flashed, slashing upward, cutting the rope. The stallion skittered to a stop, and the cow pony hurried Slocum away with renewed speed.

The Apaches were fine, fearless horsemen, too, and they pressed the chase as if they were running a steeple-chase. They all had good horses, the pick of the many they had stolen, big, strong animals, while the smaller cow pony was far more agile. Agility counted for speed on this tortuous course.

The horse of one of the last Apaches in line swung a little too far out from the curved rock wall while crossing the broken ledge part of the trail. Horse and rider went over the edge. The rider managed to jump clear of the animal, but not before he was plunging in midair. No outcry escaped him on the long way down.

The others slackened their speed not one whit as they continued the chase. They ran their mounts as fast as they could, whipping them hard with rawhide quirts.

They didn't waste any time with Terry Lee's horse. The lead riders blasted it with rifles, a rough shoot while riding bareback on a fast-moving steed. Crazed with fear and pain, riddled with bullets, the blindfolded stallion went off the edge and took the plunge.

Slocum didn't see it fall, but he heard it burst against the rocks far below with a nasty wet plopping sound.

The trail swung outward, rounding a wide curving pinnacle, momentarily exposing Slocum to the guns of the Apaches in the lead. Bullets hummed like angry hornets, buzzing inches above him as he leaned far forward in the saddle, over the horse's lowered neck. The slugs tore fist-sized chunks out of the soft black-flecked brown rocks.

It was a hot few seconds, and then Slocum was on

the far side of the pinnacle and once more safely out of range. But for how long?

Rock walls rushed apart as the gorge began widening, opening out. Slocum glimpsed daylight ahead, sky and a sweeping vista of landscape. With any luck he'd soon be out of the gorge, which meant even worse trouble. The little cow pony could outrace the pursuing horses on the twisty mountain trail, but they'd soon overtake it on more even terrain.

Slocum reined in his horse, slowing it as he neared the next curving turn. He shucked his rifle from the saddle scabbard and raised it to his shoulder and fired at the first Apache to come into view on the trail opposite him.

He shot not the man but the horse. The animal's front legs folded up under it and it crashed forward, sliding on its belly. The rider was catapulted from the horse's back. He hit the ground rolling, snatching frantically at the rocks to stop his headlong momentum, unable to stop himself before he somersaulted off the cliff.

Slocum hadn't stayed to see the finish. He got moving again as soon as he saw that his first shot had scored.

The rider had sailed over the edge but not the horse. The dead animal lay in a heap on the trail, blocking it. The next rider in line was in too much of a hurry to stop. He tried to jump his horse across the dead animal but didn't make it, and wound up riding his horse all the way to the bottom.

The rider behind him halted his horse, arresting the pursuit for as long as it took for a few braves to dismount, shove the dead horse over the side, remount, and resume the chase.

Pink Jones wasn't the sort to leave anything to chance. He, too, knew of Blacksaw Gap, thanks to the intelligence that had been collected on the region at Ma's insistence. He'd looked over the gorge from the Blood River side, but hadn't gone more than a few hundred yards into it before turning back. He rated it as highly unlikely that anyone would come through it—maybe a lone rider could make it, or a grizzled old prospector on a mule—but he never thought that a mounted force could cross the dangerous passage. Certainly the cavalry would never attempt it. If he'd known of the nearness of Sombra, he would have revised his calculations, but he hadn't the faintest notion that Apache raiders were anywhere near this part of Texas.

Even so, he'd set a couple of riflemen at the south end of the gorge, to handle any strays who might try to enter or exit the basin by that route. The sentinels he posted there were Frones and Cook, two run-of-the-mill gunmen who couldn't be trusted for any more demanding jobs than guarding a back door that Pink felt certain couldn't be opened by anything but a mountain goat. As it turned out, Frones and Cook managed to screw up this job without even half-trying.

They'd managed to smuggle a bottle of rotgut whiskey along with them when they took up their assigned post on a ledge fifteen feet above the the trail, where it broke out of the gorge into the rolling meadows of the Blood River basin. If they were caught drinking on duty, Pink might shoot them, but he probably wouldn't, because he wouldn't want to spare two other men from some more important job. Besides, if they weren't actually caught drinking, they could claim they'd boozed it up back in town, like the the boys who weren't on duty were doing every hour on the hour. So Cook and Frones spent more time watching for Pink, or one of his lieutenants sent to spy on them, than they did watching the gorge.

They were so drunk that when the shooting broke out inside the gorge, they thought it was coming from Notch Pass a half mile away. After all, there'd been plenty of shooting there earlier this afternoon, when the cavalry was wiped out. They figured that the boys were finishing off a few survivors they had flushed out, or taking some target practice, or just shooting off their guns for the hell of it. Their drunken ingenuity supplied a ready explanation for why the shots seemed to be coming from Blacksaw Gap rather than the pass, where it presumably originated: it was a trick of the echoes. These mountains were "funny that way," playing all kinds of tricks on the unwary.

Then Slocum came galloping down the trail and out of the gorge. Frones and Cook struggled to their feet when they heard him coming, accidentally overturning the whiskey bottle and causing it to break. This occasioned much grief between the two of them, since the bottle had still held a few more mouthfuls. They quarreled in sudden hot fury over whose fault it was until the fast-closing hoofbeats roused them from their dispute.

Rifles in hand, they staggered to the end of the ledge to see what all the noise was about. At first they saw only Slocum, and none too clearly, thanks to the whiskey fogging their heads. Drunk or not, they knew he shouldn't be there.

Frones fired a few shots at the intruder, some of them zipping quite close to Slocum. Slocum waved and shouted something and kept gesturing and pointing behind him. Frones, cursing, blinked groggily and peered down the rifle barrel for another shot. But it was hard for him to aim since he was seeing double. He fired anyway, and missed.

"How come you ain't shooting?" he demanded of Cook. Cook didn't answer, irking Frones, who stared sharply at him in anger and then in puzzlement. Cook stood staring with his eyes popping and his mouth hanging open.

"What's the matter with you? Shoot! Pink will have our scalps if that hombre gets clear of us," Frones said.

"My God," Cook gasped.

Frones turned to see what the other man was goggling

at, and then it was his turn to goggle, too. Slocum's pursuers had just come into view, the entire war party thundering at full tilt across the bottom of the gorge. Frones realized that what the lone rider had been shouting to them was the warning: "Apaches, Apaches!"

Not that Slocum had any interest in saving their lives. He just wanted them shooting at the Apaches instead of at him. When Frones and Cook got an eyeful of the galloping war party coming at them, for a moment they were too shocked to shoot at anybody.

"Oh, God, what do we do now?" Frones said.

Slocum came out of the gorge and swung past them, turning left, riding east toward Notch Pass. When he passed the sentries, he hung down off the far side of the horse, presenting as little a target area of himself as he could. But Cook and Frones still weren't shooting.

When they saw Slocum flash by and keep on going, the idea of flight popped into their skulls. Their horses were hitched to some bushes on the ground fifteen feet below. Cook clambered down clumsily, half-sliding, half-falling. Frones jumped, hit the ground hard, rolled, dropped his rifle.

They hadn't even reached the horses when the Apaches came racing around the bend. Four or five of the warriors in the lead blasted at them as they went by. The bullets tore through Cook but missed Frones, who sprawled facedown in the dirt.

Cook fell back against the rocks, which propped him up for a few more seconds. More slugs ripped through him. He bounced off the rocks and fell on his face, dead.

Frones had lost his rifle when he jumped, and he couldn't find it. He crouched on his hands and knees, head bowed low, looking up when a horse's four legs suddenly filled the field of his vision.

An Apache sat astride the horse, wielding not a rifle but an eight-foot lance. A brand new Winchester was slung across his back, but this warrior had a taste for making his kills according to traditional methods.

Frones forgot about his rifle and clawed for his gun, only to discover an empty holster. The gun had fallen out when he jumped.

The Apache spearman buried the blade of the lance deep in Frones's chest, so that the point burst out of his back between the shoulder blades. A deft twist of the wrist turned the lance inside Frones's guts, inflicting even more damage. The Apache pulled back on the shaft, freeing the blade from within Frones. It came loose with a sucking sound.

Frones fell and the parched earth greedily lapped up his lifeblood.

The lancer put his heels to his horse and hurried to catch up with the others, who were in hot pursuit of Slocum.

The cow pony wove speedily through the rock-strewn southern slopes of Blacksaw Mountain. These middle heights were peppered with boulders, some as big as wagons, others as big as houses. Slocum cut a zigzagging course to throw off the Apaches' aim as much as possible.

The mountain was on his left, a dark and heavy stone rampart curving up, up, up. The landscape rushed by in a blur of speed and motion. He was dimly aware of a series of long green valleys falling away in rolling terraces under a big sky to his right.

Ahead, and not too far ahead, he saw figures moving about. Abruptly, the black-flecked brown cliffs lightened to a reddish brown hue, indicating a change in the makeup of the rocks. A mass of light and space shimmered in the distance on his left where Blacksaw Mountain ended and Notch Pass began.

Slocum hadn't expected that the gorge would put him so near to the pass between the mountains. It was a lucky break and he decided to work it for all it was worth. He headed his horse straight toward the Notch.

The Apaches had forsaken stealth. They hurtled forward in full charge, the blood-curdling yips and yowls of their war cries echoing off the cliffs. Their fast horses were quickly narrowing the distance between them and Slocum, and would have already overtaken him if they hadn't been slowed by the rocky obstacles in their path.

Slocum was in a race for his life, riding hell-bent toward Notch Pass and the outlaws who held it.

Mart Kern and Asa "Ace" Teagarden were idling at their post at the south end of the pass when they saw a rider fast approaching them from the west. "Who's that in such a hurry?" Kern wondered.

"Must be one of the boys at the gorge," Teagarden said.

"Who's over there, anyhow?"

"Frones and Cook."

"Them rummies? They must have run out of likker for one of 'em to be moving so fast."

"That ain't just one or two fellows, it's a bunch of them."

"Must be our boys. Ain't nobody on this side of the mountains but our boys—alive, that is," Kern added.

"Oh, yeah? Take another look."

"Jesus jumping Christ, Injins!"

They started running for their lives even before Slocum fired his gun into the air and shouted, "Apaches, Apaches!"

Most of the Apaches held their fire, although a few shots popped, whining through the air or spanging off bullets.

"Apaches, Apaches!" Slocum swung his horse hard to the left and swept into the south end of Notch Pass with the charging war party only a few dozen yards behind him.

The floor of the pass was covered with hard-packed clay that acted as a sounding board, amplifying the pounding hoofbeats of Slocum's horse. Rumbling like a drumroll, the noise racketed off the echoing walls.

"Apaches, Apaches!"

The Apaches were close on his heels. Shots rang out, cutting off the shrieks of Kern and Teagarden as they themselves were cut down.

Outlaws in the pass ducked for cover and grabbed their guns. Others at Springshelf Station jumped on their horses and entered the pass from its north end.

Slocum realized he'd never ride clear of the pass before an Apache bullet tagged him. At least the outlaws weren't shooting at him. In the confusion of the surprise attack, they mistook him for one of their own. Indeed, some of them were even laying down covering fire to protect him.

Slocum saw a likely looking hole to hide in not too far ahead. Bullets fired from both sides whipped past him. He reined in his horse sharply, swinging clear from the saddle and running before the animal had skidded to a halt. He held on to his rifle with one hand as he hurtled across the ground in furious breakneck motion.

He dove for cover behind a pile of boulders that were part of a rock slide spilling out from the Redsaw Mountain side of the pass. There was a washtub-sized hollow behind the rocks. Slocum ducked into it, dropping his head in time to keep a bullet from taking it off.

The space was too cramped for him to properly work the lever of his rifle. He set it down beside him, drew his six-guns, and started blasting. The first man he killed was the Apache whose shot had just missed him.

The shouted word "Apache!" spread like wildfire among the outlaws. Here was a foe far more fierce and fearsome than any lawman. The worst the Law could do to them was shoot them or hang them.

The outlaws were taken by surprise. The Apaches swooped in, seemingly from nowhere, leaving the outlaws scant seconds in which to grab their guns and start shooting.

A fast and furious firefight erupted, fought at point-blank range with no quarter asked or given.

"The Gatling gun, Pink!" somebody shouted. "Blast the murdering red devils—"

The shout ended in a scream as the outlaw who voiced it was shot dead.

Gunfire boomed in the pass. Flames rimmed the muzzles of smoking guns. Apaches and outlaws both generally shunned a head-on clash against more or less equal forces, but this time, neither side had a choice.

The Apaches fanned out as they charged. The one nearest Slocum swerved even closer, leaning out of the saddle with a rifle in one hand, looking for a clear shot. Slocum fired first, shooting him off his horse. The Apache rolled to a stop only a few feet from Slocum's covert, dead.

The lancer closed on Mickey Weems, who'd broken out of Yuma prison two years before and been on the run ever since. Weems didn't run fast enough this time, and the lancer ran him through. The spearman released his weapon after the thrust. Weems staggered for some seconds with the long wooden shaft jutting from his front like a handle, then collapsed.

The lancer turned his horse to retrieve the lance, but Joe Mord shot him dead first.

Pink Jones had been on the ledge in front of the station when the shooting started. My gun! was the first and only thought to flash through his head. He jumped on the nearest horse and galloped full-tilt into the pass.

The gun wagon was still in the center of the pass where he'd left it after wiping out the cavalry unit. The Gatling gun stood atop its tripod, tilted upward, its ten barrels pointed at the sky. Pink had left it in place, planning to strip it and clean it the first chance he got.

An Apache was already in the wagon when Pink rode up, tugging at the tripod, which had been securely bolted to the planks of the wagon bed for stability. Pink pulled his sideguns and pumped hot lead into the Apache until he fell dead from the wagon.

Pink boosted himself up in the saddle and jumped into the wagon. He grabbed the gun and tried to swing it around to turn it on the attackers.

An Apache brave saw what he was doing and charged. He tried to jump his horse over the wagon at the last instant before a crashing impact, but it was too late. The horse got its front legs over the high wagon walls, but that was all. It slammed into the wagon with tremendous force, rocking it, momentarily lifting two wheels off the ground.

Pink wrapped his arms around the Gatling gun to keep from being knocked out of the wagon. The Apache drew his knife, jumped from the horse's back into the wagon, and closed with Pink.

Pink had to let go of the Gatling and grab the Apache's wrist to keep from being knifed. The Apache bowled him over, and they both fell out the other side of the wagon.

Pink fell on his back and the Apache landed on top of him, knocking the wind and the fight out of him. The Apache raised the knife. Pink opened his mouth for a great roaring shout. The Apache drove the knife through Pink's gaping mouth, stabbing him through the back of the throat so hard that Pink's head was pinned to the ground.

The Apache was still trying to free his knife when his own head was disintegrated by a shotgun blast at close range. It came from a deadly weapon wielded by Folsom, a sawed-off four-barreled shotgun. It boomed three more times, killing a man with each shot.

Joe Mord finished laying down a screen of gunfire and then saw an Apache lean far over from his horse to pluck the lance from where it sprouted from Mickey Weems's body. Joe Mord coolly leveled his pistol on the warrior and squeezed the trigger.

The hammer clicked on an empty chamber. Joe Mord jerked the trigger some more, but the gun was empty. The lance pierced his chest, pinning him against the wagon where he cowered.

The tide of battle turned. The Apaches were getting the worst of it, until few of them remained alive. They might have fought to a finish, but at that moment Folsom threw aside his empty sawed-off shotgun and hopped into the wagon and manned the Gatling gun.

Three Apaches broke for the north end of the pass and rode like the wind, escaping before Folsom could turn it on them. They didn't know that the weapon was jammed and Folsom couldn't figure out how to work it.

Two more Apaches remained on their horses. They turned and tried for the south end of the pass. Bullets in their backs dropped them well short of escape.

The fight was over. Slocum ducked down inside his covert, reloaded his guns, and stayed out of sight for the moment.

14

The horse kept screaming and wouldn't stop. Both its forelegs had been broken when its Apache rider had crashed it into the gun wagon. It lay on its side, writhing and screaming. A horse's scream is one of the worst sounds in the world.

Folsom stood in a crouch, peering through rifts in the gunsmoke, ready for the next attacker. But there was none. Wind blew the smoke out of the pass, letting Folsom see who else had survived. Besides himself, there was Lowery, McBane, and One-eyed Dick Coye. That was all. They seemed dazed, amazed to be alive. Folsom wondered if he looked the same way.

The horse kept on screaming. Other horses had been shot and mortally wounded during the fight, but this was the only one that screamed.

Folsom broke open his sawed-off shotgun and shucked the spent shells out of the four barrels. It was a lot of weapon, hard to handle except by a strong man. He had a pouchful of shotgun shells hanging from a strap on his shoulder. He loaded the weapon and closed it and went over to the screaming horse and fired a blast into its head. It was still twitching when he fired again, finishing the job.

"I hate to see a poor dumb brute suffer," he said.

It was quiet in the pass now that the horse had been silenced. They could hear the wind blow. An unseen dying man groaned, breathing heavily.

"Looks like we're the only ones who made it, boys," Folsom said.

"I can't believe it! I can't believe I ain't dead!" Dick Coye cried, carefully feeling himself all over for wounds. "I ain't even hit!"

"Careful, they might come back," Lowery said.

"Who, the Apaches? They won't be back. We whupped 'em," McBane said. He was a titan of strength and endurance. He had an Apache bullet in him but not in any vital area. It wasn't bleeding much, so he ignored his wound for now.

"They're smart. Tricky," Lowery said. He kept an eye on the pass while reloading his gun. "It's just the kind of a thing they'd do: ride off, then double back and hit us again when we've dropped our guard."

"I'm ready for them," Folsom said, gesturing with the sawed-off shotgun.

"Who's doing all that groaning?" Coye asked.

The groaner's cries of pain grew harsher with each passing instant as the victim grew more fully aware of the extent of his agonizing injuries. Folsom's thick dark brows knitted into a frown as the outcries became more insistent.

Coye followed the noise to its source. A pair of booted feet pointed toes-up protruded past the edge of a rock at the side of the pass. Coye went behind the rock, where a wounded outlaw lay with both arms hugging his belly. There was blood everywhere. Coye didn't want to get any closer for fear of getting some of it on him. The wounded man's eyes bulged as though they were about to pop out of the sockets. Veins stood out on his head and his neck was corded with strain.

"This old boy's hurt bad," Coye said, speaking loudly

to be heard over the wounded man's cries.

"Well, tell him to be less noisy about it," Folsom said. "Those bellowings of his are about to rile me."

"Who is it?" Lowery asked.

"Hard to tell, with all that blood on him. I know him, but I can't recollect his name. It's that fellow from Dakota," Coye said.

"Oh, Dakota! Sure, I know him," McBane said.

"The way he's shot, you ain't gonna know him much longer," Coye said.

"He never was much good anyhow," Folsom said.

"Take it easy, Dakota. Them hollerings of yours ain't gonna help you none anyhow," Coye said.

"Man's got a right to yell about dying," McBane said.

"Sure, but why do I have to listen to it?" Folsom said.

"You'd best just hush up now, Dakota. Folsom's getting riled and you don't want that. Hey, shut up and listen when I'm trying to tell you something, boy," Coye said.

Dakota sat up and started screaming. He was holding himself to keep his guts from falling out, and not succeeding. The sudden outburst scared Coye, who jumped back.

"That does it," Folsom said.

He stalked off behind the rock. After a pause, the shotgun boomed. Dakota's legs kicked convulsively, then were still. Folsom came out from behind the rock.

"I can't stand to see a poor dumb hombre suffer," he said.

"You did him a kindness," Coye said.

"Us, too," Lowery said. "I was getting tired of hearing that myself."

Coye went to the gun wagon and stared into the faces of the corpses heaped around it, not stopping until he found Pink Jones. His brows lifted when he saw the knife hilt sticking out from between Pink's gaping jaws, and he clutched his own throat. "Whew, that must have hurt."

"I hope so," Folsom said. "That dumb bastard! If that damned Gatling gun he was so fond of hadn't messed up we could have knocked off them Apaches one-two-three! Serves Pink right that it got him killed."

"Pink Jones dead. Who'd have thunk it?" Coye stopped rubbing his throat and started rubbing his chin. "Hmmm . . . say, there's a reward posted on old Pink, ain't there?"

"A big reward," Folsom said.

"Makes you stop and think, don't it?"

"We'd better do some thinking. Fast thinking. We've got troubles, friends," Lowery said.

"How so?" asked McBane, binding a bandana around his wounded arm. "Apart from almost getting killed, that is."

"You don't know the Joneses too well, do you, McBane?"

"Well enough to do business with, but that's about all."

"I got to know the family a little a few years back, when I was working the Mississippi steamboat run." Lowery was a professional gambler who was better with his guns than with his cards. "Nev Jones and his partner Jules were in with the rough element of the riverboat sporting crowd. As usual, the rest of the family wasn't far off, so I got to know them all fairly well. The better you know them, the more they scare you. None of them is entirely right in the head. They're all twisted in different ways. Pink here was the most normal of the bunch, and he was a double-dyed son of a bitch."

"Nev ain't such a bad sort," Coye said.

"He's a snake. He'd shoot you as soon as look at you. Sooner, after today."

"So the Joneses are skunks, Lowery. So what?"

"They're not going to like this mess, Folsom."

"I reckon I can stand it."

"Can you? Are you ready to go up against Ma and the rest of her brood?"

"Why should I? I got no quarrel with them, Lowery."

"You do, but you just don't know it yet. We all do."

"That's crazy talk!"

"Is it, McBane? The Joneses are crazy, too," Lowery said. "I know Ma well enough to tell you how her mind works: We're alive and Pink is dead. She's not going to like that from the start. Why wasn't it the other way around, she'll wonder. We're laughing and scratching and breathing but her boy is dead. Maybe we didn't do enough to save him. Maybe we ran instead of fighting. It's not true, of course, but that's how her twisted mind works."

"That ain't fair! Hell, most of this was Pink's fault! If that damned gun of his had worked like it was supposed to, he'd be alive right now!"

"You going to tell it to Ma like that, Coye?"

"Hell, no, Lowery!"

"Get the drift?" Lowery asked the others, then went on without waiting for a reply. "No matter how she figures it, every time Ma looks at us she's going to see Pink, dead. She'll get sick of the sight of us pretty fast. And when she does—well, how long do you think we'll last?"

"I ain't afraid of no old woman," Folsom said.

"No? What about Monroe?"

Folsom tapped the sawed-off shotgun. "With this on my side I ain't scared to go up against him."

"But you won't be going up against just him. You'll be bucking him and his gang and Nev and Jules and Pete Keane, too. That's a tough combination to buck."

"You ain't just talking to hear yourself talk, Lowery. You've got something up your sleeve. What is it?" Folsom said.

"If you look at this from the right angle, boys, we haven't been dealt too bad a hand."

"How's that again, Lowery? The way you was talking a second ago, the worst thing that ever happened to us was not getting killed by the Apaches."

"I'll tell you, Coye—and you, too, McBane, and Folsom. We're sitting on a gold mine."

"What?"

"That," Lowery said, pointing at the Gatling gun.

"Huh! Fat lot of good that contraption's gonna do us," Folsom said, folding his arms across his chest. "It's broke—or didn't you notice?"

"It worked against the cavalry," Lowery said.

"It wasn't broke, then."

"Maybe it's jammed."

"Unjam it, then."

"It can't hurt to take a look at it," Lowery said. He climbed up into the wagon. A dead rifleman lay curled inside it. Stepping over and around him, Lowery began examining the Gatling gun.

"Ever work one of them things?" Coye said.

"No, but I watched Pink pretty carefully while he was setting it up."

Lowery fiddled with the weapon for a minute. "What do you think? Will it work?" McBane said.

"I think I'm on the right track," Lowery said.

"Suppose it works," Folsom said. "What then?"

"We take it and get out of here while the getting is good."

"Back to town, you mean?" McBane said. Coye laughed out loud at that one but stopped laughing when McBane gave him a dirty look.

"If you want to go back to Redrock to be slaughtered Jones-style, be my guest," Lowery said. "I plan on going in the opposite direction."

"But the others are counting on us to hold the pass!"

Lowery shrugged. "Nobody figured on the Apaches

showing up. Which is another reason to make tracks. What if another war party comes? I don't intend to be around here if they do."

"What makes you think that the Gatling gun is leaving with *you*?" Folsom said.

"Because you three will be going with me. If you're smart," Lowery said. "The four of us should be able to get through. We'll take the gun and Pink's body, too. That way, if we run into any posses, we can claim we're bounty hunters bringing him in for the reward."

"All except McBane," Coye said. "There's a bounty on him, too."

"Maybe you'd like to try to collect it, little man?" McBane said.

"No thanks, McBane, it ain't worth it. It's too small."

"Once we get clear of here, we hide the Gatling gun in a safe place, then deliver Pink to the law in the nearest town and claim the reward."

"That'd be Mission Church," Coye said.

"We split the reward money four ways," Lowery said.

"Some of the other fellows scattered around here are worth money. We could take them along in the wagon, too, and claim the reward on them!"

"Now you're talking, Coye."

"What about the Gatling gun?" Folsom said.

"We sell that, too. There's plenty that would pay good money for even a damaged Gatling gun."

"You got it figured pretty good, Lowery. But what's the rest of the gang back in Redrock supposed to be doing when we ride off with the gun?"

"Dying, I hope. Or running down the river. Between the Army and the Law and the Apaches, they're not going to be able to hold the town much longer."

"Not without the Gatling gun," Coye said, laughing.

"I don't like it," McBane said.

"Why not? If the others don't get out of town in time, they're finished. If they do, they're headed on a one-way trip down the Blood and into Mexico, far from us. The way I see it, it's just about foolproof," Lowery said.

"You make it sound that way," Folsom said.

"I don't like it," McBane stubbornly repeated.

"It don't matter if you like it or not, McBane. I like it," Folsom said.

McBane backed down, didn't push it. The two bullets in him couldn't help but slow him down, perhaps fatally. Besides, Folsom had the formidable cut-down shotgun already in his hand, held loosely at his side.

"What are you fighting for? This can't miss. Like the man said, it's foolproof!"

"Thanks for the vote of confidence, Coye. And now, just to show you that your trust in me is not misplaced, I think I've found out why the gun didn't work," Lowery said.

"It's very simple, really," he continued. "You see, whoever loaded this ammunition drum was in such a hurry that he fitted it in the wrong way around, jamming it. No wonder it didn't work."

"That's all it was?" Folsom said. "Can you fix it?"

"Let's see. . . ." Lowery thumbed a switch, releasing a catching lever that allowed him to free the clip. He loaded it the right way, fitting it behind the breech, engaging the action. He put his hand on the crank handle and turned it slowly. The barrel rotated with it, spitting out slugs that spanged off the rocks.

"It works!" Coye hopped from foot to foot in a grotesque little dance of glee.

Lowery swung the gun around on its mounting, pointing it at McBane and Coye. Before they could do more than open their mouths to scream, Lowery cranked the handle, sieving them with bullets.

Folsom, off to one side, stood crouching with the cut-down shotgun covering Lowery. He held his fire.

"You were smart not to try for me, Lowery. I'd have dropped you sure. I might yet. Tell me why I shouldn't."

Lowery slowly removed his hands from the Gatling gun, gave a little shudder, and dropped his arms to his sides. "I need you alive, Folsom. I need a partner. With my brains and your muscle we'd make a perfect combination. McBane and Coye were weak, dead weight. We didn't need them."

"Funny, that's the same way I feel about you, tinhorn."

"Folsom, wait! You need me! Why, the Gatling gun wouldn't even be working now if not for me!"

"You fixed it real good, Lowery. Thanks. Now I'll fix you—"

Lowery raised his hands, as if about to plead for his life, but it was all a sham, a fake. A derringer was hidden in his palm—the seeming shudder that had ripped through him earlier had freed the derringer from its special spring holster strapped to the inside of his right forearm.

Before Folsom could realize that the object that had suddenly appeared in Lowery's hand was a gun, it shot him in the eye. His eye socket filled with blood as he staggered backward. He remembered to shoot and jerked the trigger, but by then the cut-down shotgun was already pointing into the air and discharged harmlessly.

"Foolproof," murmured Lowery, his gaze shuttling from the smoking derringer to Folsom's corpse and back to the tiny gun. It had been a close call, but then he was a gambler.

He climbed down from the gun wagon. "I bet going partners with me doesn't look so bad to you now," he said to Folsom's corpse. "Idiot."

He'd have preferred keeping Folsom around a while longer to do the donkey work. And another pair of eyes and ears with a ready gun wouldn't have hurt. He would have gotten rid of Folsom once they were clear of the danger zone.

"Hey, tinhorn."

Lowery froze at the unexpected sound of a voice coming from behind him. It hadn't come from Folsom, Coye, or McBane. He could see them. They were dead. He didn't recognize the voice.

"The derringer," it said, "drop it."

Lowery tossed the derringer away.

"Turn around slowly, and no tricks."

Lowery obeyed. He faced a stranger. The intruder wasn't one of the gang and he wasn't a settler. He looked too wild to be a lawman. He dressed like a cowboy, but he was armed with the well-tended weapons of a professional gunfighter. One of them, a Colt, was leveled at Lowery's middle.

The stranger wasn't a total stranger. Lowery had seen him before, but where and when? Then it came to him.

"I know you! You're the one the Apaches were chasing! You led them straight to us!"

"Yes," Slocum said, "and it seems to have worked out pretty well."

"Who are you?!"

"Who were *you*?" Slocum said.

Lowery got it. "Whoa, now wait a minute, cowboy—"

"I didn't want to shoot you in the back. You're facing front now."

"Hold on, mister! What're you pushing so hard for? I don't even know you! Listen, can't we make a deal—?!"

Slocum holstered his gun. "You've got a gun. Use it."

"What's the catch?"

"No catch. Go for your gun when you're ready, but make it soon."

"Let me get this straight. You're giving me a fair draw?"

"Anytime."

"You've sure got a lot of confidence, friend—"

Not a muscle in his face moved to betray him, as

Lowery plunged his hand toward his sidegun without finishing his sentence.

Slocum was faster. His bullet crashed into Lowery and knocked him down on his side. "It . . . it was a perfect plan," he whispered. "Foolproof . . ."

He tensed to lift his gun for another shot, but Slocum again shot first, finishing him off.

"Almost perfect," he said, but Lowery was beyond hearing.

Why had Slocum given Lowery a chance at a fair draw? Because he was a gambler, too. Still, he'd have shot Lowery down without warning if he hadn't been certain he could beat him in a duel. He only bet on sure things.

He found plenty of horses penned up in the Springshelf Station corral. He cut the five fastest, strongest horses out of the herd. He yoked four of them in tandem to the gun wagon. The fifth he saddled and tied to the back of the wagon with a lead rope.

He didn't break down the Gatling gun for travel but left it mounted in place on the tripod. The tripod's metal feet were solidly bolted down to the wagon bed. Slocum tied a blanket around the weapon to cushion it from the rigors of a rough ride on hard roads. He tied it so that a single slash of his knife would unwrap the package, bringing the weapon into action fast. If he was going to go to the trouble of carrying the Gatling gun, he wanted it ready for use at all times.

Folsom's cut-down four-barreled shotgun was a potent weapon, especially for close-in work. Slocum took it and the pouch of shotgun shells. He loaded it and put it inside a folded blanket beside him on the seat of the wagon. He put his loaded Winchester in the boot of the box. In addition to any outlaws he might meet along the way, there were those three Apaches who'd escaped, too.

Slocum unblocked the wheels, climbed into the wagon's front box, and released the hand brake. Taking hold of the reins, he shouted "*Haw!*" and drove the gun wagon through the pass and out its south end into the Blood River basin.

"*More* dead outlaws and I still ain't turned a nickel profit yet," Slocum said, taking a last look back at the carnage in the pass.

There was a price on Pink Jones's head, and a big one. But Slocum left the head where it was, attached to the rest of the corpse and pinned to the ground by an Apache knife stuck through the mouth. Slocum hadn't relished the thought of carting the bloody body in the wagon with him and further spooking the horses with the smell of death. Besides, on Pink that Apache knife looked good.

Having the Jones Gang behind the raid made sense. With Ma as the brains and her boys ramrodding the outlaw horde, the job could be done. So far they'd achieved all their aims: taken over Redrock, captured the pass, hit the ranches on both sides of the mountains, and destroyed the cavalry unit sent to get them. They just hadn't figured on Sombra. The Apache was the unpredictable element that could upset all their plans. Of course, Sombra hadn't figured on a head-on clash with the outlaws, either.

Sombra's body didn't lie among the dead Apaches. He must have been one of the trio who escaped. Slocum found that an unpleasant thought and one more reason not to linger.

The southern slopes beyond the pass rolled down into miles of grassy hills and valleys. The far side of the sprawling basin was marked by the pointed rows of the Hermanos mountain range, "the Brothers," so named for their fancied resemblance to a line of hooded monks. The basin drained a number of lesser streams: Quicksilver Creek, Swift Run, Polk's Creek, and the Little Blood River. With plenty of water and good grazing land came the ranchers.

The rivulets drained into Drowned Canyon on the basin floor, where Blood River took its source. The Blood ran a twisty course southeast for sixty-five miles before joining the Rio Grande at the junction of Dos Rios. Local ranchers shipped their cattle by water rather than by overland drives to the railheads. Shorthorn Point was the basin's key shipping center, and Redrock was the town that had grown up around it.

That's where Slocum was bound, to Redrock on Blood River.

As he started the wagon down the road from the south pass, he was pleased to see the cow pony browsing in a field of tall grass not far off. It was a good little horse, and he was glad to see it had come through the fight unscathed. Halting the wagon, he called to it, "Hey, you want to come along?"

The cow pony snorted, turned tail, and ran off in the opposite direction, not stopping until it had put some considerable distance between itself and Slocum.

"Animal's got more sense than I do," Slocum said. "Reckon that's why they call it 'horse sense.' Well, *Giddap*, you horses!"

The team swung into step, and the wagon rolled down the long hills under a sky massing with dark clouds that threatened a sudden spring storm.

"Looks like rain," Slocum said.

15

Emmeline Jones looked out upon her kingdom and found
it to her liking. She was the Queen of Blood River with
the absolute power of life and death over all the subjects
within her domain. She wore a black bolero hat instead
of a diamond tiara. Not a royal scepter but a six-gun and
a whip were the symbols of her authority, and they were
more than symbols, because she knew how to use both
of them and did.

She stood on the second-floor balcony of the best
suite of rooms in the Cattleman Hotel, the best hotel in
Redrock. It was twilight, and the dusk was deepened by
the heavy clouds that covered the basin like a roof. Wet
winds rose, smelling of the rain to come. The peaks of
the Hermanos were suddenly illuminated by a flash of
purple lightning.

Emmeline Jones stood with her hands on her hips,
surveying the town and the river. Redrock was built
on a flat-topped rise overlooking the stockpens and the
docks on Shorthorn Point and far enough away from
them to escape most of the noise and the stink. The
town was centered around the main drag and a couple
of cross streets. A row of stores, shops, and saloons with

wooden plank sidewalks and two-story false fronts lined both sides of Main Street. There was a bank and, farther up the road, set apart from the rest of town, a church.

She had a clear view of the church from the balcony. It was an inspirational sight, especially since that's where the women were being held.

What was left of the bank was not so inspirational. The bank president had somehow managed to close and lock the vault door even as he was being shot to death. The other employees were tortured in vain, since only the president had known the combination. Pickaxes and sledgehammers wielded by strong men failed to make a dent in the seemingly impenetrable vault. Finally, dynamite was tried. It worked all too well, blowing up not only the thick steel door but all the rest of the vault, including the money, and a good part of the rest of the bank, too.

The dynamiter survived his error only as long as it took the last scorched scrap of cremated money to flutter to earth. His enraged cohorts shot him to death. Emmeline Jones wished that he was alive again, and that bank president, too, so she could kill them again, only more slowly this time.

That was a damned shame, and expensive, too, but the rest of the raid had gone off like clockwork. The steamboat had been hijacked, then landed at a rendezvous on the river to take aboard twenty of the outlaw gang and their horses. The other half of the gang, led by Monroe Jones, began striking savagely at the ranches north of the Sawtooth Mountains on the morning of April 16. The posse left Redrock in hot pursuit.

The steamboat *Laura Lee* glided into its berth at the docks of Shorthorn Point later that day. Down came the loading ramps, unleashing a horde of mounted outlaws who thundered across the wharf, shooting everyone in sight—everyone but the women. They would be taken care of later.

Some of Monroe's gang, those whose "Wanted" circulars hadn't been posted in this part of the state and consequently could go out in the open, had been planted in Redrock ahead of time. When the raid started, they tore into the marshal's office, killing his deputies and taking him prisoner, as they had been ordered to do. The other outlaws rode through the streets, first killing anyone who showed fight, then later killing all the men, hunting each runaway down to earth.

Once the town was safely anchored, Pink Jones led his band to Notch Pass and occupied it. The Gatling gun gave him the whip hand against all challengers. With escape sealed off by closing the pass, other outlaws fanned out along the watercourses in the basin. Where there was water there would be cattle and ranches. The riders first went to the rim of the basin, then started working their way in, closing the circle. They hit the ranches and farms, killing all but the women and the girls and the very young children of both sexes. If the women were too old or ugly, they killed them, too. They spared the youngsters not out of mercy but because they could be sold.

It was a big roundup, the most bizarre the West had ever seen, a roundup not of cattle but of nubile females. Emmeline Jones had a goal: one hundred captive women, or more, but no less. That magic number would fetch her and her family a fortune down in Mexico. The Gatling gun would help ensure that they collected the money they were owed and kept it once they had it.

Anyone but a fool could plainly see that the numbers didn't add up. The sum of the sale of one hundred women divided among some forty-odd outlaws didn't leave much of a payday for anyone. Undivided, it would make a nice payday for the Joneses and a few of their closest followers, like Pete Keane and Jules. But the other outlaws, the hired hands, were fools, and Emmeline Jones was not one to protect fools from the consequences of their folly.

The darkness deepened until only a thin sliver of light remained. Electricity crackled on the undersides of the clouds. Raindrops wet her face, spattered on the balcony beneath her.

The doorknob on the far side of the room turned and before it stopped moving Emmeline "Ma" Jones stood facing the door with a gun pointing at it.

The door opened wide enough for a grizzled white-haired head to poke its way into the room. Emmeline Jones eased down the hammer and holstered the gun. "Oh, it's you. What the hell you want, Tewk?"

"Nev's wanting a word with you, Miz Jones."

"Then why doesn't he come here? I'm supposed to go to him?"

"Uh, I think there's some kind of, uh, problem, Miz Jones."

"There's always a problem. Oh, all right, I'm coming." She started across the room. Tewk began to duck his head back out of the door preparatory to leaving. "Wait a minute, you," Emmeline Jones said.

"Yes, ma'am." Tewk nearly tripped himself backing up when she flung open the door and stepped into the red-carpeted hotel corridor.

A vicious leather quirt, a cat-o'-nine-tails, hung upside-down on the left side of Emmeline's gun belt. Tewk cringed as she reached for it. "I didn't do nothing!" he cried.

"You're supposed to knock and ask for permission before entering my room," she said. "You know that."

"I did knock, I swear it! You must have not heard it! That's why I was sticking my head in the room, to see if you was inside, I swear!"

"I believe that, because I know you know better than to try to lie to me, Tewk."

"Yes, indeed, ma'am, I know that."

"Shut up." She sniffed his breath. "Phew! You're drunk!"

"Nooooooo, ma'am! I've been drinking, but I ain't drunk. There's a big difference between the two. Look at this. Take a look at this hand. It's my gun hand. Look at that hand, it's rock steady."

"Sure, but the rest of you is shaking like you've got the ague, you poor fool," she said. "Where's Pearl?"

"Huh? I don't know."

She grabbed the whip and bore down on the cowering Tewk. "What do you mean, you don't know? You've only got one thing to do to earn your keep, you stinking rum pot, and that's to keep Pearl out of trouble and now you're telling me you can't even do that?!"

"No, no! She's back in the room with Nev, I suppose; I mean, that's where she was when I left her to get you, like Nev told me to do—"

He cried out as she slashed him with the cat. He took most of the blow on his arms, which he threw up to protect his face. She slashed him again and he fell down and she slashed him again.

"That's for supposing," she said, not even breathing hard. "And Pearl had better be with Nev like you 'suppose' she is, or I'll skin you like a buffalo hide."

She started straight toward Nev's room. When she was halfway there, Jules stepped outside, into the hall. "What's going on?" he said.

"You tell me."

Jules glanced at Tewk sitting crumpled on the floor, thin red lines striping his bare arms and face. Shrugging, he stepped aside so Emmeline Jones could enter, then followed her into the room, closing the door behind them.

"Pearl's a hellcat. How's an old fart like me handle the likes of her, huh? Suppose you tell me that," Tewk said, when he was sure nobody could hear him.

• • •

The windows were open, but the air in the room was heavy with tobacco smoke and whiskey fumes. Gunsmoke, too. Someone had been using a side door for target practice. A fist-sized hole had been shot out of it where the heart of a standing man would be. A throwing knife jutted between the antlers of an a stuffed elk's head trophy-mounted on the wall.

"What's the problem, Nev?"

"Reb Dooley, Ma."

"What's that son of a bitch done now?"

"He got at one of the girls in the church. Messed her up pretty bad."

"How bad?"

"Pretty bad."

"*Damnation*, Nev—"

"Even if she lives she won't be any good to us, Ma."

She smacked a fist into her palm. It made a loud meaty sound. "How'd he manage that? Hellfire, Nev, you know those gals are strictly off limits! That's the rule! *My* rule!"

"There's nothing Nev could have done to stop it, Ma, so don't go blaming him," Jules said. That he dared to speak at all during a Jones family quarrel showed how highly they rated him. Otherwise, he'd have been shot dead for such audacity. But he was confident enough to continue.

"Neeley's the boss of the guards on this shift, Ma. He's an old pal of Reb's. And the Rebel paid for the privilege. The other guards didn't like it but what could they do about it? They didn't want to go against Neeley and Reb. They told us about it as soon as they could."

Emmeline Jones let out a long breath, pausing for a silent count of ten. "What girl?" she finally asked in a strangled voice.

"The marshal's niece. Suzanne something. I forget her last name. Reb thought it would be fun to do it to a lawman's kin, but she bit him so he pistol-whipped her. Crushed her skull. Most likely she won't last until morning," Jules said.

"*Damn* them! The *bandidos* would have paid double for the pleasure of banging that little piece! This is costing me money."

"He can't be allowed to live, of course," Nev said.

"Of course," Pearl said, then giggled.

"So there you are!" Emmeline Jones's eyes narrowed as she took a hard look at her daughter. "What's that you got on, girl?"

Pearl wore a tight red satin dress decorated with black lace and ribbons. She stood leaning provocatively against a wingback chair, strands of hair falling across her face, a half-eaten green apple in her hand.

"I found this dress in a closet down the hall. Must have belonged to a real fancy lady," Pearl said. "Like it, Ma?"

"No. It makes you look like a whore."

"Well, that's the whole idea, ain't it?" Pearl said, giggling some more.

She stopped giggling and dodged behind the chair when her mother started toward her with upraised whip.

"You little bitch—"

"Come on, Ma, save that for later. We've got business to attend to," Nev said.

"You're right, Nev. But just you wait till later, missy!" she said, shaking the cat at Pearl so that the leather thongs danced and twirled.

"I don't see what's so wrong with it. I thought it was a pretty dress," Pearl said. "You like it fine, don't you, Jules?"

"Mind your momma and do what she tells you for once in your life. That's what I'd like."

"Thank you, Jules," Emmeline Jones said.

"You're welcome, Ma."

"You're no fun, Jules. You must be getting old," Pearl said.

"I'd like to try."

"Well, what do you say, Ma?" Nev said.

"Where's Dooley now, son?"

"In the saloon with the rest of the men. He doesn't know that I know what he did. He's drunk, mostly."

"In the saloon, eh? That's good. And Neeley?"

"He's back at the church," Jules said. "The new boss of the guards is guarding him."

"Good. I'll take care of him later."

Emmeline Jones's wrathful glare swept the room, stopping at the long knife stuck in the stuffed elk's head. "Get me that knife, will you, Jules."

"Sure, Ma." Jules crossed the room, drew his gun, and fired a shot into the elk's head, knocking loose the knife. It fell to the floor. He holstered the gun and picked up the knife and gave it to Emmeline Jones hilt-first.

"Thanks. Do me another favor, Jules."

"Name it."

"Tell Reb to come up here for a minute. I want to talk to him."

"A pleasure, Ma." Jules left the room.

"Go to your room, Pearl. I don't want you to see this."

"Aww, Ma, when are you gonna stop treating me like a baby?"

"When you stop actin' like one," Ma replied.

"Ha! That's telling her, Ma!"

"Huh! As if you ain't come scratching around my door more than once, big brother, whining for some of what I got."

"I wouldn't waste my time. Maybe when you grow up, Pearl."

"Don't be talking to your sister like that, Nev, not even in fun. T'ain't fitting."

"Sorry, Ma. I was just joshing the girl."

"You wasn't joshing the other night when you tried to get into bed with me. Ask him about that, Ma!"

Emmeline Jones gave Neville a hard look. He spread out his arms palms up and gave a sheepish grin. "It was nothing, Ma. I was just tucking her in and making sure she said her prayers. That's all it was, Ma, honest!"

"When all this is over, son, I'm going to have a long talk with you," she said. "And as for you, Pearl—git!"

"What's the matter with your hand, Reb?"

"Ain't nothing wrong with it!"

"Okay, okay," the other man said, backing away, "you don't have to bark my head off."

"Nothing wrong with it," Reb Dooley said again.

But there was something wrong with his left hand. It was torn and chewed, and blood oozed through the folds of the dirty kerchief he'd wrapped around it as a makeshift bandage.

The saloon was a fancy one on the ground floor of the Cattleman's Hotel. Stock raisers, buyers, and brokers were a hard-drinking bunch, and the hotel management had arranged for them to do it in style. The long polished wooden bar had brass rails and brass spittoons. There was no sawdust on the floor, as was the custom in rowdier establishments. There were tables and chairs off to the side for those who wished to indulge in a little social gambling or go off and get drunk by themselves. The lamp fixtures hanging from the high ceiling were fancy brass-and-crystal globes trimmed with ornate little curlicues. A painting hung over the full length of the mirror behind the well-stocked bar. Its mythological subject was "Hercules Among the Amazons." Hercules was draped in a toga, the Amazons wore considerably less. The rendering of the classical theme was ripely done, but not indecent.

That was before the saloon had become the head-quarters of forty outlaws, killers, thieves, and maniacs drunk on raw whiskey and even rawer acts of murder. It now looked as if it had been hit by a tornado, and sounded like one was in progress.

The hotel was ablaze with lights while the rest of the town was blacked out. The killers were holding court. Those who weren't pulling guard duty or off raiding were holed up in the hotel saloon, roaring drunk. Some of them tried not to think of the women locked away in the church; others could dwell on nothing but that thought. All of them drank more because of it.

They were outlaws, and though they didn't like to be told what to do, they could see the wisdom of enforcing the no-women ban. But they wouldn't stand for any no-drinking nonsense, especially not when the whiskey tasted all the sweeter for being stolen. As long as they were off duty and didn't have a job to do, Emmeline Jones didn't care if they drank themselves to death. Anything that thinned out their ranks was fine with her, now that the getaway was drawing nearer.

After the messy business at the church with the little blonde bitch with the teeth, Reb Dooley had dived into the noisy chaos of the hotel saloon as if he could hide in it. In one corner of his mind he knew that he'd fucked up, but another corner belligerently insisted that Reb Dooley didn't back off from nobody, come Hell or high water.

Even with all the bottles that had been guzzled dry or blown to smithereens by drunken guns, there was still more than enough for every man. Reb got himself a bottle of whiskey. He'd have taken two bottles, but one was all he could carry, because his left hand wasn't working well and it hurt to close it.

Cobb Caswell, an Oklahoma outlaw, lifted his eyebrows when he got a good look at Reb's face. "What happened to you?" he asked. "Run into a cactus head-first?"

Reb didn't get it for a second, because his hand hurt so much he hadn't given any thought to his face. Now he did. It was all scratched up. He touched it with his good hand and came away with fresh blood on his fingers.

She'd marked him with her claws, the little bitch!

"I should have put a bullet in her," he said, turning away.

"What's that you said, Reb? Her? Her who?" Caswell said.

"Never you mind about that."

Reb's bad hand accidentally brushed his thigh, making him wince. The Oklahoman glanced down, saw it. "What's the matter with your hand, Reb?"

"Ain't nothing the matter with it!"

The Oklahoman backed off, but before going elsewhere, he said, "You'd best tend to that wound quickly, Reb. Them bites can make your hand swell up awful bad."

"Who said it was a bite?"

"Them toothmarks on the back of your hand, for one," Caswell said. "Human bite's a nasty thing. Girl bite, especially."

"Why, you—"

Reb would have gone for his gun, but he was holding the whiskey bottle instead, and by the time he set it down on the bar, the Oklahoman was lost to sight in the crowd.

"Bastard," Reb said in Caswell's general direction. He started when somebody tapped him on the shoulder from behind. It was Jules.

"You're wanted upstairs," he said. "The boss lady wants to see you."

"Me? What for?"

"How should I know? Maybe she wants to give you a promotion," Jules said. Having delivered his message, he started to move on.

"I'll be right up," Reb called after him.

"Sure." Jules didn't even look back at Reb when he said it. He crossed the room and climbed the grand staircase to the upper floor.

Reb's hand throbbed. He couldn't figure how a damaged

hand could hurt so much. He uncorked the bottle with his teeth and spat the cork out from between his jaws. He held his wounded hand out in front of him and poured whiskey over it. It burned like fire; the first rush of pain felt like it was going to take the top of his head off. Gritting his teeth, he kept pouring, soaking the bandages, saturating them.

Somebody saw what he was doing and called out, "Hey, Reb, what are you doing, trying to get your hand drunk?"

Ignoring him, Reb stopped pouring and chugged down what was left of the whiskey. When he was done, the fire inside him was hotter than the one blazing from his agonized hand.

He tossed the empty bottle in the air, drew, and fired. The bottle disintegrated in a burst of glass.

"Dang it, Reb, you almost hit me!" somebody said.

"Come out where I can see you. This time I won't miss," Reb said. "No? What's the matter, no guts?"

He twirled his gun before putting it back in the holster. He went back behind the bar, got another bottle of whiskey, and bulled his way across the room. The others gave him a wide berth.

"I'm a curly-haired wolf and tonight's my night to howl!" Reb shouted, draping himself over the banister rail of the grand staircase to keep from falling down.

He broke the neck of the bottle and drank his whiskey from the jagged edge. When his veins were full of liquid fire, he started up the stairs.

Cobb Caswell stepped out from behind a pillar where Reb could see him. When he was sure that Reb was watching, the grinning Oklahoman slowly and meaningfully drew a finger across his throat.

Reb threw the raw-edged whiskey bottle at him and missed. When Reb grabbed for his gun, the sudden motion threw him off-balance and he almost toppled over backward off the first landing. Flailing, he managed to grab the rail and held on tight.

"Coming, Reb?" said Jules, standing at the top of the stairs.

"Be right there."

A few minutes after Reb Dooley had swaggered into the manager's office on the second floor, which Nev Jones had taken for his own, a hideous shriek sounded from behind the room's closed door:

"No! Not that! For God's sake—*Noooooooooooo!!*"

The scream was abruptly silenced at the peak of its agony.

The outlaws massed on the saloon floor were hard men, but that got to them. Every face in the room turned upward, toward the top of the grand staircase. The men stood still, silent, watchful, waiting. The death scream had chilled their blood.

After a moment, a group came out of the manager's office and appeared at the top of the stairs. Emmeline "Ma" Jones stood in the middle, with Nev on one side of her and Jules on the other. The two gunfighters were empty-handed, but stood wary and watchful for trouble. Emmeline Jones was not empty-handed, though she held no gun.

The trio descended the stairs to a wide landing in the middle of the staircase. Emmeline Jones wore a black leather vest, white blouse, black gloves, and a long black leather dress whose hem brushed the ankles of her spur-heeled boots. Some wet red droplets were sprinkled on her white shirtfront. She held her right hand in front of her, away from her, with the palm up. Something raw and bloody rested on top of it. Red dripped through her black-gloved fingers.

She let them all have a good look at it before throwing it down on the bar. It landed with a wet plop beside Panther Piss Hartigan, the self-styled "Toughest Man in Texas." No man yet had challenged that title and lived.

Hartigan looked over the rim of the beer mug filled with whiskey that he was drinking from and casually eyed the thing on the bar. "Goddam!" he yelped when he realized what it was. Moving away from it, he downed in one gulp the whiskey he hadn't spilled when he first jumped back from the thing.

Others took his place, to make sure that the thing really was what they thought it was. A circle of heads closed around it, then opened as the beholders recoiled.

"That was Reb Dooley's. He put it where it didn't belong," Emmeline Jones said.

"Crazy murdering old whore!"

Jules and Nev scanned the room to see who'd spoken out. Jules spotted him first. "Blinky Arnot, Nev. When he stops blinking it means he's going to draw."

"Thanks, Jules."

Arnot pushed to the front of the crowd. He blinked fiercely, like he was trying to clear something from his eyes.

"Reb lost five hundred dollars to me in a poker game! How am I gonna collect that now?" he said.

Nev drew and fired from the hip, drilling Arnot. Arnot fell dead. "Collect it in Hell," Nev said.

"Listen up, boys!" Emmeline Jones was speaking now. "I didn't cut it off Reb because he got himself a piece of tail, even though that's against the rules. I did it because he crushed that poor little gal's skull and there ain't much of a call to buy broke-headed gals, not even in Mexico. When he ruined our chances of selling her, he was stealing from all of us—and that's just plain dishonest. We ain't risking getting shot or hanged just so's some damned fool who couldn't keep it in his pants can cheat the rest of us out of our fair share, am I right?

"As for Arnot, well, he should have talked polite to a lady. Imagine the lowdown gall of that man, calling me a whore right in front of my son! That's an insult. Hell, everybody knows I own the whole blamed whorehouse!"

Emmeline Jones threw back her head and laughed lustily. Jules and Nev joined in. "You boys aren't laughing," Nev said a few seconds later, not laughing himself anymore. The quiet menace he conveyed convinced the outlaws to muster up a few forced guffaws.

"That's more like it," Nev said.

"Drink up, boys," Emmeline Jones said. "Somebody give old Hartigan something better than the horse piss he's used to drinking. He looks like he could use it."

"I damned sure could!" Hartigan agreed.

"Here's something to celebrate: Dooley and Arnot's shares go back into the common pot, to be divided among the rest of you. That means a bigger payday for everybody," Emmeline Jones said.

"That ain't so bad," one of the outlaws allowed to a companion.

"Me, I never liked neither of them anyway," the other said.

"But that's not all," the woman's deep-chested voice boomed out. "When the rest of the boys come in for the night, I don't see why you can't have a couple of girls in the church over for a little fun. Have yourself a real party, like you deserve!"

"Now you're talking, Ma," somebody yelled, and others cheered and laughed, a more genuine laugh of relief.

"Maybe I'm drunk, but that old woman herself is starting to look good to me," Hartigan said.

"You're drunk, all right," another said.

"Man, they're ain't enough liquor in the whole wide world to get me that drunk," opined a third.

"She's had five kids from five husbands. Every man that was ever married to her is dead," the second man said. "Murdered by her," he added, lowering his voice.

"Aw, hell, that's just a story," Hartigan said.

"It is, huh? Then where are all her husbands? I'll tell you where. They're pushing up daisies in some lonely graves."

Emmeline Jones turned and climbed the stairs to the second floor, leaving behind the rowdy clamor of the riotous outlaws.

From below came a voice:

"Hey, get that pecker off the bar!"

"Idiots," she said.

She was the Queen of Blood River with the power of life and death over all within her domain.

All except for Slocum. But she didn't know about him yet.

16

There was darkness and a voice.

"How long you reckon we been locked up here in the hold, Mr. Peavey?"

It was the voice of Fluke, the slow-witted youth who did the donkey work and the dirty work on board the *Laura Lee*.

"I know you don't like me gabbing so much, Mr. Peavey. You're always telling me to keep my damned fool mouth shut. But I can't keep quiet now. Talking makes me less scared. Helps to pass the time."

He spoke in a hoarse, cracked, whispery monotone. Fluke had been rambling on for many hours, but showed no signs of stopping.

"I figure it's been a day and a half, maybe two days, since they locked us in here, right after we landed at the point. I'm just as glad they did 'cause I'd sure have hated to see what they did to that town. That's one mean bunch, Mr. Peavey."

Fluke's droning voice was accompanied by a variety of background noises: the creaking of planks and beams and hawsers, the more distant muffled gurgling of water.

"Eh? You say something, Mr. Peavey? I must have dozed off. I'm feeling poorly . . . weak, mighty weak. I keep slipping off. I don't want to sleep. I'm scared that if I do I'll wake up dead.

"I'm hungry, too. They ain't fed us since they throwed us in here. But I don't think they're fixing to starve us to death, do you, Mr. Peavey? If they was gonna kill us, they could have shot us and throwed us overboard, like they did to all them poor passengers . . . all but the females.

"But I don't reckon they'll kill us . . . not yet, anyhow. Like Captain Darby says, they's lubbers. They need us to run the boat for them. 'Course, when they don't need us no more, well, I hate to think about what they'll do then. . . .

"Thanks for letting me go on like this, Mr. Peavey, instead of saying you're going to knock eight bells out of me if'n I don't shut my damned fool trap, like you usually do. I declare, if I didn't have somebody to talk to here in the dark, like as not I'd go clean out of my head."

"Man, you sure is an ugly cuss," Bill Rigdon said. "You must have been whomped mighty hard with an ugly stick to get a pan like the one you got on you. Blowing your head off would be an improvement. What do you think about that, Admiral?"

"You won't," Captain Darby said.

"You're almighty sure of yourself, ain't you?"

"If you kill me, who's going to skipper the boat?"

"Your number two man, down in the hold."

"Mr. Peavey's in no condition to serve as the captain of this boat, nor in any other position, either, not since you shot him."

"That dopey kid, then. He can't be as dumb as he looks. He must know something about running this boat."

"Fluke couldn't sail a toy boat in a washtub. No, you need me and you know it. Besides, your boss lady wouldn't like it if you shot me."

"You're a salty cuss, ain't you, Admiral? Just keep in mind that I don't have to kill you to put a hurting on you. I could shoot your ears off, say. How'd you like that?"

Darby turned away, pointing his face in another direction from the one occupied by Bill Rigdon. That was about all he could do, since he was tied with stout ropes to a chair in the deckhouse of the *Laura Lee*. He stared at the porthole instead. There was little to see. It was night, and damp river air had fogged the glass. He wasn't seeing too well anyway, thanks to the beating he'd gotten.

"The Admiral here don't even like you a little bit, Bill," said Whiteface Ames, so-named because of his resemblance to the breed of white-faced Hereford cattle. His face was as white as it had ever been, with more than a tinge of greenness around the edges. Being on a boat didn't agree with him, not even a little bit.

"Tell you what I'm gonna do, Skipper. When this is over and we get where we're going to, I'm gonna give you a chance at a fair draw against me," Bill Rigdon said. "Now what do you say to that, Admiral?"

"I'm no gunman."

"No, you ain't, and that's a fact. You wouldn't be in the fix you're in now if you could shoot."

Rigdon took a long pull from a bottle of red whiskey. Ames, gagging, turned away.

"How can you drink that swill? Makes me sick just to watch you," he said.

"Want some?"

"Gaah! I just about lost my lunch just from sitting on this tub!"

"You're the only fellow I ever heard of who got seasick while the boat was still tied up at the dock."

"I'm a cowboy, not a sailor," Ames said. "I'll tell you this: once I get my cut, I'm heading someplace in the mountains—no, better still, the desert, where it's even drier—someplace where there ain't no more water than a chaser in a glass for as far as the eye can see!"

"Me, I'm gonna take up residence in a whorehouse," Rigdon said. "Permanent residence. Being around all them women and gals this trip and not being able to lay a finger on them has got me stoked up to the boil. All them females, and we can't touch a one of them. What a waste!"

"Makes sense, though. Untouched, they'll sell higher."

"Yeah, but how about them married women?" Rigdon argued. "They've been getting it regular. One or two more pokes ain't gonna make a difference. Their husbands won't mind, seeing as how they're all dead."

"Dead is the best way for husbands to be."

"I wish to hell I'd blown my ship sky-high before it was ever taken over by bilge rats like you two," Darby said.

"No sense rushing things, Admiral. You'll be going down with your ship soon enough," Rigdon said.

Ames took hold of a rail and held on tightly. "How can a boat that ain't moving be so unsteady?"

"If you're gonna puke again, don't do it in here."

"You're all heart, Bill."

"Here, help yourself to a chaw of this plug tobacco. It's good for what ails you."

"Now, I will puke."

Ames put a hand over his mouth and lurched unsteadily across the deckhouse floor. He flung open the door and staggered outside. The open doorway was an oblong of blackness framing him as he reeled on deck. Strings of haze, fog, floated through the air.

"Man's got a weak stomach. Some folks just can't take it," Rigdon said. He cut himself a chaw from the tobacco plug and stuffed it in the corner of his mouth.

Ames made choking, gagging sounds. "There he goes again," Rigdon said.

After a minute he glanced out the door, and saw Ames leaning over the deck rail with his head hanging down. "Don't fall in," he said. Ames said nothing.

"If you're gonna be out there for a while you might as well let Choey come in and you stand watch," Rigdon said. "If you're gonna be out there for a while."

Ames groaned, coughed, didn't move.

"Weak stomach," Rigdon said. "Guess I'll have to finish this bottle by myself."

Choey Bravo carried a gun but held it in reserve as a last resort. His weapon of choice was the knife. He was an expert knife fighter and, what was more rare, an expert knife thrower. He never missed his mark. He could have made a career performing his blade wizardry on stage or in the circus, but he preferred the real thing with human targets.

He'd had a special leather belt made for him in Durango. It was twelve inches high, circled his midriff, and held a dozen flat, balanced throwing knives sheathed to it. Choey could draw and throw a knife in the same time or less that it took a fast gunman to draw and shoot his weapon.

That was how Slocum knew him right off, by the belt. Choey stood on the afterdeck of the berthed *Laura Lee*, amusing himself by throwing his knives at the wall of a flat-roofed wooden housing covering some piece of machinery. Yellow light shone through the deckhouse portholes, beaming through clammy patches of river fog that blanketed the boat, the docks, and all of the Shorthorn Point waterfront.

A beam fell like a spotlight on the shedlike structure Choey was using for target practice. Standing as far from it as he could, outside the zone of light, he launched his whirling missiles in quick succession. Each knife struck point-first, burying itself deep in the planks with a satisfying thunking sound. The blades fell in such a tight target group that they seemed to have sprung up from a common root.

The knife-hurler was the picture of intense concentration, performing each series of actions with almost ritualized formality. His throwing arm flashed in a smooth blur of motion. His concentration did not slacken until the last of his twelve knives had left its belt sheath and flown to its target.

Thoughtful, serious, he padded light-footed to the target to retrieve his knives for another round. The blades cast long shadows thanks to the deckhouse lights. He gripped a knife properly, not at the hilt but just above where the point entered the target, to free it.

That's when Slocum got him.

He'd been hiding in the shadows, crouched behind a pile of crates stacked on deck near the machine housing that Choey was using for a target. He'd known it was Choey almost from the first instant that he'd climbed up the anchor chain out of the water and boarded the ship. That throwing knife belt of his was unique and as distinctive as a signature. More so, since Choey couldn't write his own name except as an X-shaped mark.

Set a blade to slay a blade. Slocum had a blade, too. It was the foot-long bladed spear point of an eight-foot-long Apache lance, the lance that had pinned Joe Mord to the side of the gun wagon during the fight at Notch Pass. When Slocum unpinned the dead man, it had occurred to him that the lance might come in handy later on. It could kill silently—a useful weapon indeed for a one-man hit-and-run raid on an outlaw gang that had him outnumbered forty-to-one. He'd taken it along with him in the wagon and later rigged an improvised rawhide sling for it. He strapped it across his back, leaving his arms free when he swam out to the boat and boarded it. He had his Bowie knife, too, strapped to his side, but no gun. He didn't have any way to waterproof the gun for the swim out to the boat, and a wet gun was not only useless but dangerous. Besides, this had to be done quietly.

Shirtless, barefoot, dripping wet, he skulked toward Choey. The fog deepened the darkness, there was plenty of cover on deck, and the background noises of a boat in the water conspired to mask any soft footfalls he might have made while creeping toward the target. The thing he had to be most careful of was the lance. He wasn't used to carrying one, so he took great pains to make sure that the long shaft wouldn't bump into anything and betray his presence.

He made his way with stealth to a hiding place just beyond the cone of light falling on the targeted wall, and waited. He did not have to wait long, because of the speed with which Choey loosed one blade after another.

When his belt had been emptied he went to the target to get his knives, and that's when Slocum got him.

Slocum popped up from behind the crates, holding the lance in both hands. "That you, Ames?" Choey said before looking up. Glancing to the side, expecting to see one of his partners, he saw Slocum coming at him, thrusting the lance.

Slocum speared him in the middle, in the soft spot right below the solar plexus. The shock of being speared or stabbed there often paralyzes the victim, as it did Choey. The blade pierced him with less resistance than it would have encountered from a sack of grain. Slocum kept on pushing and nailed Choey to the wall of the housing.

Choey's mouth gaped wide and his arms were spread at his sides, so that he looked as if he were about to break into song. But he couldn't move, couldn't draw a breath for an outcry.

"Greetings from Big Spring," Slocum said softly, but loud enough for Choey to hear him.

Then he twisted the spear blade inside him, and that was the end of Choey Bravo. His legs collapsed, but the lance held him pinned in place. Slocum left him there.

With Choey here, his partners couldn't be too far off. Slocum went to find them.

Before he'd gone very far, he almost tripped over a coiled rope that had been carelessly left on deck. Slocum thanked his luck that he'd seen it in time to avoid stumbling over it. A broken ankle would upset his plans, not to mention his chances of survival. He started to move on, then stopped as a thought struck him: ropes were silent, too.

He coiled up the rope, looped it over his shoulder, and went back to the attack.

"Hey, Bill, gimme a hand!"

The voice from outside the deckhouse came as a hoarse, sickly croak. Bill Rigdon glanced through the open doorway at Ames, who was still doubled over the gunwale.

"What did I tell you? Some folks just ain't got the stomach for it," Rigdon said to the captain. He wasn't expecting a response and Darby didn't make one.

"*Bill . . .*"

"All right, hold your horses, I'm coming." Rigdon got up and went out. Streamers of mist clung to his face like cobwebs.

Ames was on the dockward side of the boat, draped over the rail with his head hanging down. "Man, you is sick as a dog," Rigdon said, chuckling.

He stood behind and to one side of Ames. A rift opened in the fog, revealing the distant figures of the guards at the landward end of the dock. Then more fog rolled in, hiding them again.

"Hey, what the hell's wrong with you, boy?" Rigdon said after a long moment of silence. "You passed out or something?"

Ames did not reply. Rigdon grabbed him by the shoulder, intending to shake him, but he pulled up short when he felt something warm and wet. He grabbed instead for a fistful of hair at the back of Ames's head, knocking his hat into the water.

He jerked back Ames's head hard, and it nearly came off in his hand. Even in the dimness he could see that Ames's throat had been cut from ear to ear. Not slit— cut.

He let go as if he'd been burned. Ames's head fell forward. His neck had been sawed so deeply that he was nearly decapitated. The sudden shock of falling forward finished the job. The head tore loose and dropped into the water. It raised a little splash and then sank swiftly from sight, leaving Ames's hat bobbing on the wavelets it had made.

Something whooshed overhead, cutting the air above Rigdon. It fell on his shoulders—it was a rope loop. It was pulled taut from behind, narrowing the loop. It lifted off his shoulders, circled his neck, caught fast there, and closed still tighter.

By the time Rigdon realized that he'd been lassoed by the neck, the sliding loop had become a noose so tight that he couldn't get his fingers under it in time to stop it from cutting off his wind.

The unseen roper started reeling in his line, dragging Rigdon backward across the deck toward the wheel-house. The rope cut deep into his tender throat. He couldn't shout, couldn't breathe.

He lost his footing and fell, sitting down hard, but that only slowed his transit across the deck. His boot heels hammered the planks. His head thumped a hard projecting corner, making him see stars. Loss of breath was already dimming the edges of his vision. He didn't have a knife with which to cut himself loose. For an instant he thought about going for his gun and shoot-ing the rope apart, but when he lowered one of the hands that was fighting the noose the pressure became so unbearable that he gave up the attempt.

His head and shoulders banged into the deckhouse bulkhead, stopping his horizontal sliding motion. From here on in, the short trip took him only one way: up. And not far, either. Just enough to raise the bottom of his feet twelve inches into empty air above the deck.

The hangman stood on the flat roof of the deckhouse, wielding the rope. First, though, Slocum had crept up behind Ames and cut his throat, taking him by surprise without a struggle. He draped him over the rail, then climbed to the wheelhouse roof with the rope looped over his shoulder. Pretending to be Ames, he called out to Rigdon for help. He tied one end of the rope to a metal cleat bolted to a roof beam, put a loop in the other end, and waited for Bill Rigdon to come out. He winced when Ames's head fell off—he'd carved too deeply in the enthusiasm of the moment.

Slocum was a top ranch hand when he wanted to be, and he could throw a loop with the best of them. He roped Rigdon by the neck, dragged him across the deck, and then lifted him straight up, tugging hand over hand, body braced, feet spread wide for better balance and leverage. He wound the excess line around the cleat and snugged it in place, leaving Rigdon hanging a foot off the deck.

Rigdon kicked and jerked at the end of the rope. It wasn't pretty, and it wasn't particularly quick, but it was quiet and effective.

His struggles ceased, and Bill Rigdon became dead weight slowly twisting and turning at the end of a rope. . . .

"If anyone was ever born to hang, it was you, Bill," Slocum said.

Captain Darby was tied facing the open doorway so he'd had a front-row seat for the sudden ascension of Bill Rigdon. After Rigdon stopped kicking, a stranger suddenly vaulted into view, dropping lightly down from the roof, landing catlike on bare feet. Rising, he started for the door. The hanged man dangled in front of it like a curtain. The stranger brushed him aside and entered.

He was a tall man, broad-shouldered, deep-chested, long-limbed. His wet hair was plastered straight and his torso gleamed. He wore jeans and a long knife strapped to his side. He held the gun he'd lifted from Rigdon's holster. It was a good gun. Rigdon was a gunfighter and he had known his guns.

"You do nice work, mister, whoever you are," Darby said, motioning with his head toward the man dangling outside.

"Any more of them on board?"

"How many did you get?"

"Counting him, three," Slocum said.

"Then you got them all, unless there's others on board that I don't know about."

"I counted three. I was watching them for a while before making my move. If there was any others, I'd have seen them."

"Then again I say: you do nice work, mister."

"Thanks. The name's Slocum."

"Captain Darby, at your service."

"You're the skipper of this tub?"

"I'm the captain of the *Laura Lee*, sir," Darby said, looking pained.

"Good."

Slocum's searching gaze fell on the bottle of red whiskey that Rigdon had left behind. There were still a few mouthfuls left. Slocum took a good long pull of it, then shuddered.

"That's godawful! Warms you up inside, though," he said, then took another pull. "Takes some of the river chill out of the bones."

"Do you think you could save me a little taste of that stuff, Mr. Slocum? I haven't had a drop in two days."

"Let's get you out of those ropes first."

Slocum drew his knife, then hesitated. He had cleaned it quickly but not too well earlier after using it on Ames.

"Don't mind me; I'm not squeamish," Darby said.

Slocum cut the ropes binding Darby to the chair. The captain groaned, sagging as the severed strands fell away from him. Slocum caught him and kept him from falling.

"Easy. Here, have some of this," he said, raising the bottle to Darby's lips. Darby gulped greedily, draining the bottle.

"How long will it take to get this tub—er, this boat, moving?"

"Not long, if you just want to sink her. Just haul anchor and cut the ropes, and in a quarter hour or so we'll drift loose, and in a few more minutes after that she'll rip her bottom out on the channel rocks and sink and that will be the end of her."

"I had something a little less drastic in mind."

"Then you'll just have to wait until dawn, when there's enough light to see by. Blood River is difficult to navigate in broad daylight by an experienced crew, and Drowned Canyon is one of the most dangerous stretches of the entire run. There's crosscurrents, sandbars, and barely sunken rocks that can tear open a ship from stem to stern in the blinking of an eye."

"What you're telling me is that the ship can't sail until daylight."

"Oh, we can sail all right, Mr. Slocum, once the boilers are fired up, and that won't take long. We just wouldn't get more than a few hundred yards from shore before running aground on the rocks. Following which we would die by drowning or possibly by boiler explosion."

"Better that the ship is destroyed than the outlaws make their getaway on it."

"I quite agree. But there's easier ways to scuttle her than running her on the rocks. Just open the shuttlecocks and flood her and sink her."

"That's not a bad idea."

"Or she could be blown up. There's dynamite hidden on board. I use it to clear snags and other obstructions. The outlaws didn't find it, didn't even suspect it was here. I'll blast the *Laura Lee* to atoms before letting those devils take her again!"

"You might have to, Captain. How much dynamite do you have?"

"Plenty."

"That's good."

"There's no shortage of weapons. They've turned this ship into a floating arsenal."

"That's good, too."

"I warn you, Mr. Slocum, I don't intend to give up the ship or destroy her without a fight."

Slocum laughed. "Don't worry, Captain, you'll get your fight, I promise you that. You feel up to getting around on your feet yet?"

"It'll be a little while before I've got my sea legs back, but—yes. Just pick me up if I fall down, that's all I ask you."

"Let's get that dynamite, then—pronto."

"Let's get my crew first. They're locked in the hold."

"All right."

"They're coming, Mr. Peavey. I hear them coming for us, sure. Shhhh! Listen, you can hear them. Maybe they're just gonna feed us. Sure, that's it. They ain't gonna kill us, not yet I don't think, since we still got to get them downriver. I know this: whatever they're gonna do, we can't do nothing about it," Fluke said.

The footsteps stopped. A heavy bar was lifted on the other side of the door. A key turned in the lock. The door creaked as it was opened from without.

They were below decks. What little light there was came from the hooded lantern in Darby's hand, its shutter opened only a slit to cast a thin light. To Fluke, after countless hours of absolute darkness, the brilliance of the lamplight was dazzling, and he shielded his eyes from it.

He huddled in the cramped space of a storage locker little larger than a closet, too small to lay flat in, a close and stinking space swarming with lice and ripe with filth. Peavey was heaped in one of the corners like a pile of rags.

"Fluke! Thank God you're alive, boy!"

"Huh . . . who?"

"It's me, Captain Darby. Don't try to talk, Fluke. Save your strength. We'll have you out of there in a minute—"

A figure filled the doorway and leaned over, hooking strong hands under Fluke's arms and lifting. Fluke passed out.

When he came to some seconds later, he lay flat on his back outside the cell. Somehow he managed to raise himself on his elbows to a sitting position.

"Never mind about me. You'd best see to Mr. Peavey. He's hurt real bad, Captain."

"Hurt? He's dead! Didn't you know that, boy?"

Fluke's laugh sounded like a wood rasp. "Dead? That's the craziest thing I ever heard. I been talking to him the whole time!"

"From the looks of him, he's been dead for more than a day. Listen, Fluke. You say you've been talking to him the whole time. Did he ever say anything back to you?"

" . . . Well, come to think of it, no." Fluke chewed that one over for a moment. "Huh! Mr. Peavey dead all that time, and me thinking he was alive. . . . Huh! That's a good one on me, ain't it?"

"It's a better one on Peavey," Slocum said.

17

Bill Rigdon had a small head. Slocum had trouble fitting into his hat. He jammed it down hard, screwing it to his skull to keep it from falling off. He stuffed Rigdon's gun into the top of his pants on the left side, butt outward, for a quick cross-belly draw. He held on to Rigdon's empty whiskey bottle.

Rigdon himself went into the river, along with his partners, Choey Bravo and what was left of Whiteface Ames from the neck down. They were lowered by rope one by one off the riverward side of the boat and released to be carried away by the currents.

"A whole lot of reward money is floating down the river with them," Slocum said. "Oh well, it can't be helped."

Over his shoulders he threw a blanket that Darby had supplied and wrapped himself in serape style. Taking the empty bottle, he descended the gangplank and started toward the landward end of the long dock.

One thing he couldn't hide was his bare feet. He'd left his boots on shore, along with his guns, before taking his swim in the river. He wouldn't step into any dead men's boots, though there was no shortage of them on the boat. No shortage of dead men filling those boots, either, at least not until they went over the side and into the drink.

Some buildings showed on land at the end of the dock, long, low warehouse-type storage sheds. Two sentries patrolled the square between the dock and the shed. Their names were Dunc and Harlow. Slocum knew their names because he'd heard them talking earlier when he treaded water between the pilings under the dock before swimming to the boat.

Harlow and Dunc were still on duty, if not quite on guard. They stood with their backs to the water, facing the road that ran up the rise to Redrock. The Cattleman Hotel, headquarters for the outlaw band, was a smear of yellow light in a basin full of fog, rain, and darkness.

The rain was good to Slocum. It would wash out the tracks of the gun wagon, blotting out the trail of the Gatling gun. The rain kept the outlaws indoors and made sentries posted on guard duty like Dunc and Harlow huddle miserably under whatever shelter they could find.

Slocum had spied on Rigdon enough back in Big Spring to get to know his habits and style pretty well. As he neared the sentries, he assumed a rolling, swaggering gait, as he had seen Rigdon do. He held the empty bottle by the neck in his left hand; his right hand was under the blanket. He kept his head down, hiding much of his face under Rigdon's hat brim. The rain made that subterfuge look natural, since who doesn't duck his head in the rain?

He made noise so they would hear him coming in advance and see that he came from the boat. They didn't expect attack from that quarter; they were watching the road.

"Yo! Either of you hombres got a spare bottle of red-eye? I'm all out and I got me a powerful thirst," Slocum said in a more than passable imitation of Rigdon's voice.

"Forget it, Rigdon, we ain't got enough for ourselves," Harlow said. "Hey, hold on a minute, you ain't Rigdon!"

"No, but I'm thirsty anyway," Slocum said.

His right hand came out from under the blanket and a gun was in it. Harlow opened his mouth to say something. Slocum thrust the gun barrel hard into the pit of his belly, doubling him up. He laid the barrel hard against the side of Harlow's head, and Harlow dropped and didn't move.

It was all over in a second, and then Slocum was covering Dunc, who'd barely had time to blink. Dunc thought fast. "You can't shoot. If you do the others will hear you," he said.

Slocum snapped his wrist out almost lazily, but the effect was like cracking a whip. He backhanded the gun barrel against the point of Dunc's chin. Dunc reeled, Slocum pistol-whipped him again, and Dunc went down.

Slocum stripped their hats and coats and gun belts from them. They didn't move—they were out cold. He'd hit Harlow first, so he got rid of him first. He dragged Harlow by his heels to the edge of the dock and dumped him in the river. A moment later he disposed of Dunc the same way.

"Sorry to do you boys that way, but that's what you get for woman stealing," Slocum said.

Fluke and Captain Darby managed to limp to the end of the dock just as Slocum finished up with Dunc. "What else could I do?" Slocum said. "Waste time tying them up?"

"You're doing fine, Mr. Slocum. That's probably the first bath those wharf rats have had in years," Darby said, glancing down at the swirling black waters.

A quickly eaten meal and a few tots of some hidden rum that the outlaws hadn't found had given the captain and the cabin boy the strength to get on their feet. They still looked like the walking dead, but at least they were walking, even if they did have to brace each other to do it.

"Here, put these on. They belonged to Harlow and Dunc. With their hats and coats on you just might be able to pass for them from a distance, or long enough to use those guns if somebody comes snooping around," Slocum said.

"Don't you worry about us. I've got something better than guns."

"Oh, yeah? What's that, Captain?"

Darby spread open the flaps of his coat. Bundles of dynamite with short fuses were stuffed in the inside pockets.

"Whew! If a bullet hits you, the whole county will know it."

"That's the idea, Mr. Slocum."

"And Fluke?"

"I ain't scared, Mr. Slocum. I was scared all right when I was locked up in the hold, but I ain't scared now."

"Good man, Fluke. I'll get moving now, Captain. I can take one of the guards' horses; that'll buy me some time. I'll be back soon, if all goes well. If not—if I don't make it, blow up the ship and look to yourself as best you can."

The Gatling gun was hidden near what Slocum called the Sawmill, but before heading there he made a slight detour to fetch his boots and guns. They were wrapped up in a bundle inside his shirt and hidden beneath the rotted underside of a fallen log in a cove a quarter mile farther down the dark shoreline, past the far side of Shorthorn Point.

The point curved out from the Blood's north bank like a bull's horn that had been broken off a third of the way from the tip. The stockpens and sheds were located on the point's broad base. Stout wooden fences enclosed a large grazing field adjacent to the pens. Here was where the basin's herds were gathered for shipping down the river on cattle barges.

The pens were filled to overflowing with a few hundred head of cattle whose transshipment was indefinitely postponed due to the taking of Redrock. The lowing, milling cattle were now hungry, thirsty, and short-tempered. It wouldn't take much to set them off. The scent of the river so near must have been maddening to them. The rain had cooled them down some and temporarily eased their thirst, but it wouldn't last.

The sound of their agitated restlessness would have covered more than the slight noise Slocum made as he rode along the north shore. The outlaws had posted no guards on this lonely strip of country.

It felt good to put on a warm dry shirt after he found his bundle under the log in the cove, but it felt better to put on his own gun belt. He didn't need Rigdon's gun anymore, so he tossed it into the river.

"Take it to hell with you, Bill," he said.

He put on his boots, strapped a pair of bandoliers on crisscross over his chest, and donned his hat. He picked up his rifle, swung aboard the horse, and rode farther east along the shoreline, ready to do battle.

The outlaws hadn't bothered to post any guards here because there was nothing left to guard. They'd burned down a cluster of shacks and dugouts that had made a crude shantytown on the bank of the river. Some of its inhabitants still lay sprawled in the mud where they'd been shot down, beside the long-cool ash heaps of their torched homes. Some of the bodies had burned to charred black skeletons.

Then there was the Sawmill. It wasn't really a sawmill; Slocum just called it that because that's what it sounded like, a busy, humming, buzzing sawmill. It was a crude adobe blockhouse with its long sides parallel to the river. There'd been a mass execution inside it, where those who'd survived the first wave of slaughter, when the outlaws took over the town, had later been gathered and then gunned down in a mass. It sounded like a sawmill because of the hordes of flies swarming the remains, a Biblical plague's worth of them.

Slocum steered clear of the death house to avoid spooking the horse. But the Gatling gun was hidden in a grove upwind of the Sawmill, along with plenty of ammunition and a couple of fresh horses.

When he'd come into sight of Redrock hours earlier, he'd left the main road and swung into the middle heights of the hills to make a wide loop clear of the town until he better knew the lay of the land.

The rain was a godsend because it washed out the tracks of the heavily laden gun wagon's wheels. But even though Slocum had shaken off pursuit, the wagon was too conspicuous and unwieldy to be taken too close to town. That's why he'd hidden it in a secluded spot, unhitched the horses from the traces, and pressed them into service as pack horses to carry the Gatling gun and boxes of ammunition on their strong backs.

Riding the saddle horse, leading the pack train, he'd come down from the middle hills and into the mud flats where the shantytown had been. He picketed the horses under the dark, dripping boughs of the grove and started toward town on foot, scouting the terrain, determining the disposition of the outlaw forces, making plans.

After prowling around the outskirts of town and the riverfront, he stripped to his jeans, slung the Apache lance across his back, and waded barefoot into the shallow, mucky inlet of the cove.

Blood River was swift in places, but not close to the shore, where the currents lazed, losing their force, especially in the lee of Shorthorn Point, whose bulk served as a barrier to tame the rush of swift water.

Sticking close to the shore, Slocum made his way to the docks, then swam unnoticed by the guards out to the boat. . . .

Now, he once more returned to the docks on the point, but this time he came on horseback with a Winchester at half-cock held across the front of the saddle and a string of weary beasts of burden trailing along behind.

The fog muffled sounds, so that Slocum and the pack horses seemed to materialize like ghosts out of the swirling mists and haze at land's end.

At first he didn't see Fluke and Darby and that worried him. But they were only laying low until they made sure it was him. Then they showed themselves.

"I was starting to worry that maybe you'd jumped ship and taken off for parts unknown," Darby said.

"What, and miss all the fun?" Slocum said. "All quiet here?"

"Except for Griff."

"Griff? Who's Griff?"

"A pal of Dunc and Harlow's. He came by to pass the time with them while you were gone."

"Where is he now?"

"With his friends," Darby said, nodding toward the river.

"You do nice work yourself, Captain."

"Thanks. Griff brought his friends a couple of bottles of whiskey. Good stuff, too. Want a snort?"

"Don't mind if I do."

"Keep the bottle; I've got another. Say, maybe now you'll tell me what you're toting on those horses that's so all-fired important you had to risk your neck to get it."

Slocum hadn't told Darby what he was after. If the outlaws had somehow managed to take him alive, the riverboat captain wouldn't have been able to betray the secret of Slocum's ace-in-the-hole.

The time had come to enlighten him. "You know that Gatling gun the outlaws have?"

"Know it? Why, they smuggled it aboard my ship hidden inside a coffin!"

"Well, they don't have it anymore. I do."

18

"Where you sneaking off to down the back stairs, missy?"

"Never you mind about that, Tewk."

"Your *momma* minds. She'll have my liver for breakfast if I let you get away from me again, Miss Pearl."

"Oh, all right, come along with me then. Anything to stop your whining."

Pearl resumed her interrupted journey down the back steps of the Cattleman's Hotel. She descended quickly, curved fingers lightly trailing over the banister rail, snaky strands of hair trailing from her head like a black corona.

"But you ain't supposed to go nowhere, Miss Pearl!" Tewk called down into the stairwell. Pearl's silvery laughter floated up to him. She was getting away from him fast.

Tewk plunged after her down the stairs. He was clumsy, and his feet kept getting tangled up in each other. Once he misjudged a landing and ran face-first into a wall. He bounced off, spun, straightened out, and continued his descent.

The farther he went down in the shaft, the darker it

got. The bottom was a pit of blackness that threw Tewk
into a blind panic. Where was the exit? But the door
was opened a crack, outlined by the lesser darkness of
a rainy night. Tewk flung it open and splashed out into
the mud and the rain and the wind of a cross street. It was
a wild night made wilder and more frightening because
Pearl was nowhere to be seen.

"I know she's out here somewhere, she's got to be!"

He was close to tears and would have broken down
except that Pearl couldn't repress a fit of silvery laughter
and gave away her hiding place around the corner of
the hotel.

"You little witch! Wait, where you going now?"

"To church," Pearl said. She protected her head from
the rain with a shawl she had tossed across her shoulders
earlier, when she first set out. She raced across the road
and up the hill, splashing in the puddles.

Tewk caught up with her. "You *know* your momma
don't want you going in there, girl!"

"What can happen with you along to protect me?
Anyway, this is strictly business."

"Monkey business."

"Family business. *Jones* family business," she said.

Tewk stopped arguing because he was out of breath
and he needed some to keep up with Pearl. "Ma sure put
a hurting on old Reb," Pearl said as they neared the
church.

"Whew, I'll say! Never seen a fellow so glad to have
his throat cut, there at the end."

The church was a long, white wood frame building
with a gabled roof but no steeple. The short front end
faced the town and the river. The guards horses were
hitched nearby.

The guards were Bliss, Hovey, Gus, and Dingell. They
were each supposed to be guarding an approach to one
of the structure's four walls, but it was raining and cold
and they couldn't be bothered. They huddled on the front

steps, passing a bottle around, sheltering from the rain as best they could under the roof's overhang. A fifth man, Rollo, the boss of this detail, was inside the church. So was Neeley, Reb Dooley's associate.

So were the women.

"Let me borrow your gun, Tewk."

"What? You crazy, girl? Who you fixing to shoot?"

"Nobody. I just want to be able to protect myself. Come on, Tewkie Tewk Tewk Tewk. Let me borrow it and I'll slip you a bottle of something nice."

"What devilments are you up to?"

"Never mind. If you won't, you won't. Maybe one of those big strong cowboys will let me play with his gun, if you know what I mean."

"You'll get me a bottle, right?"

"Maybe. I don't know. I'm mad at you, Tewk."

"You said, you said!"

"Oh, all right. Give me the gun first."

She held out her hand and he placed the gun in it. She wiped the gun butt with a corner of her shawl, then hid the gun in her folded arms under the shawl.

The guards were respectful when they saw it was Pearl. They stood up and she breezed past them. "Don't mind me, boys, just go about your business," she said.

She went up the stairs and into the church, Tewk trailing after her. "You figure it's okay to let her in?" said Hovey, a worrier.

"She's a Jones. I ain't gonna try to stop her," Bliss said.

"Me, neither," Dingell seconded.

Inside the church were a hundred women and girls lost in the depths of grief, misery, and despair.

And one man: Neeley.

Pearl drank in the scene in a state of intense excitement. "Damnedest church I ever did see."

Rollo saw her and came over, hat in hand. He was a veteran gun, smart and tough, but the Joneses were too rich for his blood and he knew it. "Something I can do for you, Miss Pearl?" he said.

"Ma sent me over to take a look at Neeley, make sure you been taking good care of him, Rollo."

"Oh, he's been taken care of real good, ma'am."

"You didn't kill him, did you?"

"He should be so lucky."

"That's him over there, ain't it? I want some words with him."

"Be my guest."

Neeley sat in a side alcove, where the church ushers would be. His hands were tied and he was battered and bruised from a beating. He was cowed, hopeless, broken.

"Hey, Neeley," Pearl said.

"Hi, kid."

"Man, you really messed up this time."

"I know."

"Know what happens when you mess up?"

Neeley's apathy gave way to stark fear as Pearl brought the gun out from under her shawl and pointed it at him.

"Please, *don't*—"

Pearl shot him in the heart at point-blank range, so close that the scorch marks around the wound burst into flame and burned a hole in his shirt.

"You get dead. That's what happens when you mess up," Pearl said.

She handed the gun to Tewk, who was standing nearby. "Thanks for the loan."

Tewk took it as a matter of course, but Rollo couldn't hide his surprise. His hard-jawed face was spattered with blood but he wasn't even aware of it, he was too busy staring at Pearl.

"It's been real nice visiting with you, Rollo, but I've got to go now," Pearl said.

Rollo watched her go to the church entrance. Tewk

shrugged, then followed her out on the front steps.

Gunfire crackled somewhere in the darkness. Such outbursts by the drunken outlaws were so common as to be ignored by the others, but this was different. These shots triggered a storm.

First, it was a storm of sound, a distant rumble like a thunderclap, but instead of fading away it continued to grow. It made the earth rumble as it mounted to a roaring torrent of sound and vibration that shook man-made structures to their foundations.

Pearl stood frozen in place a few paces from the church entrance, staring in amazement as what looked like a dark river in flood rushed uphill from the waterfront and raced headlong toward the town.

"What in tarnation is that?" asked Hovey, not worried now, but scared.

"Sure wish I had that little cow pony now,'cause I've sure got plenty of cows," Slocum said.

But he needed plenty to get a good stampede going.

A few hundred head were crowded in the dockside stockpens. They'd been driven to the brink by hunger, thirst, and being crammed together nearly head to tail with scant room to move. They were spooky and wild and ready to go. It wouldn't take much to set them off.

So Slocum set them off.

He approached the fence gate on horseback. If the pens hadn't been built solid the herd would have broken out long ago. The fence enclosed a restless lake of bobbing heads and horns. A ripple of alertness ran through them as Slocum neared. They knew.

He slipped the latch loop on the fence gate and moved away fast. The pressure in the pen was so great that a mass of cattle surged through the opening as soon as it was made. The force of the rush slammed the gate back against the fence with a crack. The cattle flooded the dockside area, heads tossing, hoofs pounding, chuffing.

Their eyes were wild in their long gaunt faces.

Slocum emptied a six-gun near the edge of the mass to get them started in the right direction.

The results were immediate. The herd was galvanized into a blue funk. They lit out in a blind-panic run opposite to the direction that the shots had been fired. Slocum fired some more to encourage them.

The stampede was on. With all the curved, gleaming horns and fleet, dark coursing forms, it looked like a riot of devils in Hell.

Slocum had used a pair of outlaw's pistols to spark the charge. He threw them away as soon as they were empty and rode off quick. He cut his horse wide to the left before starting up the hill toward Redrock, keeping a safe distance from the stampede. Pushing the horse hard, he outraced the vanguard of the herd and pulled out in front of them.

He galloped past the backs of the buildings on Redrock's main street and charged the church.

The guards watched the stampede coming. Rollo and Tewk hustled Pearl into the church for her own safety. The guards saw a rider fast-approaching and thought it was one of the band come to warn them or seek shelter.

Slocum rode up, reined in, and cut loose on the guards with both pistols. Muzzle flares flashed like lightning, making the guards' long shadows caper weirdly against the church front as they spun and fell dead.

Slocum shoved the empty guns in the holsters, pulled his rifle from the saddle sheath, and dove off the horse as the church door flung open and Rollo stepped through it shooting.

He shot too high. Slocum stopped rolling, snapping off from the prone position a shot that ripped into Rollo. Rollo fell back through the door but grabbed the frame and held on. Slocum shot him again, and Rollo lost his grip and crashed inward.

Slocum came up off the ground and took the front steps two and three at a time. He came at the doorway from the side, barreling in low. His lunge carried him to the foot of the center aisle, where he crouched, looking for something to shoot.

The church was high-ceilinged, barnlike, dimly lit by a handful of lanterns that burnt with an oily, beer-colored light. Roughly one hundred ill-used females ranging in age from children to matrons were grouped in the pews, in the aisle, and on the altar. Among them were the hopeless, the defiant, and those too numb to feel.

Also among them were Tewk and Pearl.

They were behind Slocum. Tewk was a good watch-dog. When the shooting started, he had drawn his gun and grabbed Pearl, standing them both with their backs to the wall on one side of the doors.

Slocum didn't see them at first. He was trying to see everywhere at once in bad light.

"Run for it, gals!" he shouted. "Run to the boat and run hard, run for your lives! *Move!*"

Tewk leveled his gun to shoot Slocum in the back, but he'd forgotten to watch his own back. One of the captives, a brunette with a fresh knife scar marring the side of her face, came up behind Tewk with a heavy brass candlestick and brought it down hard on his head.

Tewk folded. After an instant's hesitation, Pearl dropped to her knees, scrambling for his gun. The brunette stomped on Pearl's hand, crushing it there to the floor so she couldn't raise the gun. Then some of the other captives piled on her. Slapping, scratching, punching, they bore her down.

"She's one of them; don't let her get away!"

Slocum thought he recognized the girl and stepped in to save her neck from the vengeful captives who mobbed her. It wasn't easy. These women had lost husbands, sweethearts, fathers, even their own children in some cases, murdered in cold blood. Slocum reached into the free-for-all and hauled Pearl out by her hair.

She was much the worse for wear, bedraggled, bruised, and mauled. She had a black eye, bloody nose, split lip. She was so scratched up she looked as if she'd been rolling around in thorn bushes, and there wasn't much left of her dress, either.

"Let us have her! We've got the right!"

"This is Pearl Jones. They won't be so quick to shoot when they find out we've got her," Slocum said.

"If you know who I am, you know that my momma will roast you over a slow fire, cowboy!"

"Not while I've got you, Pearl."

The outlaws poured out of the hotel into the street to investigate the source of the ever-mounting rumble that was making their heads rattle even more than the whiskey they'd swilled by the quart. Many staggered, and some were so drunk they could barely stand. Some stood in the street, staring down toward the river.

"Why, the herd is loose," one genius said mildly, so mildly that no one paid any attention to him.

Another drunk sat down in the street and couldn't get up. "Lucky the bottle didn't get broke, heh heh heh," he said.

"You'd better move, Biff," said another, who was still standing.

"Nope. Nope nope nope."

"Well then could I have a swig off your bottle?"

"Hell, no!"

The other outlaw snatched the bottle from Biff's hand and ran away.

"Hey! Hey, come back here, you thieving son of a bitch!"

Still sitting, Biff pulled his gun but never used it. The herd was upon him as they rampaged through the center of town. Biff screamed and disappeared under hoofs.

Emmeline Jones was not fooled. She suspected that

the stampede was a blind, a diversion, and when she heard the shots coming from the church, she knew it.

"It's a decoy! They're after the women! Get them, get them," she bellowed to be heard above the racketing rampage.

The gang's top gun hands, Nev, Jules, and the newly arrived Pete Keane, stood trapped on the sidewalk in front of the hotel, their guns useless against the mass of beef charging up Main Street.

"Get 'em, goddammit!" Emmeline Jones was all but tearing out her hair in frustrated rage.

The gunhawks stomped around on the boards, dashing up and down the sidewalk in search of a break in the stream of steers and not finding any.

Then somebody raced up a cross street from back behind the hotel, where the livery stables were located. "The horses just broke loose from the corral!" he shouted.

Emmeline Jones drew her gun and shot him. The outlaw, shocked, slid down the corner of the hotel and dropped out of sight.

"What did you shoot him for, Ma?"

"I'm just so damned mad I had to shoot somebody, Nev!"

Then it hit her:

"Where's Pearl?"

The captives streamed outside the church doors and ran for all they were worth. Some of the faster-thinking ones paused to grab guns from the dead outlaws spread across the stairs where Slocum had shot them. They ran downhill, screened from the view of the outlaws by the churning, charging stampede.

Slocum carried Pearl tucked under one arm. She kicked and screamed as he took her to his horse.

"Behave yourself," he said.

She tried to knee him, but he was ready for it. He made a fist and clipped her on the point of her chin, knocking her unconscious. He caught her before she fell, swooped her up across the horse, swung up himself, and rode. He rode the horse up and down the line of fleeing women, urging them to greater speed, herding in the stragglers and the strays.

The outlaws were in a state of confusion. Most of them were chasing their runaway horses, not knowing of the big breakout from the church. Some of them in front of the hotel glimpsed the fleeing forms and started shooting at them over the cattle. They weren't hitting yet.

Three outlaws galloped down the road as soon as the last of the stampede had passed. They avoided ragged lumps that once were men, now pounded to jelly by countless razor-sharp hoofs.

Slocum was waiting for them with his Winchester raised to his shoulder. He fired, and the lead rider tumbled from his mount.

The second rider swung to one side. Slocum led him a little, then fired. A fair distance stood between them, but the sound of the bullet smacking flesh was loud enough for Slocum to hear it.

The third rider reined in after seeing the other two shot down. He stopped in the middle of the street, where there was no cover. He was still looking for some when Slocum shot him down, too.

"Run, run!" Slocum held the position until the last of the captives raced past. Drumming footfalls, sobbed breathing, a child's wail marked their passage.

The outlaws were regrouping. Five more riders started down the street, and more came down from the sides. Slocum turned and rode down the hill to the foot of the docks.

Fluke stood somewhere in the middle of the dock, guiding the fugitives toward the ship's gangplank. Captain Darby stood at the top of the gangplank, ordering them to take cover behind hastily improvised bulwarks of cotton bales and crates.

The leaders among the women wasted no time in helping to organize a defense. They put the weaker ones as far out of harm's way as possible, and armed the strong ones for the fight. They were Texans, and many of them knew how to shoot and shoot well. Fortunately, there was a surplus of guns and ammunition, which the outlaws had stockpiled aboard the ship.

Outlaw gunfire was getting too hot for Slocum. He rode behind the cover of a tall stack of barbed wire rolls stacked like cordwood. Bullets started ripping into the dock, punching into planks and pilings.

The fire grew heavier and more accurate. A woman who was too slow to take cover behind a bulwark was shot in the middle. A rifle slug tore off the top of a blond head.

That shot had been fired by a sniper on a slanted warehouse rooftop. Slocum shot him. The sniper slid headfirst down the roof and crashed into the courtyard.

Another outlaw crouched behind a nearby corner. When he popped his head out in the open for a look-see, Slocum blew it off.

Other outlaws stopped shooting and ducked for cover behind barrels, crates, and bales.

Slocum blasted a few rounds to get their attention. "Tell Ma Jones I've got her girl!" he yelled.

"I know that voice," Pete Keane said.

"You do? Who is it?"

"Shhh! Hush up a minute, Jules; I want to hear this. Hey, boys, stop shooting for a minute. Cease fire! Cease fire, damn you!"

The others kept on shooting in Slocum's direction. "I've got Pearl Jones, you blasted idiots! Pearl Jones!"

That didn't cut too much ice with the outlaws.

"He got Pearl," one of them said, "he can have her."

"And welcome to her," another added.

"Amen to that."

Emmeline Jones and her henchmen finally arrived on

the scene. They sheltered under the cover of a projecting wall.

"Stop shooting!" she raged. "*Stop shooting!*"

The outlaw fire petered out after that, except for one fellow working a hot gun aimed at where he thought Slocum was hiding.

"The Widow says hold your fire, Sid," the man nearest him said.

"Like hell! I got the range on that honker, I tell you. Watch me get him on this shot."

Sid fired, missed. "This one for sure," he said.

Emmeline Jones came up behind him and shot him in the back.

"What are you, deaf?"

"Take it easy, Ma."

"When I give an order I mean it!"

"Sure, Ma, sure, but it's not helping to shoot our men for no good reason. We might need them."

"Nev, son, that's your little sister they got down there."

"Now, we don't know that, Ma."

"I'll damned well find out," she said. "Hey, you, cowboy! You hear me down there?"

"They can hear you clear to Mexico," Slocum said. "Oklahoma, too."

"You bastard . . ."

"I didn't get that," Slocum said.

"You got my girl?"

"Yeah!"

"Let me hear her say something, prove it's her. Prove she's alive. Pearlie, darling, say something to Momma, sweetie."

Slocum poked Pearl in the rump. "I didn't hit you that hard. Say something."

"I'd like to claw out your eyes and piss in the sockets!"

"Nice. Only say it to your ma, not to me."

She told Slocum what he could do to himself.

"That's not nice. You hear that, Widow Jones?"

"I don't hear nothing, cowboy! By God, if this is a trick—"

"If they don't believe you're here they'll start shooting and you've got as good a chance of getting hit as me, Pearl," Slocum told the girl.

"Damn you!"

"Especially with that big fat ass of yours making such a fine target, I don't see how those old boys can miss."

"*Damn* you! All right, let me up and I'll say something."

"You can say it just as well hanging upside-down across a horse."

"It's me, Ma!" she shouted. "Pearl! Come and get me and kill them, kill them all!"

"I will, honey, I swear it!"

"Pearl gets the first bullet," Slocum said.

"I *know* that voice!" Pete Keane said.

"Listen up, mister. Hurt one hair on my little girl's head and I'll slaughter every living soul on that boat!"

"The others won't like that. You can't sell a dead woman," Slocum said.

"This is bad," Pete Keane said.

"Who is it, Pete?" asked Jules.

"I'm going on board, Pearlie and me," Slocum said. "Don't anybody shoot or I might get scared and drop her on her head."

"What now, Ma?" Nev said.

"Hold your fire! Hold your fire, everybody!" Emmeline Jones said.

Slocum dismounted, tossed Pearl over his shoulder, and wove his way through the maze of unloaded cargo littering the decks toward the ship. He used her as a human shield.

He felt most exposed and vulnerable while climbing the gangplank, but none of the outlaws fired at him. The lesson of Reb Dooley was still fresh and raw in their minds.

"They can't move until first light without wrecking the boat on the rocks. I'll think of something by then," Emmeline Jones said.

19

"Stupid little bitch!"

"Don't talk about your sister like that, Nev."

"If it wasn't for her, there'd be no problem. We could just go in shooting and rush the boat. What've they got, two, three men, no more, and the rest women. We could take them easy!"

"Sure, and Pearl dies."

"That's her tough luck."

Emmeline Jones lashed at him with the nine-tailed cat. Nev took the blow on his upraised arm.

"Are you crazy?" he said.

"We'd best hang together, folks," Pete Keane said quietly. "The rest of these old boys will run wild if they see us falling out."

"You're talking sense, Pete," Nev said, breathing hard.

"Riders," a lookout shouted, "lots of them, coming this way!"

"Theirs or ours?"

The outlaws sweated until the reply:

"They're ours, ours! It's Monroe and his bunch! Monroe's back!"

This was welcome news. Monroe was a cruel and deadly gun, the only one in the family besides his mother to attract his own following. The guns who rode with him were the same type: fast, bold, and vicious. Among them were mountain man Matt Skimmerhorn, Johnny Drago, Earl Green, Marut Bauer, Grenville Sykes, and Del Hogan.

Monroe resembled the impossibly idealized hero of a dime novel. He was a coldly handsome giant with long hair the color of tarnished bronze and the physique of a Hercules in buckskin and blue jeans. He wore two fancy guns and rode a white horse.

He took a long look around and then said to his riders, "More bad news."

"What do you mean, more bad news?" Nev said.

"I'll tell you later. Now you tell me."

"Something's wrong, son," Emmeline Jones said, closing a fist over her heart. "Something's wrong, I know it, I feel it!"

"Pink's dead," Monroe said.

Emmeline Jones's face scrunched up and she pounded her chest over her heart. "Oh, Lord, my poor son Pink!"

"Now for the bad news: the Gatling gun is gone."

Emmeline Jones let out a howl of loss and pain that made the first one seem tame.

" 'Paches done it," Earl Green said, sending a chill through those who were first hearing the news.

"Apaches!" somebody echoed, shocked.

"They did for Pink, but he did for plenty of them. Not enough, though. He's dead and they got the gun," Monroe said.

"The hell you say! Them savages wouldn't know what to do with it if they had it," Emmeline Jones said.

"Some would. Some of them know as much about guns as any white man going, and maybe more," Pete Keane said.

"Where's Pink? I don't see his body nowhere. Didn't you bring him home with you, son?"

"What for? He's dead, Ma. Now what the hell's going on here? I wish somebody would tell me."

They told him. When he got the picture, his dark dead eyes rolled.

"Where's Tewk?" was the first thing he said after being told.

"Here he is." Johnny Drago, Monroe's right-hand man, held Tewk by the collar and dragged him into the scene.

Tewk was in a sorry state. Drago had to hold him up. Dried blood masked half his face.

"They hit me from behind, derned near split my skull! I never even got a look at them," Tewk said. "Lucky I wasn't killed!"

"Lucky, he says," Drago said.

"You messed up, old man."

"I done the best I could, Monroe, I swear!"

"The family's been carrying you for years when you should have been sent to the glue factory, you old fool. All you had to do to earn your keep was look after the girl and you couldn't even do that right."

"You got no call to talk to me like that, Monroe Jones! I know I done the best I could!"

"A toothless watchdog's no good to me," Monroe said, and shot him.

Monroe's gun was back in the holster before Tewk hit the ground.

Emmeline Jones gave a stricken cry. She went to Tewk and stood over him, almost bent double. She didn't touch him; she just stood over him, wheezing and shaking.

"What the hell are you carrying on for?" Monroe said, mildly surprised. "It's only Tewk."

"You shouldn't have done it, son. You shouldn't have

killed him. No good can come of it. You've jinxed yourself now, put on a curse that will last until the end of your days."

"From killing that old rumpot? We're better off without him. I should have got rid of him years ago."

"You fool," Emmeline Jones said, shoving her teary face at him, half-sorrowful, half-triumphant. "You poor fool! He was my first husband, only none of you ever knew it. I kept it a secret from you. Tewk was *your father,* Monroe. You just killed your own father!"

Monroe flinched. "My God!" Neville said, white-faced. Nobody else dared to speak.

Monroe finally broke the silence. "Never tell that lie again, old woman. If you do, I'll kill you where you stand."

"I run this bunch from here on in," he said to the others. "I make the laws. Anybody objects, speak up now so I can get the killing over with."

No one objected. "Silence means consent, big brother," Nev said.

"That a yes?"

"So say we all."

"All right. We need that boat and we need those women. We can't risk the outfit just for one person. Pearl will have to take her chances, same as everybody else. Agreed?"

"I don't see any other way around it," Nev said.

"All right then. The less time wasted the better. One good rush and we can take the boat. The bitches are already aboard and we run them down to Mexico for a big payday. Let's get to it. Now how do you like them apples, old woman?"

"What are you asking me for, Monroe? Like you said, you run this bunch now."

"You're damned right I do."

20

"You on the boat, hear me good! This is Monroe Jones speaking. Maybe you heard of me. Any of you people that's got a lick of sense will jump in the river and drown before I get you!"

"You must not like your sister much," Slocum shouted back, "not that I blame you. She's tied up here by the deckhouse, out in the open so you can see her and not forget what she looks like. She's gagged so we don't have to hear her. Be real careful with those bullets, boys, I know how much you'd hate to have to lose her."

"You got a name, stranger? Or are you just going to keep on hiding behind a bunch of women's skirts?"

"Funny you should say that, Monroe, considering. The name's Slocum."

"Slocum," Pete Keane said. "Sure, I knew it."

"I'll see you soon, Slocum. Too bad all them women and kids are going to get hurt."

"That never stopped you before, Monroe."

"Enough talk," Monroe said to his men. "It's butt-whomping time."

Pearl Jones had a bird's-eye view of the preliminaries. She was tied standing up to the rail of the apron extending from the wheelhouse some fifteen feet above the deck. She was tightly gagged so she couldn't reveal the nature of the defenses.

Ashen gray predawn light lit the hazy, unreal scene as the attack began. Monroe had divided his forces into two groups. The main body, split into smaller squads, huddled behind bales of cotton, which they used as moveable barricades. Squads of riflemen and *pistoleros* behind shields of burlap-wrapped cotton advanced up the dock toward the ship.

The second, smaller group, consisting mainly of the elite gunmen, was made up from all of Monroe's inner circle and a handful of lone wolves. They boarded two longboats and rowed toward the ship from its riverward side.

As the front ranks of the cotton-bale barricade crept closer, Slocum passed the word to the women crouched behind the ship's bulwarks:

"Don't shoot until I give the signal, or you'll spoil the surprise. And keep your heads down!"

"They're getting closer, Mr. Slocum!"

"Steady, Fluke."

"They're almost on us!"

"Steady—"

The attackers opened fire, peppering the dock side of the boat with a hot fusillade.

"Here they come!"

Shouting, whooping, the outlaws rushed out from behind the barricades and charged the ship, laying down murderous fire.

When a mass of them surged across the open dock in close ranks, Slocum gave the signal:

"Now!"

Rifle barrels, six-guns, and shotguns poked out from firing slots running along the side of the ship. The women were at the guns, and they opened fire with a stinging volley that started knocking men down.

"Hell's fire, them females is shooting at us—*Ugh!*"

The women kept blasting. Lead sleeted down into the charging ranks, thinning them.

An outlaw's leg was shot out from under him, and he fell down. A man near him was hit in the chest, the bullet kicking up a puff of dust from the back of his shirt as it drilled clear through him. Others shrieked, spun, then stretched their length on the dock, dead.

Some of the outlaws made it to the relative safety below the ship's curving hull, protected from the overhang. Soon they were emboldened to attempt to scale the sides.

One man reached the top of the rail, threw a leg over it. A rifle barrel was shoved in his face. He grabbed it with both hands as its wielder pulled the trigger. He back-flipped off the boat and hit the dock.

Now the outlaws who'd been held in reserve during the first wave rushed to the attack. There must have been two dozen outlaws or more, clearing the way with a storm of lead to overwhelm the ship's defenders through superior firepower and sheer brute force of numbers.

That was Slocum's cue to swing into action. He'd been held in reserve, too, until the enemy was totally committed in full strength. The Gatling gun was mounted on its tripod up on the wheelhouse walkway, and Slocum was manning it.

The ten-barreled gun swung around and down to cover the mass rush on the dock. Slocum turned the handle, cranking out mass death.

The Gatling gun cut down the outlaws like a hailstorm leveling a cornfield. No man could stand against its inexorable firepower. It was wholesale slaughter, doubly effective since it was completely unexpected.

Slocum worked the crank, sweeping the barrel from side to side, raking the foe. He opened up big gaps in their lines, and the gaps grew until the dock was virtually clear of standing men.

"Slocum! Over here!"

Slocum darted to the river side of the boat to see why Darby had alerted him. Bullets from down below in the water tore into the side of the deckhouse, stinging his face with wood chips.

The two longboats with the outlaws' most deadly killers were about to close with the *Laura Lee*. But Monroe's boarding party was made up of gunhawks, not sailors, and their clumsy rowing had delayed them from launching a simultaneous attack with the men on the docks.

Captain Darby touched the lit end of his cigar to the fuse of a bundle of dynamite and tossed it over the side at the nearest longboat. He missed by a wide margin, but the blast was tremendous, throwing up a twenty-foot water spout that nearly swamped the longboat.

"Let me try," Slocum said.

When the fuse was lit and sputtering on the next bundle of explosives, Slocum popped up, pitched it into the longboat, and ducked for cover.

The men in the boat saw it coming, but there was nothing they could do about it but scream. The blast came a split second later: short fuse.

Blood River hurled up a high and grisly column of water thick with dark shapes and bits and pieces of the longboat and its crew. They rained down on the other boat.

"Row faster, damn you!" Monroe said. "If we get close enough to the ship they can't bomb us for fear of sinking themselves!"

"Shut up and row!"

"We ain't gonna make it," Earl Green sobbed. "We got to jump, swim for it!"

"I'll shoot any man who tries," Monroe said, and proved it by plugging Earl Green when he stood up in the boat. Green clutched himself and fell sideways into the water.

Monroe sat at the stern facing the ship, so he was the only one who saw the next sputtering bundle of dynamite come arcing down from the deckhouse on an irresistible trajectory.

His reflexes were so quick that he actually jumped clear of the longboat before the dynamite dropped in near the bow.

The blast disintegrated the forward half of the long-boat and all the men in it. The others hit the water in various states of wholeness. Some were too damaged to stay afloat, others too stunned.

Mighty Matt Skimmerhorn was paralyzed by the shock wave. He was conscious, fully aware, but his body refused to respond to his will. His eyes were open, so he watched himself sink below the surface, into the cold black depths of the Blood. . . .

A few others were able to stay afloat for a time, tread-ing water, but they were too weak to swim to safety and were swept away.

The last surviving outlaws on the dock made a final, desperate last-ditch attempt to board the ship. Some of them made it, swarming over the side and throwing themselves on deck for a do-or-die effort.

It was mostly die. The female defenders knew it was life or death for them, too. They were beyond fear, they wanted revenge, they had plenty of guns and ammu-nition—the outlaws' own supplies—and they had the better strategic position.

This was war. It was kill or be killed.

The fighting was at too close quarters for Slocum to bring the Gatling gun into play. He grabbed the four-barreled cut-down shotgun and went downstairs to the main deck, where the weapon would be of best use.

An outlaw suddenly stepped into view at the far end of the companionway. His gun was pointing at Slocum even as Slocum squeezed one of the twinned double triggers of the shotgun. The blast cleared the way like a cannonball.

The battle neared its finish. Outlaws and defenders hammered away at each other at point-blank range, so close that they could look the enemy in the eye before shooting his—or her—face off.

Pete Keane couldn't believe his luck. He was shot in the thigh and the shoulder, losing a lot of blood, but still able to stay on his feet, even do a little walking. Slocum had come down from the deckhouse without seeing him, but he'd seen Slocum, and even better, he was behind Slocum's back with a loaded gun in his hand.

"Slocum," he said, whispering so Slocum wouldn't hear him.

He didn't see the wiry and intense blond teenager crouched over to one side of him.

She saw him, though. She was Karen Ingram and she had a gun. She held it out in front of her with both hands and emptied it into Pete Keane.

He wasn't so lucky after all. He lay on his back, motionless, with the life gushing out of him through six .44 holes.

Slocum whirled at the sound of the first shot, spinning low in a crouch, but Pete Keane was already pretty much history. He met Karen Ingram's eyes, knew who she was, and knew that she knew him.

"Much obliged," he said.

Gunfire ebbed, dying away. The groans of the wounded and the dying were loud in the sudden lull. There weren't many outlaws left alive, and those there were had stopped fighting and started running.

Gunfire came crackling down Redrock Road, growing louder and nearer, massive firepower wielded by a large and determined group of mounted men.

"My God," Darby groaned, "are there still more of them?"

"Take another look, Captain. That's the Texas Rangers and the U.S. Cavalry riding to the rescue. Ben Bowman must have gotten through after all," Slocum said.

"They sure took their damned time about it!"

Pete Keane didn't look as if he could lift a finger, but Slocum was careful to pry the gun from his nerveless hand anyway. His eyes opened when Slocum's shadow fell across his face.

" . . . Slocum."

"Pete."

"How—How'd we ever wind up like this? How'd we get to here, anyhow?"

"You sided with the wrong bunch, Pete."

"Well, it don't matter. I'm dead now," he said, and was.

"Slocum!"

Monroe Jones stood swaying on the other side of the deck, looking like some man-shaped monster that had been spit up from the mucky ooze at the bottom of the Blood. He was soaked, stunned, shaken, suffering from internal bleeding, and scorched and deaf in both ears thanks to the dynamite blast.

A normal man would have been dead from his injuries, but Monroe had a lot of hate in him and it kept him going. He was soaking wet and still dripping after just managing to clamber aboard.

He had his gun in his hand, and he pulled the trigger even as he shouted Slocum's name. He couldn't hear himself because he was deafened, but his head vibrated with the power of his primal roar.

The gun roared, too. There was water still in the barrel from the dunking it had gotten. Some of the water had run out but not enough, not nearly enough.

The barrel peeled backward like a metal flower as it exploded from the backblast, pulping Monroe's gun hand into a mangled red mass.

Slocum cut loose with a double-barreled shotgun blast and then fired a third for good measure. Monroe Jones was a hard man to kill, and Slocum was taking no chances. Three loads of buckshot mangled what was left of him and swept him clean off the deck and over the side into the water. He sank down, down, down into the Blood.

Emmeline Jones and Nev watched the bitter end from the safety of a distant ridge between the Little Blood River and Quicksilver Creek. They sat on fast horses between the crest of the ridge and a stand of dark, overgrown timber. Down in the basin, the Rangers and the Cavalry were hunting down the last scattered remnants of the outlaw band. The authorities were not overzealous about taking prisoners.

"That's their finish. I reckon Monroe wasn't as smart as he thought he was," she said.

"That's water under the bridge, Ma. The question is, what do we do now?"

"Run for it. What else? Least, that's what I'm gonna do."

"Come on, Ma, don't be like that."

"I didn't see you lift a finger to defend your mother."

"And get shot down by big brother? Nobody bucks Monroe, Ma. You of all people should know that. Nobody bucks that killer."

"Somebody did," she said. "Well, let's get gone. It's all over but the hangings."

"Which way, Ma?"

"We'll strike out along the Little Blood and cross the Hermanos, I reckon."

"I don't know. . . . That takes us way out in the middle of nowhere."

"Nowhere is where we want to be. It'll be a long time before this blows over."

"The law will never stop looking for us."

"We ain't hung yet. Let's vamoose, son."

"Okay, Ma."

They turned their horses away from Redrock and toward the Little Blood River. Two Apaches on horseback emerged from behind a spur of timber and halted, facing the Joneses, mother and son.

One of the Apaches fired a rifle into Nev, killing him. Nev fell off the horse and lay there, leaking red into the green grass. The Apaches remained motionless, watching the woman to see what she would do.

Emmeline Jones drew her gun and charged the Apaches, shooting at them. They were too far away for her gunfire to hit with any accuracy; their rifles had the range in this unequal contest.

They didn't fire them. Emmeline Jones was shot in the back at close range by the third Apache, Sombra, who'd crept up close for the killing shot earlier and hidden in the brush nearby without his prey ever sensing his nearness.

The Apaches stole the Jones's guns and horses and rode out along the Little Blood. This raid was ended; there would be others. It was said that Geronimo and his cousin Juh were forming a warrior band somewhere in the desolate mountains of Sonora. . . .

21

Ben Bowman had liberated an unbroken bottle of whiskey and two tumblers from the wreckage of the Cattleman Hotel, and now he and Slocum sat at a crude table made of logs and held together by rawhide thongs. They sat outside, in the shade of a largely intact building that had escaped the fires and general devastation of Redrock.

Bowman topped off the tumblers with the precious amber liquid. "Let's drink to Terry Lee. He planned on having this drink with you," Slocum said.

"I'll drink to that."

The tumblers were empty when they set them down, and Bowman refilled them to the brim. "This manhunting is thirsty work," he said.

"Profitable, too, if you kill the right people like I did."

"Well, now, Slocum, that's something I wanted to talk to you about. You've earned yourself some reward money, and no mistake. You done good, son."

"Better pour me another one because this soft soap sounds like it's going to cost me money, and I need another drink to face that."

"You know what your trouble is? You done too good."

"I don't follow you."

"Let's break it down to simple arithmetic. Now, the Apaches and the outlaws mostly killed each other and there ain't no bounty paid out on them. You can see that, can't you?"

"I can't see it for a hill of beans, Ben."

"That's the way of it anyhow. Here in Texas we got us something called the burden of proof. You need ironclad, rock-solid evidence that'll hold up in a court of law if you expect to get paid for collecting a bounty. Now, when all is said and done, the plain solid truth when we get right down to the nut cutting is that the only outlaw you can prove you killed is Monroe Jones. There's witnesses saw you finish him. Oh, you might have bagged a few other small fry, penny-ante stuff, but Monroe is the only big fish in your creel."

"I believe I'll have another drink, Ben."

"Whoa, now, easy does it. Good whiskey is scarce in Redrock since those owlhoots drank up everything in stock."

"What about the bonus the Army is paying for getting their Gatling gun back? I figure I'm in line for that, too."

"So, you heard about that, too, did you? You get around, Slocum. Say, where do you hail from, anyway?"

"Georgia."

"Well, you ain't no Texan, but at least you're a Southern boy, you ain't no damned Yankee."

"Thanks."

"Here, make yourself comfortable and have another drink—why, I see you already helped yourself. Good, Now that I got you in the right frame of mind, I want to run something by you. Hear me out before you answer."

"Shoot."

"You ever considered a career in law enforcement, son?"

"No."

"Maybe you should."

"No, thanks. I get shot at enough without wearing a badge for a target."

"Hold your horses, Slocum. I ain't talking about hiring on as some piss-ant town marshal or a politicking butt-kissing county sheriff's deputy. I'm talking about becoming a part of the hardest-riding, straightest-shooting body of peacekeepers the world has ever seen, the Texas Rangers!"

"You want me to join the Rangers?!"

"Why not? You'll get shot at, but you're used to that. And the pay ain't much, but hell, you're used to that. But what money can't buy is the pride of wearing the badge of Texas's best, and there ain't nothing nowhere that's better than that."

"That's real flattering, Ben. You've given me something to think over, yes, sir."

Slocum sat silently, watching cloud shadows glide across the basin. "You know, that little Pearl Jones sure is a fool for luck," he said after a while.

"Eh? What's that? Well, I reckon she is at that, being tied up in the middle of that whole shooting match and coming out of it without a scratch."

"I wasn't talking about that, Ben."

"No? Then what was you talking about?"

"I just saw her climb out the back window of the building you locked her in and run over to the stables."

"What?!"

"She's probably saddling a stolen horse right now. If you move fast, you still might be able to catch her."

"Dang it, Slocum! Why didn't you say something sooner?"

"I must have been dazzled by that bright future you've been promising me."

Bowman leaped up from the table and ran down a cross street toward the stables, only to slow to a stop in puzzlement when he saw a group of rangers out in front of it, unconcernedly tending to their horses.

She couldn't have broken out this way, he thought, the boys would have seen her! Something's fishy here. . . .

He turned and retraced his steps, but when he got back, Slocum was nowhere in sight—and neither was the last bottle of good whiskey in town.

"Gone! And my whiskey's gone, too! He stole it, the skunk," Ben Bowman said. "Oh, well, I guess he earned it at that."

America's new star of the classic western

GILES TIPPETTE

author of *Hard Rock*, *Jailbreak*, and *Crossfire*,
is back with his newest, most exciting novel yet

SIXKILLER

Springtime on the Half-Moon ranch has never been
so hard. On top of running the biggest spread in
Matagorda County, Justa Williams is about to become
a daddy. Which means he's got a lot more to fight for
when Sam Sixkiller comes to town. With his pack of
wild cutthroats slicing a swath of mayhem all the way
from Galveston, Sixkiller now has his ice-cold eyes
on Blessing—and word has it he intends to pick the
town clean.

Now, backed by men more skilled with branding irons
than rifles, the Williams clan must fight to defend
their dream—with their wits, their courage, and their
guns. . . .

Turn the page
for an exciting preview of
SIXKILLER
by Giles Tippette

Coming in May from Jove Books!

It was late afternoon when I got on my horse and rode the half mile from the house I'd built for Nora, my wife, up to the big ranch house my father and my two younger brothers still occupied. I had good news, the kind of news that does a body good, and I had taken the short run pretty fast. The two-year-old bay colt I'd been riding lately was kind of surprised when I hit him with the spurs, but he'd been lazing around the little horse trap behind my house and was grateful for the chance to stretch his legs and impress me with his speed. So we made it over the rolling plains of our ranch, the Half-Moon, in mighty good time.

I pulled up just at the front door of the big house, dropped the reins to the ground so that the colt would stand, and then made my way up on the big wooden porch, the rowels of my spurs making a *ching-ching* sound as I walked. I opened the big front door and let myself into the hall that led back to the main parts of the house.

I was Justa Williams and I was boss of all thirty-thousand deeded acres of the place. I had been so since it had come my duty on the weakening of our father,

Howard, through two unfortunate incidents. The first had been the early demise of our mother, which had taken it out of Howard. That had been when he'd sort of started preparing me to take over the load. I'd been a hard sixteen or a soft seventeen at the time. The next level had jumped up when he'd got nicked in the lungs by a stray bullet. After that I'd had the job of boss. The place was run with my two younger brothers, Ben and Norris.

It had been a hard job but having Howard around had made the job easier. Now I had some good news for him and I meant him to take it so. So when I went clumping back toward his bedroom that was just off the office I went to yelling, "Howard! Howard!"

He'd been lying back on his daybed, and he got up at my approach and come out leaning on his cane. He said, "What the thunder!"

I said, "Old man, sit down."

I went over and poured us out a good three fingers of whiskey. I didn't even bother to water his as I was supposed to do because my news was so big. He looked on with a good deal of pleasure as I poured out the drink. He wasn't even supposed to drink whiskey, but he'd put up such a fuss that the doctor had finally given in and allowed him one well-watered whiskey a day. But Howard claimed he never could count very well and that sometimes he got mixed up and that one drink turned into four. But, hell, I couldn't blame him. Sitting around all day like he was forced to was enough to make anybody crave a drink even if it was just for something to do.

But now he seen he was going to get the straight stuff and he got a mighty big gleam in his eye. He took the glass when I handed it to him and said, "What's the occasion? Tryin' to kill me off?"

"Hell no," I said. "But a man can't make a proper toast with watered whiskey."

"That's a fact." he said. "Now what the thunder are we toasting?"

I clinked my glass with his. I said, "If all goes well you are going to be a grandfather."

"Lord A'mighty!" he said.

We said, "Luck" as was our custom and then knocked them back.

Then he set his glass down and said, "Well, I'll just be damned." He got a satisfied look on his face that I didn't reckon was all due to the whiskey. He said, "Been long enough in coming."

I said, "Hell, the way you keep me busy with this ranch's business I'm surprised I've had the time."

"Pshaw!" he said.

We stood there, kind of enjoying the moment, and then I nodded at the whiskey bottle and said, "You keep on sneaking drinks, you ain't likely to be around for the occasion."

He reared up and said, "Here now! When did I raise you to talk like that?"

I gave him a small smile and said, "Somewhere along the line." Then I set my glass down and said, "Howard, I've got to get to work. I just reckoned you'd want the news."

He said, "Guess it will be a boy?"

I give him a sarcastic look. I said, "Sure, Howard, and I've gone into the gypsy business."

Then I turned out of the house and went to looking for our foreman, Harley. It was early spring in the year of 1848, and we were coming into a swift calf crop after an unusually mild winter. We were about to have calves dropping all over the place, and with the quality of our crossbred beef, we couldn't afford to lose a one.

On the way across the ranch yard my youngest brother, Ben, came riding up. He was on a little prancing chestnut that wouldn't stay still while he was trying to talk to me. I knew he was schooling the little filly, but I said, a little impatiently, "Ben, either ride on off and talk to me later or make that damn horse stand. I can't catch but every other word."

Ben said, mildly, "Hell, don't get agitated. I just wanted to give you a piece of news you might be interested in."

I said, "All right, what is this piece of news?"

"One of the hands drifting the Shorthorn herd got sent back to the barn to pick up some stuff for Harley. He said he seen Lew Vara heading this way."

I was standing up near his horse. The animal had been worked pretty hard, and you could take the horse smell right up your nose off him. I said, "Well, okay. So the sheriff is coming. What you reckon we ought to do, get him a cake baked?"

He give me one of his sardonic looks. Ben and I were so much alike it was awful to contemplate. Only difference between us was that I was a good deal wiser and less hotheaded and he was an even size smaller than me. He said, "I reckon he'd rather have whiskey."

I said, "I got some news for you but I ain't going to tell you now."

"What is it?"

I wasn't about to tell him he might be an uncle under such circumstances. I gave his horse a whack on the rump and said, as he went off, "Tell you this evening after work. Now get, and tell Ray Hays I want to see him later on."

He rode off, and I walked back to the ranch house thinking about Lew Vara. Lew, outside of my family, was about the best friend I'd ever had. We'd started off, however, in a kind of peculiar way to make friends. Some eight or nine years past Lew and I had had about the worst fistfight I'd ever been in. It occurred at Crook's Saloon and Cafe in Blessing, the closest town to our ranch, about seven miles away, of which we owned a good part. The fight took nearly a half an hour, and we both did our dead level best to beat the other to death. I won the fight, but unfairly. Lew had had me down on the saloon floor and was in the process of finishing me off when my groping hand found a beer mug. I smashed him over the head with it in a last-ditch effort to keep my own head on my shoulders. It sent Lew to the infirmary for quite a long stay; I'd fractured his skull. When he was partially recovered Lew sent word to me that as soon as he was able, he was coming to kill me.

But it never happened. When he was free from medical care Lew took off for the Oklahoma Territory, and I didn't hear another word from him for four years. Next time I saw him he came into that very same saloon. I was sitting at a back table when I saw him come through the door. I eased my right leg forward so as to clear my revolver for a quick draw from the holster. But Lew just came up, stuck out his hand in a friendly gesture, and said he wanted to let bygones be bygones. He offered to buy me a drink, but I had a bottle on the table so I just told him to get himself a glass and take advantage of my hospitality.

Which he did.

After that Lew became a friend of the family and was important in helping the Williams family in about three confrontations where his gun and his savvy did a good deal to turn the tide in our favor. After that we ran him against the incumbent sheriff who we'd come to dislike and no longer trust. Lew had been reluctant at first, but I'd told him that money couldn't buy poverty but it could damn well buy the sheriff's job in Matagorda County. As a result he got elected, and so far as I was concerned, he did an outstanding job of keeping the peace in his territory.

Which wasn't saying a great deal because most of the trouble he had to deal with, outside of helping us, was the occasional Saturday night drunk and the odd Main Street dogfight.

So I walked back to the main ranch house wondering what he wanted. But I also knew that if it was in my power to give, Lew could have it.

I was standing on the porch about five minutes later when he came riding up. I said, "You want to come inside or talk outside?"

He swung off his horse. He said, "Let's get inside."

"You want coffee?"

"I could stand it."

"This going to be serious?"

"Is to me."

"All right."

I led him through the house to the dining room, where we generally, as a family, sat around and talked things out. I said, looking at Lew, "Get started on it."

He wouldn't face me. "Wait until the coffee comes. We can talk then."

About then Buttercup came staggering in with a couple of cups of coffee. It didn't much make any difference about what time of day or night it was, Buttercup might or might not be staggering. He was an old hand of our father's who'd helped to develop the Half-Moon. In his day he'd been about the best horse breaker around, but time and tumbles had taken their toll. But Howard wasn't a man to forget past loyalties so he'd kept Buttercup on as a cook. His real name was Butterfield, but me and my brothers had called him Buttercup, a name he clearly despised, for as long as I could remember. He was easily the best shot with a long-range rifle I'd ever seen. He had an old .50-caliber Sharps buffalo rifle, and even with his old eyes and seemingly unsteady hands he was deadly anywhere up to five hundred yards. On more than one occasion I'd had the benefit of that seemingly ageless ability. Now he set the coffee down for us and gave all the indications of making himself at home. I said, "Buttercup, go on back out in the kitchen. This is a private conversation."

I sat. I picked up my coffee cup and blew on it and then took a sip. I said, "Let me have it, Lew."

He looked plain miserable. He said, "Justa, you and your family have done me a world of good. So has the town and the county. I used to be the trash of the alley and y'all helped bring me back from nothing." He looked away. He said, "That's why this is so damn hard."

"What's so damned hard?"

But instead of answering straight out he said, "They is going to be people that don't understand. That's why I want you to have the straight of it."

I said, with a little heat, "Goddammit, Lew, if you don't tell me what's going on I'm going to stretch you out over that kitchen stove in yonder."

He'd been looking away, but now he brought his gaze back to me and said, "I've got to resign, Justa. As sheriff. And not only that, I got to quit this part of the country."

Thoughts of his past life in the Oklahoma Territory flashed through my mind, when he'd been thought an outlaw and later proved innocent. I thought maybe that old business had come up again and he was going to have to flee for his life and his freedom. I said as much.

He give me a look and then made a short bark that I reckoned he took for a laugh. He said, "Naw, you got it about as backwards as can be. It's got to do with my days in the Oklahoma Territory all right, but it ain't the law. Pretty much the opposite of it. It's the outlaw part that's coming to plague me."

It took some doing, but I finally got the whole story out of him. It seemed that the old gang he'd fallen in with in Oklahoma had got wind of his being the sheriff of Matagorda County. They thought that Lew was still the same young hellion and that they had them a bird nest on the ground, what with him being sheriff and all. They'd sent word that they'd be in town in a few days and they figured to "pick the place clean." And they expected Lew's help.

"How'd you get word?"

Lew said, "Right now they are raising hell in Galveston, but they sent the first robin of spring down to let me know to get the welcome mat rolled out. Some kid about eighteen or nineteen. Thinks he's tough."

"Where's he?"

Lew jerked his head in the general direction of Blessing. "I throwed him in jail."

I said, "You got me confused. How is you quitting going to help the situation? Looks like with no law it would be even worse."

He said, "If I ain't here maybe they won't come. I plan to send the robin back with the message I ain't the sheriff and ain't even in the country. Besides, there's plenty of good men in the county for the job that won't attract the riffraff I seem to have done." He looked down at his coffee as if he was ashamed.

I didn't know what to say for a minute. This didn't sound like the Lew Vara I knew. I understood he wasn't afraid and I understood he thought he was doing what he thought was the best for everyone concerned, but I didn't think he was thinking too straight. I said, "Lew, how many of them is there?"

He said, tiredly, "About eighteen all told. Counting the robin in the jail. But they be a bunch of rough hombres. This town ain't equipped to handle such. Not without a whole lot of folks gettin' hurt. And I won't have that. I figured on an argument from you, Justa, but I ain't going to make no battlefield out of this town. I know this bunch. Or kinds like them." Then he raised his head and give me a hard look. "So I don't want no argument out of you. I come out to tell you what was what because I care about what you might think of me. Don't make me no mind about nobody else but I wanted you to know."

I got up. I said, "Finish your coffee. I got to ride over to my house. I'll be back inside of half an hour. Then we'll go into town and look into this matter."

He said, "Dammit, Justa, I done told you I—"

"Yeah, I know what you told me. I also know it ain't really what you want to do. Now we ain't going to argue and I ain't going to try to tell you what to do, but I am going to ask you to let us look into the situation a little before you light a shuck and go tearing out of here. Now will you wait until I ride over to the house and tell Nora I'm going into town?"

He looked uncomfortable, but, after a moment, he nodded. "All right," he said. "But it ain't going to change my mind none."

I said, "Just go in and visit with Howard until I get back. He don't get much company and even as sorry as you are you're better than nothing."

That at least did make him smile a bit. He sipped at his coffee, and I took out the back door to where my horse was waiting.

Nora met me at the front door when I came into the house. She said, "Well, how did the soon-to-be grandpa take it?"

I said, "Howard? Like to have knocked the heels off his boots. I give him a straight shot of whiskey in celebration. He's so damned tickled I don't reckon he's settled down yet."

"What about the others?"

I said, kind of cautiously, "Well, wasn't nobody else around. Ben's out with the herd and Norris is in Blessing. Naturally Buttercup is drunk."

Meanwhile I was kind of edging my way back toward our bedroom. She followed me. I was at the point of strapping on my gunbelt when she came into the room. She said, "Why are you putting on that gun?"

It was my sidegun, a .42/40-caliber Colts revolver that I'd been carrying for several years. I had two of them, one that I wore and one that I carried in my saddlebags. The gun was a .40-caliber chambered weapon on a .42-caliber frame. The heavier frame gave it a nice feel in the hand with very little barrel deflection, and the .40-caliber slug was big enough to stop any thing you could hit solid. It had been good luck for me and the best proof of that was that I was alive.

I said, kind of looking away from her, "Well, I've got to go into town."

"Why do you need your gun to go into town?"

I said, "Hell, Nora, I never go into town without a gun. You know that."

"What are you going into town for?"

I said, "Norris has got some papers for me to sign."

"I thought Norris was already in town. What does he need you to sign anything for?"

I kind of blew up. I said, "Dammit, Nora, what is with all these questions? I've got business. Ain't that good enough for you?"

She give me a cool look. "Yes," she said. "I don't mess in your business. It's only when you try and lie to me. Justa, you are the worst liar in the world."

"All right," I said. "All right. Lew Vara has got some trouble. Nothing serious. I'm going to give him a hand. God knows he's helped us out enough." I could hear her maid, Juanita, banging around in the kitchen. I said, "Look, why don't you get Juanita to hitch up the buggy and you and her go up to the big house and fix us a supper. I'll be back before dark and we'll all eat together and celebrate. What about that?"

She looked at me for a long moment. I could see her thinking about all the possibilities. Finally she said, "Are you going to run a risk on the day I've told you you're going to be a father?"

"Hell no!" I said. "What do you think? I'm going in to use a little influence for Lew's sake. I ain't going to be running any risks."

She made a little motion with her hand. "Then why the gun?"

"Hell, Nora, I don't even ride out into the pasture without a gun. Will you quit plaguing me?"

It took a second, but then her smooth, young face calmed down. She said, "I'm sorry, honey. Go and help Lew if you can. Juanita and I will go up to the big house and I'll personally see to supper. You better be back."

I give her a good, loving kiss and then made my adieus, left the house, and mounted my horse and rode off.

But I rode off with a little guilt nagging at me. I swear, it is hell on a man to answer all the tugs he gets on his sleeve. He gets pulled first one way and then the other. A man damn near needs to be made out of India rubber to handle all of them. No, I wasn't riding into no danger that March day, but if we didn't do something about it, it wouldn't be long before I would be.

A special offer for people who enjoy reading the best Westerns published today.

WESTERNS!

NO OBLIGATION

Mail the coupon below

To start your subscription and receive 2 FREE WESTERNS, fill out the coupon below and mail it today. We'll send your first shipment which includes 2 FREE BOOKS as soon as we receive it.

- - - - - - - - - - - - - - - - - - -

Mail To: **True Value Home Subscription Services, Inc. P.O. Box 5235**
120 Brighton Road, Clifton, New Jersey 07015-5235

YES! I want to start reviewing the very best Westerns being published today. Send me my first shipment of 6 Westerns for me to preview FREE for 10 days. If I decide to keep them, I'll pay for just 4 of the books at the low subscriber price of $2.75 each; a total $11.00 (a $21.00 value). Then each month I'll receive the 6 newest and best Westerns to preview Free for 10 days. If I'm not satisfied I may return them within 10 days and owe nothing. Otherwise I'll be billed at the special low subscriber rate of $2.75 each; a total of $16.50 (at least a $21.00 value) and save $4.50 off the publishers price. There are never any shipping, handling or other hidden charges. I understand I am under no obligation to purchase any number of books and I can cancel my subscription at any time, no questions asked. In any case the 2 FREE books are mine to keep.

Name
_____

Street Address _____ Apt. No. _____

City _____ State _____ Zip Code _____

Telephone
_____

Signature
_____
(if under 18 parent or guardian must sign)

Terms and prices subject to change. Orders subject
to acceptance by True Value Home Subscription
Services, Inc.

425-13273-0